FORSAKEN

THE THOMAS WOLSEY TRILOGY

LAURA DOWERS

Blue Laurel
Press

Paperback: 978-1-912968-33-6

eBook: 978-1-912968-34-3

CHAPTER ONE

1521

Thomas Wolsey touched the tip of his quill to each line of his account ledger, his mouth moving as he added up the figures. He reached the end of the column and tutted at the total. His household expenditure for the past twelve months had been over a third more than it had been the previous year. He hadn't lost money, but his annual spending was eating deeper and deeper into his revenues, and that wasn't good.

Thomas knew where the money had gone; everything was itemised and accounted for in his ledgers. The building works at Hampton Court had cost an absolute fortune, and his grand meeting at the Val d'Or the previous summer had been his biggest expenditure to date, creating an enormous hole in his personal coffers. He didn't begrudge the money, though. Hampton Court was turning into his masterpiece, and the Val d'Or…, well, that had been an event that would go down in history for its splendour, if for no other reason. But something would have to be done to replenish his coffers, and that was a fact.

Thomas dragged over another of the heavy ledgers,

this time, the one he didn't let his secretaries or clerks see, for it recorded all the monies he received from foreign sovereigns in recognition of his excellent service. Not that he was doing anything underhand by taking pensions – it was understood that men in positions of authority and influence received such retainers – but he saw no reason why anyone should know just how much he collected.

He checked the dates of his last pension payments. Several were overdue, and he made a note to chase up on those, but even those payments wouldn't be enough to make up the shortfall. He would have to keep an eye out for Church positions becoming vacant and snap them up before anyone else could get their hands on them.

Thomas closed the ledger, threw down the quill, and rubbed his hands together. He'd been writing for so long his fingers were cramping. The cold weather didn't help. Oh, how he longed for the spring, when the days grew longer, and he wouldn't need to wear three layers of woollen hose to keep the chill out. *When did I become old?* Thomas wondered. *I never used to mind about the cold when I was young.*

Grey daylight was bleeding through the frosted windows and Thomas leant forward to blow out the candle that was almost down to the stub. His stomach growled, protesting at the lack of sustenance. Rising at five, he had said his prayers and come straight to his office, not bothering to break his fast. He looked over at his secretary's desk in the corner of the room. There was a plate of almond biscuits on it, left over from the day before.

Thomas rose, groaning as he arched his back and his bones clicked into place. Moving around his desk, he made for the biscuits and snatched one up. It was a little dry, but better than nothing. When his secretary came in, he would order something more substantial. A few slices of the venison the king had sent him, perhaps, and some manchet bread with cheese.

He turned towards the door at the sound of raised voices. One belonged to Brian Tuke, his secretary, arriving to begin the day's work. The other Thomas recognised as the voice of Thomas More.

The door opened and Tuke's head appeared. 'Good morning, Your Eminence. Master More is here, insisting on seeing you. I've told him he must make an appointment, but he is adamant he cannot wait.'

Thomas swallowed down the last of the biscuit and moved back to his desk. 'It's all right, Brian, I'll see him.'

'Very good, Your Eminence.' Tuke opened the door wider and Thomas More strode in, tossing the book he held onto the desk. It landed with a thump beneath Thomas's nose.

'I want to know what you're going to do about that,' he declared.

A little annoyed by the lawyer's manner, Thomas picked up the book, opening the cover to examine the frontispiece. *De captivitate Babylonica ecclesiae praeludium*, read the title and he understood why More was so angry. If there was one thing guaranteed to ignite the saintly More's fury, it was a heretical work by Martin Luther. He closed the book and looked up at More.

'What am I going to do? Luther is being dealt with by the pope. He's issued a bull against him and all his works.'

'I know what the pope has done.' More plumped down on the stool by Thomas's desk. 'But what about here in England? We must prevent this filth from spreading.'

'I have issued a ban on the importation of all of Luther's books,' Thomas said patiently. 'I have instructed the port authorities to be on the lookout for copies being smuggled into the country and to impound any they find.'

'A ban? Is that all?'

'What else would you have me do?'

More slammed his hand down on the desk in irritation. 'You do know Luther is being read at Cambridge and Oxford, don't you? Our young scholars are having their heads filled with this… this… shit.'

Out of the corner of his eye, Thomas saw Tuke's eyebrows rise at the use of the expletive. 'Yes, I am aware of that, and once the ban has been publicly declared, their reading will cease.'

More grunted. 'That's not good enough.'

Thomas's expression hardened. 'I'm afraid it will have to do.'

More and Thomas stared at each other for a long moment, then More reached over the ink pot and snatched up the book. 'Then you leave me no choice. I shall speak with the king.' He rose, tucking the book into a leather satchel that hung beneath his cloak. 'I'm sure he'll be more interested in stopping Luther than you seem to be.'

'And I can assure you, Master More, the king will be content to leave Luther to me.'

More looked down his nose at Thomas. 'I think you're wrong about that. I've talked with the king. I know how he feels about that lousy little friar.'

'I'm sure His Majesty is outraged by Luther,' Thomas agreed, 'but what do you imagine he can do that I cannot?'

'That's something I shall find out, isn't it? Unless you mean to prevent me from seeing the king?'

Thomas shook his head. 'I wouldn't dream of preventing you. I know how fond the king is of you.'

More's eyes narrowed. 'I will see the king about this, Your Eminence.'

'I believe you, Master More. Now, if you will excuse me.' Thomas gestured at the papers before him. 'I have much to do.'

More looked at the papers disdainfully. 'I'm dismissed, am I?'

'You did not have an appointment.' Thomas picked up his quill. 'Be grateful I saw you at all.'

'Good day to you, then.' More turned on his heel and exited as furiously as he had entered.

Tuke closed the door after him. 'I never thought I'd hear Master More speak so crudely.'

Thomas chuckled. 'That was nothing, Brian. You should hear Master More when he really gets going about Luther and any other person he considers a heretic. He detests heretics and Martin Luther is the biggest heretic of all. I should have known he would turn up here sooner or later, making demands I do something about him.' A sudden pain pierced behind his droopy eye and he cried out.

Tuke drew near. 'What is it, Your Eminence?'

Thomas pressed two fingers to his twitching eyelid. 'Just the usual headache, Brian. It will pass.'

'Perhaps a compress would help.'

'The only thing that helped were Joan's simples,' Thomas said, then cursed inwardly for mentioning his former mistress's name.

It had been several months since Joan Larke had left him, but he still felt her absence keenly. Thomas hadn't blamed her for leaving. He knew he had taken her for granted, expecting her to put up with a hidden life, never allowed to come out into the open, never to be acknowledged as meaning anything to him. It had been asking too much and Joan, quite rightly, had decided she'd had enough and moved back to Ipswich.

'We could write to Mistress Larke for the recipes,' Tuke suggested. 'I'm sure one of the household women could replicate them.'

'Aye, maybe,' Thomas muttered as the pain receded, and he waved Tuke back to his desk. 'Get a message to one of my people in the king's privy chamber. I want to know when More meets with the king.'

Tuke scribbled a note. 'You're not worried about More talking to the king of Luther, are you? After all, the king isn't likely to do anything.'

'No, he isn't likely to do anything,' Thomas agreed. 'Henry will listen, he will sympathise, he will agree something must be done, and then he will talk to me about Luther. I will tell him what steps I have put in place, and the king will believe he has done all he can. Even so, I would prefer it if More did not trouble the king with such trivialities. He will have put an idea in his head, and once an idea is in Henry's head, it is very difficult to remove it, and it may keep cropping up when he and I should be concerned with more important matters.'

'I'm sure you'll be able to persuade the king he can leave the matter to you, Your Eminence,' Tuke said. 'You know how to manage him. You know him so well.'

Thomas raised his eyes to the portrait of Henry that hung on the wall opposite his desk. It was a poor representation of the king, a copy of a copy, and the artist had caught nothing of the king's charm, certainly nothing of the freshness of his countenance. The skin was dull and bore no trace of the girlish pinkness that often coloured Henry's cheeks, while the eyes held no life but squinted out of the flesh like a man twice his age. He knew he should have a better portrait of the king on his wall, but he just hadn't had time to commission a more competent artist to paint one.

'You're right, Brian. I do know him well. In fact,' he said, smiling to himself, 'I probably know him better than he knows himself.'

CHAPTER TWO

It was three days later when Thomas received word from one of his informants in Henry's privy chamber that Master More had met with the king. More had said nothing Thomas had not expected, and he had also been proved correct about Henry's response. Henry had been interested in what More had to say, had been outraged by Luther, and had promised the saintly More that he would speak with his beloved Wolsey about the matter.

So, when Thomas arrived at Greenwich for his weekly meeting with the king, he knew what to expect. As he was led along the corridors, courtiers backing up against the walls and bowing as he passed, Thomas considered how he would deal with the matter of Luther. Should he tell Henry he agreed with More but that there was nothing more he could do? Or should he tell the king More exaggerated the situation, that Luther was nowhere near as dangerous an influence as he made out and that he would soon be nothing more than a memory, despite what More said?

Discrediting More might not be a wise move. The king was very fond of the lawyer, and Thomas did not want to appear to be antagonistic towards a man Henry rated highly. But then, there really was nothing more to be done about Luther than he was already doing. What a nuisance More was, making him waste his time on matters beyond his control. There was nothing for it, Thomas decided. He would simply have to play it by ear.

Henry was in the chapel, and Thomas entered quietly, seeing the king was on his knees, those bony joints pressing into a red velvet cushion before the chapel's altar. Thomas stayed by the doors while the king murmured his prayers.

'Amen,' Henry said a minute later, making the sign of the cross over his broad chest before pushing himself up onto his feet with an ease Thomas envied. 'Ah, Thomas, there you are.'

'Yes, Your Majesty,' Thomas agreed, 'here I am.'

Henry gestured Thomas towards one of the wooden pews, then slid in beside him. The odours of musk and bergamot wafted over him, and Thomas noted the king had changed his perfume.

'Tell me, how stands my realm?'

The question was mostly rhetorical. Henry didn't really want to know. All he wanted was for Thomas to assure him he had everything in hand.

'Your realm stands in good order, Your Majesty,' Thomas said, giving a variation of the reply he always gave. He told Henry a few of the most important matters he had dealt with since their last meeting, just so Henry felt he had a hand in the business of running the country. But there were plenty of other matters he had dealt with that Henry didn't need to know, and Thomas kept silent about those.

'That is all excellent, Thomas,' Henry said when he had finished, 'but there is one matter you haven't mentioned which I feel compelled to discuss with you.'

'Martin Luther, Your Majesty?'

Henry's face registered surprise. 'Well, yes. By God's bones, have you taken to reading minds?'

Thomas smiled, thinking what a useful skill that would be for a man in his position. 'Indeed not, Your Majesty, but I had the pleasure of a visit from Master More earlier this week and he was so good as to tell me of his concerns regarding Luther.'

'Valid concerns,' Henry said earnestly, and Thomas's heart sank a little. Had he underestimated the power of More's oratory? Was Henry going to insist he do something? 'But More said you didn't share them.'

'I fear Master More does me an injustice,' Thomas protested. 'I am very concerned about Luther's influence, but I have faith the pope can deal with him.'

'That's all very well,' Henry said, shaking his head, 'but should we not do what we can to check him? I have the welfare of my subjects to consider.'

Thomas cleared his throat. 'As I informed Master More, all that can be done has been done, at this time. And if you will forgive me for saying so, he should not have bothered you with this. It is for the Church to deal with Luther. He is a renegade foreign priest, not your subject.'

'I understand that,' Henry said, 'but I still feel I have a duty towards the Church to do something, and I have been thinking. You know of the book I have been writing?'

Oh yes, Thomas knew about the book. Henry had been working on his great theological book for the past two years, and Thomas had serious doubts that the blasted thing would ever be finished. Writing a book required discipline and commitment, two traits Henry lacked. If progress had been made with the book, Thomas suspected it was only because More had been encouraging Henry.

'Master More suggested I use my book to refute Luther's allegations,' Henry continued. 'Perhaps I could devote one chapter to that? What do you think?'

'I think that is an excellent idea,' Thomas said, putting as much enthusiasm as he could muster into his words.

Henry grinned. 'Then that is what I shall do. And you will help me, won't you?'

Thomas suppressed a groan. *As if I don't have enough to do.* 'Of course,' he nodded, smiling, 'I will give you any help you require, Your Majesty, though I fear my efforts can be nothing but feeble. I am no scholar.' A sly thought occurred, a petty way of paying More back. 'But, of course, Master More is a brilliant scholar. If I might suggest, More is the man you need. He has the words for such a worthwhile endeavour. Mine are not so persuasive nor so erudite as his.' Henry's face had fallen a little and Thomas, eager not to appear reluctant to assist, quickly added, 'But if you will allow, Your Majesty, I would be honoured to pen a preface to your book. I would not wish my inferior words to take up any more space than that.'

Henry's mouth widened into a smile. 'I shall look forward to reading it. I intend to have my book finished within two months. Every day that passes is another day Luther has an opportunity to corrupt feeble minds.'

There was fervour in Henry's voice. Perhaps he did mean to complete it in two months, though Thomas would only believe that when he held the finished manuscript in his hands.

'I will have my preface written within the next few days and sent to you with all speed,' he promised. 'Now, if that is all, Your Majesty.' Thomas half rose, but Henry put out a hand and he was obliged to put his backside back on the wooden seat.

'There is one other matter I wish to discuss with you,' Henry said, his face all seriousness. 'Have you been keeping a watch on those nobles I asked you to?'

Thomas hesitated. This was one question he hadn't been expecting. When Henry had first said to Thomas – when had it been? A year ago, two? – that he had his suspicions about the loyalty of some of his nobles and that he wanted them watched, Thomas had been taken aback. He was used to thinking the dukes and earls of England were conspiring against him, but for Henry to think they were plotting against their king was so very out of character. That realisation had been surprising enough, but when Henry had said he was worried about the loyalty of Charles Brandon, Thomas had been struck dumb. If anyone was loyal, Thomas had supposed, it was Henry's brother-in-law.

'Yes, Your Majesty,' Thomas said, 'I have watchers in their households, as you asked.'

'And you have heard nothing?'

'Nothing of any consequence. Why? Have you?'

Henry rose and moved into the aisle. He put his hands on his hips, pushed out his bottom lip and stared at the flagstones in deep concentration. 'No, but suspicions plague me, Thomas. Keep watching them, especially Buckingham, if you are not already. My nights are troubled with evil dreams of him.'

Not only Brandon, but Buckingham too, now! But at least a fear of Buckingham made sense. If there was one noble who had the potential to be a traitor, it was the man with Plantagenet blood running through his veins. Though Thomas had never told Henry, he had had watchers in the duke's household for many years before ever the king had spoken of disloyalty.

'I will see to it, Your Majesty,' he said, and took his leave, hurrying from the chapel, wondering what there was in Henry's dreams to worry him so about Edward Stafford.

Edward Stafford, duke of Buckingham, raised his cup in the air and waggled it at his servant to refill it. The servant pushed himself away from the wall, emptied the contents of his jug into the cup and readied a new jugful, believing this night would be no different from other nights when his master seemed determined to drink his wine cellar dry.

'And I tell you,' Buckingham said, wiping his mouth with the back of his hand, 'I was damn glad to get out of London. It's sickening to see how much sway Wolsey holds over the king. When I see Henry fawning over that knave, it makes me sick to my stomach. God only knows what the foreign ambassadors think and report back to their kings.'

Lord Montague frowned and shared a glance with the third man at the table. Lord Abergavenny jerked his eyebrow at Montague, a shared understanding of just how much in his cups their host was.

'I thought the king always presented a most princely air,' Montague said, brushing crumbs from his long black beard.

Buckingham banged his empty cup on the table. 'Oh, Henry looks the part, I'll give him that, but they all know who's really in charge. Do you know what they call Wolsey on the Continent? The *alter rex*.'

'Oh yes,' Montague smiled, 'the other king. But that is just flattery, do you not think? A means by which they can ingratiate themselves with Wolsey.'

'Ha,' Buckingham cried, 'the best way they can ingratiate themselves is to…,' he rubbed his fingers together, 'pay up. There's nothing Wolsey loves more than money.'

'What man doesn't?' Abergavenny murmured so low Buckingham didn't hear.

'And I'll tell you something else,' Buckingham went on, 'there's nothing he won't do to get it. He'd even sell our king to the Spanish or the French for the right price.'

'Oh, Edward, come,' Montague said, shaking his head, 'if there is one thing you cannot accuse Wolsey of it is failing to serve his king.'

Buckingham's top lip curled in disdain. 'Well, if I were king, I wouldn't let a butcher's cur rule over me, I promise you that.'

'If you were king, Edward?' Abergavenny asked, his cup paused halfway to his mouth.

'And why not?' Buckingham glared at him. 'I could be king. I should be king. The blood of the Plantagenets runs in my veins, does it not?'

Abergavenny spread his hands. 'That line of kings, alas, fell with King Richard.'

'And what a sorry day that was.' Buckingham punched his chest to bring up a belch. 'That we should come to this, having the country ruled over by a common dog like Wolsey.'

Abergavenny glanced at Montague. The wine had loosened the duke's tongue, and he was saying things he would do better to keep to himself. 'But does Wolsey do such a poor job of it?' he asked, his fingers stroking the tapestry tablecloth.

'Are you serious?' Buckingham demanded. 'You only have to look at that farce last year in France.'

'The Val d'Or? Why do you call it a farce?' Montague asked.

Another bang on the table, making both men jump. 'God blind me,' Buckingham cried, spittle falling onto his beard, 'that's what it was. Tournaments, wrestling, dancing, masques.' He shook his head in disgust. 'All of us prancing around, bowing and kissing hands with the pox-ridden French. And don't tell me it was done for the benefit of England. That ridiculous spectacle was done for one reason and for one reason only – the glory of Wolsey.'

'It is true,' Abergavenny conceded to Montague. 'The cardinal was in his element.'

'And how much did it cost to glorify His Eminence, eh? Answer me that.' Buckingham was slurring his words a little now. 'It near ruined me, that I do know. And it's all come to nothing, despite all the cardinal's bluster. Peace?' He threw his arms wide, smacking Montague on the shoulder. 'What peace? Are we at peace? Is Europe?'

'We are not at war,' Abergavenny pointed out.

'Not yet, but we will be, I guarantee you that.' Buckingham wagged a finger at him. 'And why do we want peace with France, anyway? The French are our enemies. Always have been and always will be. That's the proper order for you. Not all this kissing palms and making bows. Shall we all be French from now on? Shall we all go around waving silk handkerchiefs, dabbing perfume behind our ears?' He made a noise of disgust. 'I am an honest Englishman, and I will always be an honest Englishman. And that, my friends, is what this country needs in its king.' He held up his cup and the servant obligingly refilled it.

Thomas had been dreaming about Joan again. She was in the kitchen, stirring a pot of herbs over a chafing dish, and telling him he was working too hard. He was sitting at the kitchen table, something he had never done, and listening to her going on while the cooks and spit-boys bustled around him as if he wasn't there. Joan had poured out the sweet-smelling mixture into an earthenware cup and was handing it to him when Thomas was rudely awoken.

'I am so sorry, Your Eminence.' George Cavendish's pudgy face was a picture of anguish. 'But Lord Montague is here to see you.'

The name took a few moments to register in Thomas's sleep-befuddled brain. 'What does he want?' he asked, rubbing sleep out of his eyes.

'He didn't say, but he apologises for the early hour. Will you dress?'

There seemed to be no doubt in Cavendish's mind that Thomas would see Lord Montague. And, of course, Thomas thought ruefully, he was right. For Montague to come to him at so early an hour could only mean he had a matter of importance to tell. Thomas sat up and swung his bare legs to the floor, shivering at the sudden chill upon his skin. Cavendish swiftly bent and forced Thomas's feet into his silk slippers.

'No, I shall not dress. Lord Montague must take me as I am.'

He stood and moved behind the wooden screen that sectioned off his close stool from the rest of the room. He emptied his aching bladder and told Cavendish to show his visitor in.

'Well, my lord,' he said, tying the belt of his dressing gown as Montague entered, 'to what do I owe this honour?'

Montague glanced nervously at Cavendish.

'You can leave us, George,' Thomas said, and waited while Cavendish exited. 'Secrets, my lord?'

Montague shrugged. 'The matter is sensitive.' He pointed to a chair by the fireplace. 'May I?'

Thomas nodded, and Montague strode over to the chair, snatching his cap from his head and scrunching it up in his hand. Wondering what was worrying the lord so, Thomas took the chair opposite. 'What have you to tell me?'

'I've come from Thornbury,' Montague said.

Thomas's ears pricked at the mention of Buckingham's country estate. He kept silent and waited.

'I thought I ought to tell you what was said while I was there.' Montague sighed. 'Edward Stafford is a friend, of course, and one doesn't like to tell tales…'

'But?'

'But he's been getting worse of late, and you need to hear what he's been saying before he gets himself into trouble.'

Thomas sat back in his chair, wishing he had ordered the fire to be lit before dismissing Cavendish. 'You had better tell me what he said.'

'You must understand,' Montague said, 'he had been drinking very heavily, so perhaps we shouldn't lend too much weight to his words. After all, we all say things in our cups that we wouldn't dare speak aloud when sober.'

'Quite,' Thomas agreed. 'But what did he say?'

Montague looked embarrassed. 'He spoke ill of both you and the king.'

'I am aware of the duke's low opinion of me. He has made his feelings plain on several occasions.' *Like last year,* he mentally added, *when he poured a bowl of scented water over my shoes in front of the king and the emperor of Spain and called me knave.* 'You need not tell me what he said about me.'

'I know there is no love lost between you, but I haven't heard him speak so ill of the king before,' Montague said. 'True, he has never cared for any of the Tudors, but I believed he always respected their right to sit on the throne. Now…,' he threw up his hands.

'Has the duke spoken treason?' Thomas asked quietly.

Montague bit his bottom lip. 'That is for you to judge, not I. He said if he were king, he would not allow you to rule him as Henry does. He said he should be king.'

Thomas was disappointed. 'Is this all?'

'Isn't that enough?' Montague cried. 'God's Death, in the late king's time, such words would have been enough to have the duke's head from his shoulders, and mine too, for listening to it.'

'The king is not his father,' Thomas pointed out. 'But tell me, did he actually threaten the king's life?'

Montague hesitated before shaking his head.

'My lord?' Thomas prompted.

'Well, I heard him say once how easy it would be to kill the king, but it was after Henry had received a great many people and he had allowed them to draw so close. The duke thought he was being dangerously foolish to allow strangers so near and he showed how Henry could be killed.'

'How could he be killed?'

Montague sighed. 'Apparently, it was an idea his father had to kill King Richard. He would kneel and take Henry's hand to kiss. With the other, he would draw out a dagger and, as he rose to his feet, it would be no effort at all to slip the blade beneath the king's ribs. I'm sure he wasn't suggesting that is how he would do it, just how it could be done, and so easily.'

'Why did you not report this to me before?' Thomas asked sharply.

Montague looked worried. 'I thought little of it at the time. And there were others who heard him say so. You may as well ask them why they didn't report his words to you. But I feel I have done my duty to you and to the king by coming to you now.'

Thomas nodded and smiled, deciding not to pursue the point. 'Indeed. I thank you, my lord, for bringing me this intelligence.' He clapped his hands down on the pommels of his chair and rose.

'What will you do with it?' Montague asked, following suit.

'I'm not yet sure,' Thomas said. 'The duke's words could be considered treasonous, but they may just be drunken ramblings, as you say.'

'Will you tell the king?'

'I shall take some little time to consider that, my lord. But, in the meantime, I hope your conscience has been eased.'

Montague slapped his cap against his other hand. 'Not as much as I had hoped,' he muttered, and took his leave a moment later.

Thomas didn't suppose his conscience was eased. Lord Montague might have just handed his friend over to the headsman and he knew it.

CHAPTER THREE

Thomas was still debating what to do about Buckingham when, a few weeks later, Tuke waved a letter at him.

'The pope's secretary has written again, Your Eminence.' He broke open the huge red seal of the papal office, unfolding the letter and skimming the contents.

'What does he want this time?' Thomas asked, not looking up from his work.

'"Following his excommunication of Luther," blah, blah, blah,' Tuke read, '"it is our desire that his works be publicly burned, and a decree passed banning their reading." I wonder if Master More wrote to him.'

Thomas held out his hand for the letter, and Tuke put it in his palm. 'This is no more than I expected from the pope,' Thomas said, giving the letter only a cursory glance, 'whether or not Master More had a hand in it.' He tossed the letter aside.

'So, where and when for the burning?' Tuke asked, snatching up his pen to make a note. He frowned as Thomas didn't answer, and followed his master's gaze to the window where a pigeon, perched on the sill, was sticking its beak into its feathers to clean them. Surely, it wasn't the bird that was claiming his master's attention so wholeheartedly. 'Your Eminence?' he prompted.

'I'm thinking, Brian,' Thomas said.

'You are not minded to burn Luther's books?'

'I have nothing against burning them.'

'Then—?'

'But why should I?' Thomas mused, tapping his fingers against his lips.

'Because the pope requests it.' Tuke picked up another letter from before him on the desk. 'As does Archbishop Warham. He has written too.'

Thomas waved Warham's letter aside, having no desire to read the old man's ramblings. 'But the pope offers me nothing.'

'Then what are you thinking, Your Eminence?'

'That my legateship is due to expire soon.'

Tuke nodded, understanding. 'And you'd rather like it to continue?'

'I think that if the pope wants me to burn Luther's books, then the least he can do for me is renew my legateship for another…' he paused, considering.

'Two years, Your Eminence?' Tuke suggested.

Thomas grinned. 'Yes, another two years. Let us write back to the pope and say I am perfectly willing to perform a public burning of Luther's works, but that, as I will soon be deprived of my legateship, I fear I lack the necessary authority. However, if the pope can see his way to renewing my legateship for another two years, I will feel secure I do have the power and the book burning would be performed at the earliest opportunity. And… no, wait,' he halted Tuke as he began to write. 'Say it would be better if the renewed legateship had an unlimited authority. That way I need not bother His Holiness with frequent enquiries but may do as I see fit in the best interests of the Church.' There was no sound of quill on paper, and Thomas looked over to his secretary to find out why. Tuke's mouth was hanging open. 'You have some objection to writing that, Brian?'

'Your Eminence,' Tuke exclaimed, 'you are black-mailing the pope.'

'What a thing to say. I am negotiating a better position for myself, that is all. Now, if you please. ' He pointed at Tuke's pen. 'Write.'

'Yes, Your Eminence, of course,' Tuke said, and scribbled, head bent over the paper.

It was too cold to be sitting outside. Even the fire wasn't fierce enough to warm him. *That's what comes of burning Luther's books*, Thomas thought wryly, shoving his hands further up his sleeves. *All show, no substance.*

The pope had agreed to Thomas's demands, renewing the legateship for two years and giving him unlimited authority during that tenure. Thomas now had no reason or excuse not to burn Luther's books. It had taken weeks to gather enough books to make a bonfire, and the pile had been sitting in a Tower chamber. When they had been thrown down at the base of the cross and a torch put to them, the pages were so damp they hadn't been able to catch the flames, and kindling had to be thrown on top. It all felt to Thomas a little ridiculous.

He had expected a sizeable audience, but not that so many people would halt work to watch Luther's works go up in flames. It looked like all of London had come to St Paul's Cross to witness the conflagration. The people were below him as he sat on the dais beneath his canopy of estate, flanked by Archbishop Warham, Bishop Tunstall, the Imperial ambassador and the papal nuncio, who, Thomas knew, would report back to the pope as soon as it was all over. Well, the papal nuncio could write that Thomas had done his bit, that he'd burned the bloody books and issued an importation ban, and that the pope could stop bothering him about Luther.

Thomas squeezed his buttocks to encourage some feeling into them as Bishop Fisher's lectern was manoeuvred into position. Fisher looked happy. He hated Luther even more than the pope, even more than Master More, if that was possible, and he seemed to relish the opportunity to denounce the heretic.

Thomas cast a weary gaze over the crowd and unwittingly caught the eye of More, who was standing at the front of the crowd, arms folded, a smile on his face as the books went up in flames. More ambled over to Thomas, making only a token genuflection as he approached.

'You look cold, Your Eminence,' More said. 'Is this splendid fire not enough to warm you?'

'The fire can barely stay alight,' Thomas muttered. 'Enough to warm me? Not at all.'

'But hot enough to burn Luther's filth.'

'For all the good it will do.'

'It will do a great deal of good. This will tell the people the pope forbids the reading of Luther and such heretical works.'

'You think so? You do not think this sort of display only makes people curious? "What are we not being told?" they'll wonder, and they'll want to find out.'

'But if the books aren't there to be read, they can't read them, can they?' More persisted.

'There are a thousand ways books can enter this country, you know that,' Thomas said testily. 'This will not stop Luther being read entirely.'

'You must have faith, Your Eminence.'

'I have plenty of faith,' Thomas growled, sinking his chin into his collar, 'just not in the worth of this.'

'I agree that this is a mere drop in the ocean. If I had my way, it would be Luther himself in the flames.'

Thomas winced. 'Could you really watch a man burn to death?'

'Such a man as Luther, aye, and take pleasure in it.'

Thomas grimaced, hoping More would wander back to the crowd and leave him in peace. 'Quiet now,' he said. 'Bishop Fisher is about to speak.'

Fisher had grabbed the lectern with both hands and raised his chin to look over his audience. His dark eyes were like coals in his white face, and the strength of his voice as he began his address belied his seventy-odd years.

Thomas had forgotten how much Bishop Fisher liked the sound of his own voice and realised with dismay that they were in for a very long sermon. Fisher first praised Martin Luther for his learning and his desire to seek theological truth; then came the meat of his argument, when he denounced the monk's pride in believing he had the right to criticise the Church. He had much to say on this topic, and as the hours dragged by, the crowd thinned. Even Fisher realised he was losing his audience and cleared his throat to deliver his conclusion.

'Know this,' he said, pointing to the spectators who remained, 'I have warned you about the danger of heeding Martin Luther. If, despite this, anyone of you gives faith to him or any other heretic rather than to Jesus Christ and to the spirit of truth, or spreads Luther's vile teachings, then that person is sure to never pass through the gate to ever-lasting rest, which is every Christian's desire. Remember this day. May God watch over us, for ever and ever, Amen.'

The crowd repeated, 'Amen' and Fisher stepped aside, accepting the offer of a stool from one of his servants. He fell down onto it with a loud grunt of relief. Fisher was, Thomas mused, too old a man to be on his feet for so long.

He nodded a congratulation to the bishop, then got to his feet. Bidding his companions a good day, and deftly avoiding an invitation from Warham to join them for refreshments, Thomas made his way back to York Place.

'How did it go, Your Eminence?' Tuke asked as Thomas entered the office. 'Was Master More suitably mollified?'

'Master More was extremely happy, Brian, and only wished he could throw Martin Luther on the fire, too. But at least the pope can stop pestering me now. Luther's books were burned. Eventually. Like Luther, they resisted punishment. They were damp and needed more than a little encouragement.'

'So that's why you were so long. I did wonder.'

'No, what took so long was Bishop Fisher's sermon,' Thomas said with a sigh. 'It lasted four hours.'

'I'm surprised the old man had the strength to stand for so long,' Tuke laughed.

Thomas frowned as he took his seat at the desk. 'You'd be surprised at what old men are capable of, Brian,' he said sternly. Tuke was getting a little over-familiar of late, speaking without being spoken to first, making derisive comments about his betters, and Thomas thought he should probably do something about his secretary's lack of respect. It didn't do to let inferiors think they could treat their masters as equals. He sniffed, and his nose wrinkled at the smell of smoke on his silken robes. He doubted if his laundrywomen could get rid of the smell without damaging the silk. 'Is there anything to eat? My stomach has been grumbling for the past hour.'

'Here and waiting for you, Your Eminence,' Tuke said, depositing a tray beside Thomas. He whipped off the covering cloth to reveal a plate of manchet bread, a wedge of cheese and four slices of pork. 'Wine?'

Thomas nodded and picked up the bread, tearing it apart and biting off a mouthful as Tuke put a cup of wine on his desk. 'Anything important this morning, Brian?'

'A person turned up about an hour after you left for St Paul's, wanting to see you. I told him he would have to wait and that you'd see him upon your return.'

'How many times must I tell you?' Thomas snapped. 'I will see no one without an appointment. I can't just have people turning up and demanding I see them. It throws my whole day out.'

'I know that, Your Eminence,' Tuke said, contrition in his voice, 'but I thought you would want to see this man. You see, he was the duke of Buckingham's chancellor.'

Thomas looked up, his eyes narrowing. 'Was?'

'It seems the duke has dismissed him, but he didn't say why. His name is Robert Gilbert. Do you know him?'

'No, I don't think so,' Thomas said. 'You better show him in.'

Tuke hurried into the outer office, returning a moment later with a man who snatched the cap off his head and bowed to Thomas.

'Thank you for seeing me, Your Eminence,' he said.

Thomas jerked his head at Tuke. Tuke scurried to his

desk and took up his quill, ready to make notes of this meeting. Thomas studied his visitor. Robert Gilbert had evidently been on the road for at least two days, for his cloak was damp and muddied, and his jaw was dark with stubble.

'My secretary here tells me you were the duke of Buckingham's chancellor but have been dismissed from his service. Is that right?'

Gilbert nodded. 'I was dismissed two days ago.'

'Why were you dismissed?'

'Because I suggested to His Grace that he moderate his spending.'

Thomas's eyebrow rose. 'And you considered it your place to do so?'

Gilbert swallowed nervously. 'I was his chancellor, Your Eminence. He entrusted his accounts to me and his coffers were running dangerously low. Also…'

'Also?' Thomas prompted.

'It was what his money was being spent on that concerned me most. You see, much was being spent on liveries for his servants.'

'Personal liveries?' Thomas's tone was sharp. 'Despite the king expressly forbidding nobles from dressing their retainers in their own liveries?'

Gilbert nodded. 'That was the point I was trying to make to His Grace. But he said he would dress his servants how he pleased and to hell with the king.'

Both of Thomas's eyebrows rose. 'He said that, did he? Anything else?'

'Gambling debts.'

Thomas was disappointed. 'All nobles gamble.'

'His debts are excessive,' Gilbert protested. 'The duke simply cannot afford to lose money so profligately.

I sought to bring this to his attention and he dismissed me.'

Thomas studied him with curiosity. 'What do you expect me to do for you?'

'I had hoped…' Gilbert coloured and hung his head.

'That I would find you a position?' Thomas suggested.

'Is that not possible, Your Eminence?'

'Anything is possible, Master Gilbert.' Thomas considered. By informing on his former master, Gilbert had proved he could not be entirely trusted. *But then*, Thomas mused, *who could these days?* 'Something shall be found for you,' he decided. 'In the meantime, my steward will see you lodged and fed.' He nodded at Tuke, who took Gilbert's elbow and steered him out of the room.

'You already knew about the liveries, didn't you, Your Eminence?' Tuke asked as he closed the door.

Thomas nodded. 'Sir Charles Knyvet informed me a month ago, but it is good to have it confirmed by another party. I know the duke has spoken against the king on several occasions in the company of friends, as I've received a letter from another of my informants. Here.' Thomas held out a letter. 'Read for yourself.'

Tuke took it. '"The duke has been heard to say the king is cursed because of the execution of the earl of Warwick at his father's hands and will never have a male heir. That the king has no right to sit on the throne being descended merely from a Welsh steward. That Your Eminence has used sorcery to ensnare the king and that you act as his bawd and procurer, and that he will, given the chance, have you beheaded."' Tuke folded the letter back up and whistled. 'This is slanderous, Your Eminence.'

'Slanderous? Is that what you call it?' Thomas cried, annoyed by the whistle. 'The duke has spoken against the king. He has impugned the honour of his chief minister. He discredits the entire Tudor bloodline and suggests the king is not fit to sit on the throne of England. By God, Brian, I call that treason, not slander.'

'Of course, you are right, Your Eminence,' Tuke agreed, swallowing nervously. 'But he is the premier duke in this realm. We cannot bring a charge of treason against him lightly. Can we?'

'You rush ahead, Brian,' Thomas said. 'I cannot bring a charge of treason against anyone. I will inform the king of this latest information from Gilbert and he will decide what to do with the duke.'

'In that case, should I order your barge to be made ready?'

'Well, yes, Brian,' Thomas said in a tone that suggested the secretary shouldn't need to ask, 'I rather think you should.'

Henry was pacing up and down the privy chamber, cursing and raging.

Thomas glanced at Katherine sitting by the window, embroidery lying forgotten in her lap, her expression pained. She must have felt Thomas's gaze upon her for she turned her head towards him. He found her accusatory stare distinctly uncomfortable.

'My lord,' she called to Henry, 'please, do not upset yourself so. All you have been told is nothing, I am sure.'

'Nothing!' Henry yelled, storming over to her with such ferocity that she shifted back in her chair as if fearful of being struck. 'Buckingham is speaking falsehoods against me, challenging my right to sit on the throne of

England, calling my right hand a procurer of whores for my bed, and you call that nothing?'

Katherine reached up to touch his hand. 'I just meant that all this so-called evidence of Buckingham's treachery comes from dismissed servants and his,' she glared at Thomas, 'informants. We cannot trust such men to speak the truth. They will say anything, especially if they are paid to do so. And, my lord, you know Buckingham. You know he is loyal.'

Henry snatched his hand away. 'Oh yes, I know Buckingham. I know he hates me, resents me. Do you not recall last year when I visited him at Penshurst? He had given one of my servants his own livery to wear.'

'Yes, and you rightly reprimanded him. But it was done in error, my lord. Buckingham had not realised the man was your servant.'

Thomas could be silent no longer. Katherine was talking nonsense and he would not have Henry swayed by it. 'Forgive me, madam, but the duke could hardly have been ignorant of the fact. The man would have presented himself to the duke wearing the king's livery. The duke would have asked who his previous employer was and why he was no longer in his service.'

Katherine turned pointedly away from Thomas and back to Henry. 'You cannot believe everything this man tells you. He loathes the duke.'

'Are you quite mad? I think you must be to accuse Thomas of lying. Thomas is the only man I can trust,' Henry said, moving away to touch Thomas's arm.

Thomas thanked him with a smile. 'How do you wish to proceed, Your Majesty?'

Henry moved to the window and stared out of it, lost in thought. Thomas heard him tapping the windowsill, the rings on his fingers making a metallic knock with each beat. Thomas waited, glancing at Katherine out of the corner of his eye. She was waiting, too.

'Arrest him,' Henry said after a long moment. 'Arrest the duke.'

Thomas saw Katherine open her mouth to speak, probably to protest, but closed it again. He had expected Henry's decision, and he agreed with it. The duke had been a nuisance for too long. A spell, perhaps a long spell, under arrest would teach him not to push his luck any further. Then Buckingham could be released with a warning to behave, and he could scuttle off back to Thornbury and bother them no more.

Thomas bowed. 'I shall see to his arrest at once, Your Majesty.'

CHAPTER FOUR

Thomas had summoned Buckingham to London in the king's name, and Buckingham had come, suspecting nothing. He had even stopped at York Place to avail himself of Thomas's fine wine cellar. As he climbed back into his barge, intending to make for the court at Greenwich, Sir Henry Marney, the captain of the king's guard, got in with him. Placing him under arrest, Marney escorted Buckingham to the Tower.

Thomas watched the drama unfold from his office window. As soon as he received word from Marney that Buckingham was securely locked up, he set out for Greenwich to inform the king.

He found Henry in the garden with a bow in his hand. A small group of courtiers clustered around him, and they muttered disapprovingly as Thomas drew near. He was used to muttering courtiers and paid them no attention.

Henry lifted the bow and looked down the shaft of the arrow. Drawing the string back to his jaw, his eyes narrowed, lining up the tip of the arrow with the target set two hundred yards away. Instinctively, Thomas held his breath as the king loosed the arrow, and he watched it fly towards the butt. He had never learnt how to handle a bow, it not being required of scholarly priests at Magdalen College, and he felt a pang of envy as the arrow thudded into one of the target's inner rings. He doubted he would have had Henry's talent for archery, but it would have been pleasant to try.

A ripple of applause came from the courtiers, and Henry turned to Thomas with a satisfied smile on his face. 'Thought I saw you there.' Henry held out his arm, and a page hurried to take the bow from his hand and untie the leather guard around his forearm. 'You have news for me, Thomas?'

'I do,' Thomas nodded, and gestured with his eyes at the hovering courtiers to suggest his news was not for their ears.

Henry nodded and turned to the path. Thomas joined him.

'Buckingham?' Henry asked.

'The duke is in the Tower, awaiting your pleasure.'

'My pleasure is that he stands trial.'

Thomas halted. This was not what he had expected Henry to say. 'To stand trial, Your Majesty? On what charge?'

'On a charge of treason, of course. What else?'

'I understand his offences do tend towards treason,' he said, concerned by the turn this conversation had taken, 'but if his peers were to find the duke guilty, then the penalty would have to be death.'

'Do you think my mind is failing, Thomas, that you remind me of that?'

'Not at all, Your Majesty,' Thomas said hastily, 'but are you certain this is how you want to proceed? The duke is the realm's premier nobleman, second only to yourself. His execution may not go down well with certain members of your court.'

'You mean the Howards won't like it,' Henry grunted. 'To the devil with them. I am king here, Thomas, am I not?'

'Indeed you are, Your Majesty.'

'Then I will have my way. How soon can he be sent to trial?'

Thomas's mind was racing. This wasn't what he had wanted at all. 'The lords who will sit in judgement on him will need to be summoned. Many are in the country, so that will take at least a week. The witnesses to the duke's treasons will need to be brought to London and their statements taken, the indictment read…,' he trailed off, his mind busy with all that would have to be done. 'A month from today, I should say.'

'And will you hear the case in Star Chamber?'

'No, Your Majesty, the duke should stand trial in the court of the Lord High Steward of England at the Guild Hall.'

'Wherever you say, Thomas. Just tell me when so I know to be there.'

'You don't mean to appear at the duke's trial?' Thomas asked, horrified.

Henry glared at him. 'Of course I intend to appear. I want to look that devil in the eye.'

'Your Majesty, I don't think that would be wise. It is not the custom.'

'To hell with custom!' Henry cried. 'There has to be a first time for everything.'

'But it may look as if you are attempting to influence and intimidate the witnesses.'

'Me?' Henry cried incredulously, seemingly unaware of how imposing a figure he represented.

Thomas held up his hands. 'It would be better for you not to attend. I beg you not to. Rest assured, I will provide you with a full report on the trial.'

'Very well,' Henry said grudgingly, 'but it's a pity. I would like to see Buckingham's face when the guilty verdict is delivered. It will be a guilty verdict, Thomas?'

'Oh yes,' Thomas said with a sigh, understanding that was what Henry wanted and would be satisfied with none other. 'The duke will be found guilty.'

Thomas had made his way secretly to the Guild Hall, this being no day for pomp and ceremony. His scarlet robes had been replaced by a brown woollen cloak and his head covered by a black cap borrowed from Tuke. It had been many years since Thomas had worn such clothes and he rather resented the necessity, but he had no more business at the trial of the duke of Buckingham than Henry, and it was important not to be noticed. He could have stayed away, but curiosity had got the better of him.

And so he was closeted in a room above the main hall, alone, with only a jug of wine and a plate of almond biscuits to pass the time until eight o'clock. He paced the small room, unable to settle into his chair with its plump, inviting cushions that Tuke had so thoughtfully provided, until he heard movement below. Then he opened the door a crack, wincing as it creaked, and looked out.

Benches for the spectators were being set out. The wooden bar for the prisoner was put before the benches facing a long table and chairs where the twenty lords summoned to pass judgement on the duke would sit.

It was not long before those lords entered and took their seats. Suffolk, Dorset, Shrewsbury, Worcester, Oxford, Essex. These and lesser lords all took their places. Thomas Howard, duke of Norfolk, took the centre seat as befit the Lord High Steward of England, and Thomas squinted to examine his expression. It was decidedly grim, and Thomas knew that Howard, like so many of his peers, took no pleasure in the trial of one of their own.

Thomas returned to the chair, adjusting the cushions to support his lower back, and reached for the plate of biscuits. He had a little while before the trial would begin, and as he rested his head on the back of the chair, his mind turned to the Val d'Or. Despite the splendour of the occasion, despite the congratulations heaped upon Thomas by foreign kings, it had been a grave disappointment. All his hopes of creating something original and great between the powers of Europe had been dashed because of three men he could not control: his own supremely vain king, a serious young man of Spain with unlimited imperial ambitions, and a French popinjay. He shook his head. *Stop thinking about what might have been*, he chided himself. Peace simply wasn't possible, especially not now, with Henry's latest instructions to pursue a secret accord with Spain so they could one day fight the French together. *And*, Thomas thought ruefully, *if Henry changes his mind tomorrow and decides he wants to be friends with the French instead, I must endeavour to make it happen and act as if nothing is amiss.*

Thomas gave a deep sigh. It was so tiring, trying to keep up with the king's likes and dislikes these days, his changes of moods, his whims, his indulgences. What was the reason for this change? he wondered. Was it because Katherine had failed to give Henry an heir? Henry complained often to Thomas that he had no son to carry on the Tudor line and swore the fault lay with his wife. Katherine had certainly failed in her queenly duty. Though she had given the king several children, only one had survived, and that one a girl, useful only for making a good marriage. But Thomas suspected the age difference between Henry and Katherine was also now playing a part in driving them apart. When they had been younger, six years had seemed nothing. Katherine had been comely and pretty then, and Henry, amorous and chivalrous, keen to play the lover and gallant knight rescuing the poor maiden. But Katherine had grown fat, and his spies told him her menses had become irregular. How much longer did Katherine have to provide Henry with an heir? One year, two? Not long enough, and certainly not without danger to herself. Not that it would matter if she didn't survive. Queens died in childbirth as easily as common women, and they could be just as easily replaced. Now, there was an idea!

A banging of wood on stone brought Thomas back to himself. He rose and put his eye to the crack in the door. Buckingham had been brought to the bar and the king's counsel was standing, a long sheet of parchment held out before him. His stentorian voice carried to Thomas's ears up in his eyrie.

'Edward Stafford, duke of Buckingham, you have been indicted for high treason. That you have traitorously imagined and conspired against your king to shorten his life. How say you to this charge?'

Buckingham gripped the bar with both hands. 'The charge is false. I never conspired to bring death to the king.'

'Witnesses have come forward to testify to your treasons. They have given statements as to what you said and did in their hearing and sight.'

'What witnesses?' Buckingham scoffed. 'Bring them before me. Let them dare recount their lies to my face.'

Thomas, expecting the duke to demand he be allowed to face his accusers, had prepared the witnesses, telling them how to behave, what to say, and to give their testimonies without fear. Knyvet, Gilbert and the others Thomas had collected were called in, and one by one gave their testimony. Not one of them met the duke's eyes, though he seemed to try to bore into their very souls with his. They spoke of conversations they had heard, during which the duke had complained the king preferred to reward his favourites, callow youths of no good station, rather than his faithful and experienced nobles, and that the king's lack of an heir was God's punishment for Henry VII's killing of the young and innocent earl of Warwick when he took the throne from Richard III.

And then they told of the conversations that made Thomas's blood boil, when the duke had declared that he, Cardinal Wolsey, had acted as the king's pimp and procurer, finding women to warm Henry's bed and keep him occupied, leaving Thomas to do as he pleased, and that Thomas had such hatred for all the king's nobles that he would do all he could to bring them down.

Though he had heard the accusations already, to endure their public recitation made Thomas's fists clench. Calumny. They were vile and vicious accusations with absolutely no foundation. Had the king's bedfellows ever been his concern? What did it matter to him who the king consorted with? He just had to deal with the unfortunate consequences of Henry's lust, as he had with that poor, stupid girl, Elizabeth Blount, when she fell pregnant with

Henry's child. Packed off to have his son in secret, then sent away to marry with a commoner, of no further interest to the king.

It took Buckingham a full hour to answer all the charges made against him. He spoke well, Thomas acknowledged, so well indeed that many of those listening had tears in their eyes and shook their heads that the duke should be brought to such a pass.

But the time came for the lords to retire and consider their verdict. Thomas watched as they filed out of the hall to a private chamber just beyond and the door close upon them. He turned his gaze back to Buckingham, who was hunched over the bar, head down. Where was the proud duke now? Thomas mused.

The lords did not deliberate for long. Less than an hour later, the chamber door opened, and they trooped out to take up their seats once more. Buckingham got to his feet.

Howard cleared his throat and addressed his fellow judges. 'You have now heard the charges laid against the prisoner. What say you of Edward Stafford, duke of Buckingham, touching these high treasons? Is he guilty or not guilty?'

One by one, the lords put their right hands to their hearts and solemnly declared, 'I say he is guilty.' Some were so choked up they could barely get the words out, others rushed over them, as if they wanted to get the hateful sentence out of their mouths.

Howard turned to Buckingham, who was staring at his fellow peers in disbelief. 'Edward Stafford, you have been found guilty of high treason by your peers.' He broke off, putting a hand to his mouth, then astonished everyone by suddenly bursting into tears. He drew a handkerchief from his sleeve and wiped his tears away. Sniffing loudly, he blinked a few times, then began again. 'You will be taken to Tower Hill tomorrow morning, there to be hanged, cut down while still alive, your member to be cut off and cast into the fire, your bowels burned, your head severed and your body quartered, the four parts to be divided and displayed according to the king's will. May God have mercy on your soul. Amen.'

A Yeoman Warder lifted the axe that had been on the table before Buckingham during the trial and turned the blade deliberately towards the condemned man. Buckingham let out a wail, then grabbed the bar once more.

'I am no traitor, my lords,' he cried desperately, 'but I do not blame you for the verdict you have delivered here today. May God forgive you for my death, as I do.'

Guards led him away, sobbing, and Thomas noted that not one of his peers was able to watch him go. That boded ill, Thomas thought. The trial of Buckingham was supposed to terrify them into having absolute loyalty to the king; instead, Thomas feared it had made them mutinous.

Gathering up his cloak, Thomas hurried down the back stairs. He had to see Henry without delay.

Henry rushed towards him as Thomas entered the privy chamber.

'Is it over? What happened? What did Buckingham say?'

'Yes, it's over,' Thomas said. 'The verdict has been given.'

'And?' Henry demanded impatiently.

'Guilty, as you instructed.'

Henry drew back, frown lines creasing his forehead. 'I

did not instruct, Thomas. His peers found Buckingham guilty because he is guilty.'

'Of course,' Thomas said, bowing his head at his slip. 'I spoke amiss. Forgive me, it has been a long few days.'

Henry grunted and moved away.

'The duke has been sentenced to be executed tomorrow morning at eleven,' Thomas continued. 'That is, if Your Majesty means to have his head off.' *Please, please, say you just mean to frighten him by keeping him imprisoned for a while.*

Henry grinned, fell down into his chair, and hooked his right leg over the arm. 'You want me to pardon him, don't you?'

'I assumed you always meant to,' Thomas lied.

'You're too keen to make assumptions about me, Thomas,' Henry chided. 'Why do you care whether the duke lives or dies? You have no reason to love him, especially after the way he's treated you.' He chuckled. 'Remember the time he poured a basin of water over your shoes in front of me and the emperor?'

'Yes, Your Majesty, I remember,' Thomas said tightly. 'And you are correct, I have no love for the duke. But I have a great love for you, and I speak in the duke's defence only for your benefit.'

'My benefit?'

'Your nobles were not at all happy to find the duke guilty of treason. My lord of Norfolk wept when he sentenced him, and the other lords were much moved by his declaration of innocence.'

'Norfolk wept?' Henry scoffed. 'What the devil has got into the man?'

'And as I left the hall,' Thomas went on, 'the people were muttering foul words.'

'Against me?' Henry was indignant.

'No,' Thomas admitted, 'against me. They blame me for the duke's downfall. Oh, that is nothing,' he hastened to say as Henry's expression darkened, 'I am used to being disliked, but it does make me wonder if they will move on to speaking disparagingly of you if the duke is executed on the morrow. No doubt they believe you will pardon him.'

Henry's foot tapped the air as he considered these words, and Thomas kept quiet, hoping the king would see sense.

'No,' Henry said eventually.

'No, Your Majesty?' Thomas queried uneasily.

'Let the people say what they want. I want the duke dead, Thomas. He's been a constant thorn in my side. My father would have had his head long before now had he still been here. I have been merciful long enough. Buckingham will die tomorrow.'

There was something in the way Henry said those words that told Thomas there was no point in arguing. 'And what of his family, Your Majesty?' he asked. 'The duchess, his child?'

'What of them?' Henry asked irritably. 'I don't mean to have their heads too, if that's what you're thinking.'

'No, I wasn't thinking that. I mean, will you be writing the customary condolence letters to them?'

'Condolence letters? Why the devil should I? I'm not at all sorry he'll be dead.'

'I think, if you will forgive me, Your Majesty, that regardless of your feelings, it would be wise to write letters of condolence to the duke's widow and son.' *Just write the damn letters,* Thomas willed irritably. 'It is but a little thing to do, Your Majesty, and it would look well to your other nobles. Were you not to write those letters,

42

letters of sympathy to a woman and child who have done you no personal wrong…' Thomas spread his hands as if the rest of his sentence didn't need to be said.

Henry made a face. 'I am no tyrant, Thomas. I don't hold grudges against women and children. I'll write the letters.'

Thomas said a silent prayer of thanks. 'And if I may make a suggestion, Your Majesty? It would be most magnanimous of you if you were to grant the duke's widow a pension for the rest of her life.' He hurried on before Henry could voice a protest. 'The duke's profligacy has left her coffers in a parlous state. It would do your reputation no good if you were to allow the duchess to become destitute.'

Henry nodded. 'I would not see a lady come to such a pass. See to it, Thomas.'

'I will, Your Majesty. Thank you, Your Majesty.' Thomas bowed and backed out of the room, disappointed he hadn't been able to persuade the king to pardon the duke and trying to work out when Henry had become so cruel.

As the doors closed upon Henry, the answer came to Thomas. Henry had not become cruel; he had always been so. Had he not executed his father's tax collectors, Empson and Dudley, when he ascended the throne merely to curry favour with the people? Yes, cruelty had been in him then. It was just that Henry had fooled everyone into thinking he was a kind and merciful prince.

And I have been fooled more than anyone, Thomas thought miserably as he made his way down the corridor. *But my eyes are open now. It's clear Henry will not allow himself to be crossed any longer.*

CHAPTER FIVE

'Are these reports accurate?' Louise de Savoie asked, peering at the papers her son had given her to read.

'I am assured they are, Mother,' King Francis said. 'All the reports we have received say the same thing. Spain is planning to move against us, and with the pope's support. Both Charles and His Holiness have their sights set on capturing Milan.'

Louise groaned and cradled her stomach as a pain shot through her insides.

'Mother?' Francis said, reaching out to touch her hand. 'What's wrong?'

'It's nothing, darling,' she said with a wan smile. 'It will pass.'

Her words didn't reassure her son, and she cursed herself for letting him see her pain. He had enough to worry about without fretting over her. But why, why must there always be conflict between their country and others? What was it about men that always made them want more than they had? Oh, how pleasant it would be to have peace for a little while. A thought struck her. There was one man living who she knew would rather have peace than war.

'Cardinal Wolsey,' she declared. 'He will not want the pope and Charles in an alliance any more than we do. He will help us.'

Francis frowned. 'How can Wolsey help us?'

'The Treaty of London,' Louise cried, shaking her head at her son. 'We all signed that treaty, didn't we? Remember the terms, Francis. If any one country takes offensive action against any of the signatories, the other signatories must come to that country's aid. Spain has taken offensive action by entering into an alliance with the pope against us. The treaty compels England to stand with us.'

Francis made a face. 'Charles obviously doesn't care about that treaty. He will find some way to wriggle out of it. And Wolsey, Mother, is adept at wriggling, too.'

Louise shook her head. 'Wolsey wants peace, my boy.'

'So you say, but remember what happened last year after our meeting in the Val d'Or. The minute we parted, Henry and Wolsey were off to have a secret meeting with Charles.'

'Not so secret,' Louise pointed out with a wry smile. 'But anyway, that meeting was Queen Katherine's doing, not Wolsey's. I have it on good authority that Wolsey tried to persuade King Henry not to go, but Katherine insisted, and the cardinal had no choice but to comply.'

'Since when does Wolsey do anything he doesn't want to do?' Francis scoffed.

'Ah, that's where you've read him quite wrong, my boy,' Louise said. 'True, Wolsey always looks out for Wolsey, but he never forgets who he serves. In the end, he will always do what Henry wants, even if he thinks it a bad idea. Do you want my advice?'

'Always, Mother,' Francis said, taking hold of her hand and pressing it to his cheek.

She smiled and brushed her fingers against his warm skin. 'We cannot rely entirely on support from England, I agree with you there, but we must make use of Wolsey and ask for England's support. But in the meantime, we must do what we can ourselves. So, we build ships. In that way, when Charles makes his move – and he will move against us, my boy, make no mistake – we are able to respond in kind. And while we're waiting for that to happen, I don't think it would hurt if we made a few aggressive gestures of our own.'

'How do you mean?'

'You have ordered your nobles not to encroach upon Spanish territory, lest it provoke reprisals. Rescind that order. Let your nobles off their leashes. Let them loose wherever they wish to roam. They'll enjoy that, and it will enable us to test just how good Spain's military capabilities are. They may not be nearly as advanced as we've been led to believe.'

'Allowing my nobles to raid Spanish-held lands might lead to all out war, Mother,' Francis warned.

Louise sighed and leant back in her chair. 'Yes, my boy, I'm afraid it might. But then, isn't that the way of the world?'

Thomas bounced on the balls of his feet impatiently. He had been standing in the Presence Chamber at Greenwich for the past hour, long past the time Henry was supposed to meet with the Spanish ambassadors to discuss the current European situation, and Thomas could sense their irritation as they talked amongst themselves at the opposite side of the room.

It was foolish, he thought, to keep them waiting for such a petty reason; Henry had decided to have his dinner before meeting the ambassadors rather than after, as Thomas had planned. It was so frustrating. Did Henry not realise the gravity of the situation between France and Spain? Both Charles and Francis, quarrelling amongst themselves, were pressing for England to honour the terms of the Treaty of London and support them. It didn't matter to either that both could be considered aggressors; they each believed themselves to be injured parties and looked to Henry to make all well again.

Thomas signalled to the pageboy standing by the doors, and the boy hurried over. 'Go to the king's apartments,' he told him. 'Send my compliments and remind the king the Imperial ambassadors are waiting to see him.'

The boy scurried away to deliver the message. Thomas noticed the ambassadors were looking in his direction and made his way towards them.

'Your Eminence,' one of them said at his approach, 'where is the king?'

'The king has been unavoidably detained, Your Excellency. I am sure he will be here soon.'

'I hope so. My master will be displeased if he feels we are being ignored.'

'I assure you, the king is most eager to receive you. Ah,' Thomas held a hand to his ear at the sound of voices in the corridor beyond, 'I believe the king is coming now.'

They turned and Thomas saw with relief that Henry had indeed arrived, flanked by Compton, Bryan and Carew. It was probably they who had convinced Henry the ambassadors could wait on his leisure. Thomas excused himself and hurried over to Henry.

'Your Majesty, you are more than an hour late for this meeting,' he chided.

Bryan stepped forward, pushing in between Thomas and Henry. 'Do you know, that sounds like you're telling the king off, Your Eminence? What do you say to that, Your Majesty? Do you think it right?'

Thomas cursed himself; Bryan spoke true. What was he thinking to rebuke the king so? He knew he should have chosen his words more carefully, but frustration had got the better of him. Henry was looking at Bryan with interest and Thomas knew he must right the wrong he had committed.

'Forgive me, Your Majesty. It is, of course, for you to decide when you grant an audience, but the gentlemen are growing restless, and I know how eager you are to calm this situation between France and Spain.'

'I'm here now,' Henry said, ignoring the blatant untruth Thomas had just spoken. 'Let's get on with it, shall we?' He moved to the chair set beneath his canopy of estate and sat down expectantly.

Thomas waved the ambassadors over and they came a little stiffly, as if determined to show the delay had annoyed them. He cleared his throat and addressed Henry.

'Your Majesty, the Emperor Charles has sent his ambassadors to inform you of the recent territorial encroachments made by certain French subjects into Span-ish-owned territory. Henry d'Albret has taken possession of Navarre, which, as we all know, was land claimed by King Ferdinand of Spain, and Robert de la Marck has declared war on the emperor and invaded Burgundy.'

The ambassador cut in. 'We are here to remind Your

Majesty that according to the terms of the Treaty of London, England is duty-bound to intervene and support Spain in this uncalled-for aggression by France.'

Henry frowned, and Thomas hoped he hadn't forgotten what they had agreed in their meeting that morning. 'As I understand it, sir,' Henry said, 'these encroachments are the work of but two men acting alone. We have no proof King Francis had anything to do with them.'

'What evidence do we need?' the ambassador cried. 'King Francis has not condemned their actions nor ordered them to withdraw. That is proof enough he has sanctioned them.'

'I do not deny the encroachments are uncalled for,' Henry conceded. 'The French are damnably unruly, are they not, Your Eminence?'

This was Thomas's cue. 'Indeed, Your Majesty. And of course, we will speak with the French about this matter. In the meantime….' His eyes widened at Henry meaningfully.

'Yes,' Henry nodded, 'in the meantime, Your Excellency, we advise Charles remains on the defensive until we have talked some sense into the French. In fact,' and Henry narrowed his eyes at Thomas, 'we shall send His Eminence to talk to them.'

Thomas's breath caught in his throat. This wasn't part of the plan. They had never discussed him being sent to talk sense into the French. 'I, Your Majesty?'

'Yes, Thomas,' Henry said with enthusiasm. 'If you were to go to Calais and meet with Francis, I'm sure we could clear this matter up in no time at all.'

Henry's friends were sniggering. Was this their idea? Thomas wondered. Was this why Henry had insisted on having his dinner before meeting with the ambassadors, so they could play a trick on him? To hell with them. Yes, he didn't want to go, and yes, it would be a complete waste of time, but he was damned if he was going to give them the pleasure of seeing him plead with the king not to be sent to Calais.

Thomas smiled at Henry and turned to the ambassadors to smile at them too. 'If that is your wish, Your Majesty, of course, I will go and do what I can. It will be an honour.'

Henry and Thomas said goodbye to the Spanish ambassadors and retired to the privy chamber. Henry headed straight for the table by the window where there was a pack of cards and a pile of gold pieces. He sat down and shuffled the cards while Thomas hovered nearby.

'That went well, didn't it?' Henry said.

'Yes, although I wasn't expecting to be sent to Calais, Your Majesty,' Thomas said stiffly.

Henry chuckled. 'I know, but the idea just came to me. Call it a moment of inspiration. What better representative to send than you, Thomas? Both Charles and Francis hold you in such high regard that every word you utter is heeded.'

There was no persuading him, Thomas could see that, and resolved to not even try. 'You do wish me to persuade both of them to stop provoking one another with these petty skirmishes, then?'

'Well,' Henry said with a shy grin, 'I'm not sure we should go as far as that. Just make a good show, that's all.'

Thomas was confused. 'A good show of what?'

'Thomas,' Henry said in an exasperated tone, 'are you being deliberately obtuse?'

Thomas opened his mouth to reply, but Henry went on.

'You make a good show of doing all you can to reconcile Francis and Charles to putting up with one another.'

'Forgive me, Your Majesty, but that implies you wish them not to be reconciled.'

'Why the devil would I wish that?' Henry grinned.

'Then on whose side will we fall?'

'With Charles, of course. Francis has played right into our hands with this unprovoked aggression of his nobles.'

Thomas nodded. 'I see.'

'Come now, Thomas, don't be so glum,' Henry chided. 'The plain truth of the matter is that we cannot trust Francis. The way he behaved at the Val d'Or last year proved that.'

You mean when you challenged him to a wrestling match, and he beat you, Thomas thought bitterly. *You'll never forgive that blow to your pride, will you?*

'It was an admirable ambition, your universal peace,' Henry said. 'How I wish it could come true, but there can be no peace with France, not now. Charles knows it, the pope knows it. Time you realised it too, Thomas.'

'But what about the Treaty of London?'

'A piece of paper, Thomas, nothing more.'

'So, when I arrive in Calais, you wish me to, what, exactly?' Thomas asked, trying not to let his disappointment show.

'Delay matters,' Henry said. 'Allow the French to think we are doing all we can to reconcile them with Spain. Make them think Spain wants to negotiate. Meanwhile—'

'Meanwhile, Charles will be doing all he can to make war against France,' Thomas finished sadly.

Henry grinned. 'You see, Thomas? I don't need to tell you anything.'

. . .

Thomas sorted through the papers stacked on the large table by the window, making a pile of some, discarding others on the floor to be cleared up later. He was probably taking too many documents with him, but it was impossible to know which he would need and which he wouldn't while he was away.

He looked up as Tuke came into the office. 'Brian, I want regular reports. What's happening in the palace, what's happening in the law courts, what's happening in the country. You understand? I've arranged for all despatches to come to me at Calais first, then to be forwarded here for you to deal with as appropriate. I'm sure there's much I've forgotten to do, but we'll have to deal with those matters as they arise.'

Tuke said he would do as instructed, then studied Thomas for a long moment. 'You don't want to go to Calais, do you?'

Thomas sighed and threw the papers he held onto the table. 'No, I don't. Oh, God, it's all going to be such a waste of time.'

'But I would have thought you would be in favour of trying to calm things down between France and Spain.'

'I am all for that, but the king does not share my desire.' Thomas wiped his damp forehead with a clammy hand. 'The king wants an alliance with Spain. He's not interested in peace with France.'

'Because of the queen's influence?' Tuke wondered. 'She wants England to have an alliance with her nephew and is doing all she can to promote it?'

That thought had crossed Thomas's mind. Even though he had closed most of her channels of communication with her relatives abroad, Thomas knew Katherine still managed to smuggle out messages to them, and there seemed to be nothing he could do to stop her.

'Perhaps,' he said, 'but the king is not such a fool as to let blood interfere with policy. He knows the pope is siding with the emperor and Henry would rather be the friend of a friend of the pope than a friend to Francis who has the pope and the emperor against him.'

'Is there not sense in that?'

'You might think so, Brian, and yet you might think it makes more sense to not take sides at all.'

'I don't think we live in that kind of world, Your Eminence.'

'I agree. We must take a side. I just need to work out which one. Oh well, I better get on.' Thomas went to the door and opened it. He paused, his hand on the handle. 'Before I forget, Brian. Give me the Great Seal.'

Tuke stared at him. 'The Seal, Your Eminence?'

'Yes. I'm taking the Seal with me.'

'But the Great Seal is not supposed to leave England.'

'Just get me the Seal.'

'But I cannot—'

'Enough!' Thomas yelled, slamming his hand against the door frame. Twelve pairs of eyes turned on him from the outer office and Thomas closed the door on his clerks. 'I will take the Great Seal with me to Calais, Brian. I will be away for weeks, perhaps months, and I dare not leave it here. God knows what might happen in my absence, what foolish laws or edicts the king's friends may convince him to enact. If the Great Seal is not here, nothing can be ratified.' Tuke still looked unsure and Thomas's anger cooled, understanding the position he might put his secretary in when it was discovered the Great Seal was gone. 'It will be on my responsibility, Brian,' he promised. 'Now, please, give it to me.'

Tuke fetched the velvet bag from the box he kept locked beneath his desk. He handed it gingerly to Thomas. 'What shall I say if anyone should ask for it?'

'You tell the truth. You say I have it in Calais.' Thomas smiled and shook his head. 'No one will ask for it, Brian. Don't worry.'

CHAPTER SIX

'Still feeling poorly?' Thomas More asked, coming up to stand beside Thomas as he leant over the side of the boat and retched into the sea. 'I don't know why being on the water troubles you so much. It never bothers me.'

Thomas straightened slowly, eyes closed, his head swimming. 'If I'd know you were going to gloat, Master More, I should not have asked you to come.'

More grinned and turned his face out to sea. 'It's not even that rough.'

A napkin suddenly appeared in front of Thomas and he pushed the hand that held it away angrily. 'God's Death, George, must you shove it in my face?'

'My apologies, Your Eminence,' Cavendish said, his face colouring. 'I thought… you're rather flushed… you're sweating—'

'Yes, yes,' Thomas said irritably, 'I'm… oh, God…,' and he bent over the rail to vomit again. When there was nothing left to come up, Thomas straightened and Cavendish tentatively offered the napkin again. Thomas took it and wiped his mouth, thanking his gentleman usher with a nod.

'I can see Calais,' More said, squinting into the distance. 'Another fifteen minutes, I should say, and we'll be there.'

'Thank God for that,' Thomas muttered. 'Help me below, George. I must tidy myself before we disembark. I cannot be seen in this state.'

Cavendish gave him his arm and steered Thomas down the stairs and into his cabin. Thomas sat on the edge of the bunk and watched him pour water into a silver bowl and sprinkle in a handful of rose petals. He set a clean linen towel by the bowl and brought it over to Thomas.

'I had not realised how badly sea travel affects you, Your Eminence,' Cavendish said as Thomas dipped his hands in the water and patted his face. 'I recall Master Tuke telling me how you were accustomed to suffer when at sea, but he must have rather understated the matter.'

'I don't remember ever feeling this bad,' Thomas said, wiping his face with the towel.

'And yet Master More is right. The sea is not so very rough. Perhaps it is not seasickness, but something else.'

Thomas was about to contradict Cavendish when he considered his words. He recalled he had been feeling under the weather – tired, sweaty – before he ever stepped foot on the ship. Was George right? Was this not seasickness at all, but something else, something worse?

Thomas took the clove-studded orange Cavendish held out to him. He put it to his nose and breathed in, hoping the fresh citrus scent would make him feel better. It didn't, and he closed his eyes and prayed. *Oh God, don't let me be ill. Not now.*

Cavendish broke into his thoughts. 'Who will be at this arbitration, Your Eminence? Anyone we know?'

Thomas smiled at his servant's use of 'we'. 'The Imperial ambassador, Gattinara, whom I have not yet had the pleasure of meeting, and the French ambassador, Duprat, whom I have.'

'Neither King Francis nor the Emperor Charles will be present?' Cavendish sounded disappointed.

'This isn't a matter for kings to discuss in person.'

'That's a shame. If they were both present for the discussions, with your help, an agreement would soon be reached and your universal peace idea could be allowed to flourish.'

'What faith you have in me, George.' Thomas took a sip of the wine Cavendish offered. 'You must lower your expectations of our mission here. We are here to delay an inevitable war between France and Spain, and to prevent England from being dragged into it. My hope for peace in Europe...' he shrugged, wincing as his muscles protested. 'It was a good idea that has come to nothing.'

'I am sorry for it. I thought it a most laudable ambition.'

'Bless you, George,' Thomas said, patting Cavendish's arm. 'If only there were more men like you, the world would be a better place.'

Within the fifteen minutes More had predicted, the ship dropped anchor in the harbour and Thomas and his party clambered into a small boat to be rowed ashore. Thomas kept his eyes closed, feeling his stomach lurch with every rise and fall the boat endured, and wished fervently for solid ground beneath his feet. It seemed an eternity but was probably no more than five minutes before the rowboat bumped against the jetty. Thomas climbed out, not waiting to be helped, desperate to make it onto land. His legs were unsteady as he stepped onto the wooden planks of the jetty, and he held onto the end post until his head stopped swimming.

'Better now, Your Eminence?' Cavendish asked.

Thomas shook his head, convinced now what he was suffering from was not simple seasickness. 'I need to get to the governor's residence with all haste.'

'Are you truly ill?' Cavendish asked, worry in his voice. 'It wasn't just the sea?'

'I think I've been poisoned, George,' Thomas said, and heard Cavendish's astonished gasp.

A litter was waiting for him on the dock and Cavendish bundled him into it, exhibiting a quite astonishing confidence Thomas had not thought him capable of by ordering the servants to make all haste in conveying its occupant to the residence in a loud, authoritative voice. Thomas lay back on the cushions, taking deep breaths, the smell of Calais bringing back memories he'd rather forget. It was an unpleasant smell, arising from the detritus left behind by the ships that loaded and unloaded their cargo in Calais. Time was when it was Thomas's business, as secretary to the governor, to know the details of every barrel and crate that went on and came off the merchant ships. What a tedious time that had been.

But not a waste of time. He had learnt an enormous amount about commerce and how the common man thought, which gave him an advantage over his fellow councillors on the Privy Council. They were all nobles and knights who had no idea about trading in commodities, no notion what it was like to have to worry about harvests or diseased livestock, to negotiate prices and understand supply chains, to know how much cargo a ship could carry and where the hidden compartments for smuggled goods were. Commonplace knowledge, certainly, but valuable.

It took almost half an hour to reach the residence, a half hour of spasms in his stomach, pains in his head, and aches in his bones. The litter was set down and Cavendish enlisted men to haul Thomas out and onto his feet.

'We're here,' Cavendish said, putting Thomas's arm around his shoulders without asking permission. He led him inside the residence. Their feet echoed on the flagstones and every step jolted through Thomas's body.

'Get me to my bed,' Thomas croaked, 'and fetch the doctor.'

'Your Eminence!' a voice cried.

Thomas looked up and saw Antoine Duprat, his arms spread wide in greeting, coming out of a doorway to their left.

'What is this?' The French ambassador asked, looking Thomas up and down. 'Are you not well?'

It was Cavendish who answered. 'Forgive me, sir, but I must get His Eminence to bed.'

Duprat stepped forward to block their way. 'But this is grave news, indeed. Will you be well enough to meet—?'

'Sir, I must protest,' Cavendish began, but Thomas gave his hand a feeble squeeze.

'It's all right, George,' he said. 'My dear Antoine, I shall be well enough when I have had a little rest.'

'That is a great relief,' Duprat said. 'It is urgent I speak with you. The Imperial ambassador—'

'Antoine,' Thomas snapped, feeling as if the floor was moving beneath him, 'I cannot talk now.'

'You will excuse us, sir,' Cavendish said, and pushed Duprat out of the way.

That was the last thing Thomas remembered distinctly. What followed was a blur, from climbing the stairs to the bedchamber prepared for him to being put into bed. The next thing he knew, he was opening his eyes and looking at a man standing by the window staring into a pisspot.

'Have I been poisoned?' Thomas croaked.

Cavendish appeared out of nowhere and gently lifted him up into a sitting position to put a horn cup of water to his lips. 'The doctor thinks not, Your Eminence,' he said, gesturing at the man by the window.

The doctor came towards the bed. 'I see no sign of poison in your urine nor in your stool.'

Thomas had no memory of visiting the close stool, and he wondered with some embarrassment if he had soiled himself in his sleep. He glanced up at Cavendish and his usher's avoiding eyes confirmed this to be so.

'Then what is it?' Thomas asked, easing himself back against the goose-feather pillows. 'What's wrong with me?'

'Your man here tells me you suffer from seasickness, Your Eminence,' the doctor said.

'This is more than seasickness,' Thomas said, nodding for another sip of water.

The doctor set the pisspot down. 'Do you have a particular reason to fear poisoning?'

'A man in my position always has enemies, doctor.'

'Well, I admit my knowledge of poisons is scant, but I believe that if you had been poisoned, you would be dead by now.'

Thomas realised the doctor was right. Poisons were

fast acting, and he had taken no antidote. 'So, I will recover?'

The doctor nodded. 'With rest, I believe you will.'

Thomas laughed, a weak, scornful noise. 'Rest is one luxury I do not have.' He told the doctor he could go, and Cavendish showed him out. An image came back to Thomas. 'I seem to remember Duprat wanted to talk to me, or did I dream that, George?'

Cavendish made a face. 'You didn't dream it. He's been here, knocking on the door every hour to see how you fare. I've kept him out so far, but he may force his way in if he doesn't see you soon.'

'Keep him out for as long as you can,' Thomas said, closing his eyes as he leant his head back. 'I do need to rest a little longer.'

'More than a little, Your Eminence,' Cavendish said sternly. 'At least until tomorrow.'

How like Joan he sounds, Thomas thought as he drifted off. 'Whatever you say, George,' he murmured. 'I put myself entirely in your hands.'

Tomorrow seemed to come too soon, but Thomas could not allow himself to lie abed any longer and he threw back the bedclothes and called Cavendish to help him dress.

'Are you certain this is wise, Your Eminence?' Cavendish asked, looking at him askance. 'You still look very pale.'

'Wise or not, I cannot be seen to be unfit to conduct this wretched business.' Cavendish held out his dressing gown and Thomas slid his arms into the sleeves. 'I actually seem to have something of an appetite, George. I think I could manage a small plate of meat.'

61

'At once, Your Eminence.' Cavendish made for the door, but then hesitated, his hand on the knob. 'If you are intent on returning to work, I suppose I should give you this.' He reached inside his doublet and drew out a letter.

Thomas stared at the red wax. 'That is an Imperial seal, George.'

'It arrived yesterday, but you weren't well enough to read, so I kept hold of it.'

Thomas snatched the letter out of his hand. 'It is not for you to decide when I look at my letters. Do you understand me, George? You are my gentleman usher, not my secretary, not my wife, not my father, not my king.' Cavendish's shoulders drooped and he hung his head. Thomas sighed. He could never stay angry at Cavendish for long. He broke open the seal and unfolded the letter. 'Just don't try to do my thinking for me, George, that's all I ask. Now, bring me that food.'

Thomas moved back to the bed to read the letter. Cavendish returned a few minutes later with a tray bearing a gold plate of beef, a gold jug of wine and a goblet. He set the tray on the bed and placed a napkin over Thomas's shoulder.

Thomas cursed and Cavendish asked, 'Is something wrong, Your Eminence?' glancing worriedly at the tray. 'Have I not brought what you asked for?'

'The food is fine, George,' Thomas assured him. 'It's this letter. The emperor wants a private meeting in Bruges as soon as possible.' He refolded the letter and put it to one side. 'I shall have to go, though what Duprat will say, I don't know. Send my secretary to me so we can begin making the travel arrangements, and then bring Duprat here.'

'He's outside, asking to see you.'

'Then show him in, George.' Thomas took a bite of the beef, chewing slowly, testing his stomach. Duprat entered.

'At last,' the French ambassador cried. 'I've been asking that man of yours,' he jerked his head at Cavendish, 'to see you for days.'

'I've been ill, Antoine. I haven't been well enough to see anyone.' Thomas gestured for him to take a seat.

'But you can continue?' Duprat asked, looking him up and down.

'I am,' Thomas nodded, aware Duprat was not concerned for his health, just for his ability to mediate, 'but there will be some brief delay before we can begin.'

Duprat frowned. 'There has already been a delay.'

'Alas, I cannot help it. I must leave soon.'

'But you've only just arrived. Your king cannot want you back already.'

'Not to return to England,' Thomas said, deciding it was best to tell Duprat the truth about where he was going. 'I have to leave for Bruges today.'

Duprat's expression darkened. 'The emperor, I understand, is at Bruges.'

'He is, and he has requested that I meet with him there.' Thomas held up his hands. 'I know what you are going to say, Antoine, but I truly believe it is for the best.'

'How can it be for the best?' Duprat spluttered indignantly.

'You and I both want the same thing. If not peace, then a truce. And the only way I can achieve this is to keep everyone talking. If that means I have to go to Bruges, I will do it. If King Francis asked me to go to Paris to see him, I would do that too.'

'But King Francis isn't asking you to go to Paris,' Duprat protested. 'He trusts me to speak for him, as Señor

Gattinara is supposed to do for the emperor. Why then is he asking to speak with you in private?'

'Until I have spoken with the emperor, I cannot say. But I assure you, I will not allow him to prejudice the situation in any way before you and I, and Gattinara, have had a chance to sit down and talk.'

Duprat looked unconvinced. 'You promise?'

Thomas put his hand on his chest. 'I swear it, Antoine.'

Thomas rode up to the city gates of Bruges. He wasn't sure what kind of reception to expect and was surprised when the gates opened and the emperor himself trotted out on his mare. *Is this a sign that he needs me more than I need him?* Thomas wondered as he reined in his mule and waited for the emperor to draw near.

Charles presented a very different image to both Francis and Henry. Where those two kings dressed in the finest silks and decorated their clothes with jewels, Charles adopted an almost austere look, choosing to wear black rather than bright colours and disdaining ornament.

Charles drew rein alongside him, his mare sniffing the nose of the mule. He studied Thomas for a moment, then leant over and put his arms around him.

'I thank you with all my heart for your coming to me here. All this talk, ambassadors sitting around a table.' Charles shook his head dismissively. 'I tell you, you and I will achieve more in a day than my ambassadors will do in a month in Calais.'

'I am glad to have this opportunity to meet with you, Your Imperial Highness,' Thomas returned with a smile, flattered by the compliment. 'Though I must confess, I had some difficulty in convincing the French ambassador it was for a good cause.'

Charles's lip curled. 'Never mind the French. You came, that is all that matters. We have much to discuss. But first,' he gestured back at the gates, 'we feast.'

The feasting was done, and Charles had taken Thomas to his apartments to talk in private.

'France cannot be allowed to continue to harass my territories, Your Eminence,' he said. 'That is the matter in its simplest form.'

'I agree France and her allies have been provocative,' Thomas said, 'but so far, their provocations have been minor incursions into disputed territory.'

'Minor or not, they are clear violations of the Treaty of London, and King Henry must uphold the terms of the treaty and support Spain against an aggressor.'

Thomas held out his hand, asking for calm. Despite Henry's desire, Thomas wasn't ready to commit England to war with France just yet. At least, not until it was worth his while. 'My king and I do not deny that France has pushed the boundaries of acceptable behaviour as signatories of the Treaty of London, but we are not ready to denounce her because of what amounts to nothing more than skirmishes by men acting on their own authority.'

'Then what will it take?' Charles demanded.

Thomas drummed his fingers on his stomach, feeling his insides squirm. He had eaten too much, and he should have known better, the doctor having warned him before he left Calais to eat only plain food until he was fully recovered from his illness. He would have preferred to have had this conversation in the morning, but Charles was impatient and he dared not put him off.

'If England were to join with you against the French, what would we get?' he asked, running his finger along his top lip.

'Terms, Your Eminence?' Charles smiled coldly. 'In the treaty, there was no mention of conditions.'

'We would be risking a great deal, Your Imperial Highness. To declare war on France is no small thing, at least not for us.'

Charles nodded. 'Very well. Marriage between myself and the Princess Mary would be the principal term.'

'Such a marriage has been suggested before,' Thomas said, knowing Katherine had been a staunch advocate for marrying her daughter to her nephew, and had nagged Henry often to consider it. 'What kind of dowry would you ask for?'

'A million ducats,' Charles said without hesitation.

Thomas caught his breath. 'That is a little on the high side. I would suggest sixty thousand.'

Charles shook his head. 'That is too little. No, Your Eminence, one million ducats.'

'Seventy-five,' Thomas suggested.

'Ninety-five,' Charles countered.

'Eighty thousand ducats.' Thomas held up his hands. 'That is my final offer.' *And you'll accept*, he thought as he studied the man sitting opposite, chewing on his bottom lip, pretending to consider. He knew this man, knew what he wanted, what he needed. *Oh yes, you'll accept.*

Charles nodded. 'Agreed.'

'The marriage to take place when?'

'Do not be so impatient,' Charles chided with a smile. 'The princess is not yet of marriageable age, so there's no need to hurry. Before we agree on a wedding date, I wish to discuss military matters.'

'Of course, Your Imperial Highness,' Thomas said, gesturing for Charles to continue.

Charles uncrossed and recrossed his legs before speaking. The buckles on his shoes glinted in the sunlight. 'I require England to prepare for an invasion of France.'

Thomas frowned, dismayed at Charles's urgent desire for war. 'Such preparations will take time, and this is the wrong time of year to start. Winter is just around the corner. I would say that we cannot think of declaring war until two years hence. I know that sounds like a long way off, but it is the best I can offer at this time.'

'I appreciate the difficulties,' Charles nodded, 'and that nothing can happen immediately. It will be enough to have your assurance that it will be so when the time comes.'

'You have my assurance, if I can be assured of a certain matter.'

Charles's eyes narrowed. 'Of what matter do you speak, Your Eminence?'

Thomas kept his eyes on the table before him. 'It is but a trifling matter when compared to talk of war between countries, but it is of no little importance to me personally. You see, Your Imperial Highness, by England declaring war on France, I will lose the pensions gifted to me by King Francis. He will not continue to pay me those pensions when England has become his enemy. I will be, if I may be so crude, out of pocket by agreeing England will war against France with Spain.'

Charles's mouth curved up at the corners. 'But, of course, I would not wish you to lose by this arrangement. I am sure you can be compensated for those pensions lost to you. Perhaps I should discuss the matter with King Henry's Privy Council?'

Thomas's lips pursed, knowing Charles was teasing him. 'That will not be necessary. If I have your assurance I will be compensated, then you have my assurance that England will be by your side when the times comes to invade France.'

'Excellent.' Charles held out his hand and Thomas shook it. 'What will you tell the French when you return to Calais? I assume you will be returning to Calais?'

'Yes, I will go back. For the sake of appearances, you understand, I will continue with the arbitration. We do not want the French pre-empting us and mounting an attack before we are ready.'

'They do not have the means,' Charles said dismissively.

'Nevertheless, it will be best to continue talks,' Thomas said.

The truth was he hoped all this talk of war would remain just that – talk. Much could happen in two years. It was possible the marriage with the Princess Mary would fall through and that the French would reconsider their provoking behaviour against the Spanish. It was also possible Charles might die or Francis might die, or the pope might die, and then none of this would matter one jot.

As far as Thomas was concerned, it would be far better if he could keep everyone on a piece of string dangling from his finger. It seemed an impossible task, but Thomas wasn't about to let that stop him trying.

CHAPTER SEVEN

Thomas wasn't sure how much more he could take.

He had left Bruges almost a month before, having enjoyed Charles's hospitality for two weeks before returning, rather reluctantly, to Calais. It didn't take long for him to realise that all Charles's talk of agreeing to wait for England's readiness to go to war and Spain doing nothing to aggravate the situation with France was just empty words. Almost as soon as he stepped foot inside the governor's residence, Thomas received a report that Imperial troops had besieged the French town of Mezieres, a flagrant act of unprovoked aggression that Duprat insisted required an English response.

Thomas knew he had to tread carefully. He needed to keep up the pretence to Duprat that a peaceful resolution between France and Spain was still what England wanted, while not offending Charles by siding too obviously with the French. What was he to do?

The solution came to him as Cavendish poured out a cup of wine. Thomas knew the English merchant fleet was due to sail to Bordeaux to collect their cargoes of wine in the next two months. If he brought that forward, however, and ordered them to sail in the next week and anchor off the coast of France, this small fleet of ships would show English willingness and ability to aid the French yet not make any move that could be considered aggressive by the Spanish. It was a neat manoeuvre, Thomas thought, and he hoped it would work.

It did, for a week or so, at least, for the besiegers at Mezieres retreated. But then he learnt Imperial troops had raided Ardres, another French town, this one insultingly close to the Pale of Calais. Duprat was furious.

'My king is convinced you are colluding with the emperor against him,' Duprat declared. 'That you never intended to arbitrate at all. You just wanted to stall, to keep me here while the emperor and your king plan war against France.'

Duprat has found us out, Thomas thought ruefully, watching the ambassador pace up and down. He held up his hands in an attempt at pacification. 'My dear Antoine, how can you say this to me? Did I not despatch our English merchant fleet to show the emperor what friends your king has in England?'

'Yes, yes,' Duprat waved his words aside impatiently, 'but the fact remains there are Imperial troops in French territory and you are doing nothing to remove them.'

'I am doing what I can. Please, Antoine, I pray you, take some wine and sit down. You are making me quite dizzy with all this pacing.'

Reluctantly, Duprat sat and snatched at the goblet Cavendish proffered. He gulped down a mouthful.

Thomas continued. 'Now, I shall speak with Gattinara

and see what we can do about this sorry affair in Ardres. For all we know, rogue elements within the Imperial army have undertaken this raid, and Charles knows nothing about it.'

Duprat considered, 'Very well. But something has to be done or there is no point in my staying here and I will return to Paris.' He set his cup down and strode out.

Thomas was sick of Calais, sick of the endless sitting around tables with ambassadors trying to come to agreements, sick of the lies he was having to tell and sick too of knowing that anything that was agreed amongst them would be undone the moment he left the room.

He had retired to his private chamber for the night, what there was left of it, and cast a wistful glance at the bed. There was no point in slipping between its silk covers for he would be in bed for no more than two hours before he had to rise to meet with Gattinara before mass. And besides, he would only lie there wide awake, the wording of treaties and letters going around and around in his head.

Letters! He hadn't opened the latest parcel of personal letters to arrive, and he knew there would be one from Joan amongst them. Thomas sorted eagerly through the pile on the small table beneath the window, angling the fronts of the letters to the moonlight to read the handwriting. There it was, Joan's scrawl. He threw the other unopened letters on the table and took Joan's back to his chair by the fire, breaking the seal eagerly.

Joan wrote of domestic matters, how her herb garden was growing, what new concoctions she had made and how her family fared. The very normalcy of Joan's life, the simplicity of it, soothed Thomas, though it also made him yearn for her presence. But it wasn't just her presence he missed. He missed the freedom of confession. Not the type of confession he made to a priest, but the type one could make to the person who understood you best and didn't judge you. He could never admit to Tuke or Cavendish how weary he felt, how worried he was, the pressure he was under. To them, he had to appear invulnerable, to never show a chink in his armour lest some rogue drive a dagger into it. But he had always been able to unburden himself to Joan, able to acknowledge his errors and admit his fears.

And he would do so now, he decided. He got up from his chair and moved to his bed, lying back against the goose-feather pillows. He dragged his writing slope onto his legs, laid a clean sheet of paper upon it and began to write.

My dearest Joan. Thank you for your letter. I cannot tell you what joy it is to receive a communication that is not concerned with treaties or foreign raids or any of the thousand and one things I am forced to deal with in Calais. I am so tossed about in my mind by the contrariness of the people I have to deal with here, all of them putting so many difficulties in my path that there is no possibility of a truce being achieved or of war being avoided, that I have no rest, night nor day. My mind cannot sleep, my body cries out for repose, and, you will laugh, my dear, I have quite lost my appetite. I daresay you think that no bad thing, that my stomach will thank me, but what other pleasures do I have? None, now that you are gone.

What news can I tell you? The king has finally finished his book, and the papal nuncio suggested to me I present a

copy to the pope in Rome. Knowing the king would be flat-
tered by this, I agreed it was an excellent idea, and had a
jewelled copy made to be presented to the pope by our
ambassador in Rome, Master John Clerk. Master Clerk
reported that the pope was delighted with the book, and
that he has bestowed upon the king the title Defender of
the Faith. This has made the king very happy, as you can
imagine.

Well, I could ramble on about this and that, but I do
not wish to bore you. Write to me when you can. I know
you are busy with your family and business, but I do so like
to hear from you.

Just one thing more. Please tell no one what I write to
you. My letters to you contain much about me I would not
have anyone but you know.

Bless you, Joan.

With fondest love, Thomas.

He put his quill down and read the words he had written. Had he said too much? Had he given too much away?
Would Joan understand he wanted her back?

Before he could change his mind, Thomas folded up
the letter and dripped red wax over the flap. Tugging off
his seal ring, he pressed the seal into the cooling wax. He
would have it sent on the next ship leaving for England.

If only I could go with it, he mused.

A few weeks later, Thomas got his wish.

His mission was over. There was no point in staying in
Calais; Gattinara had departed and Duprat had swiftly
done the same, recalled to Paris by King Francis, who had
finally realised that England meant to do nothing to stop
the Spanish.

Going home meant he had failed, of course, but at least he wouldn't go home empty-handed. He had the Treaty of Bruges to show the king and the Privy Council. It was a grand name for something not at all grand, but it was an alliance, signed and sealed, and Thomas expected Henry would like it. As he read and reread the official document, Thomas realised the piece of paper represented not only an end to his hope for peace, but the impossibility of economic stability for England. How much would this war against the French cost his little country? Many hundreds of thousands of pounds, at the very least, money England could ill afford. And yet, Henry would insist he find the money somehow. That would be his next mission, Thomas supposed as he boarded the ship that would take him back to England. He had a feeling getting the money was going to be even harder work than Calais had been.

'So, you're back.' Henry clamped his huge hand down on Thomas's shoulder. 'How was it?'

For the briefest of moments, Thomas considered telling Henry exactly how the last few months had been for him. How he had had to endure ill health, fractious ambassadors, constant twists and turns in policy, threats to his personal safety, and so much more, but he knew Henry didn't want to know about his troubles, so simply said, 'Not as successful as I hoped.'

'Oh, I don't know about that,' Henry grinned. 'We got what we wanted, didn't we? Katherine is overjoyed with this Treaty of Bruges you've brought back, and so am I. I can't say I wanted my dear little Mary married to the Dauphin. Far better Charles has her.'

'I am glad the queen is glad,' Thomas said, 'though the

marriage has not come cheap. Her nephew insisted on a million ducats for a dowry.'

Henry's eyes widened. 'God's Death, Thomas!'

'But I got him to agree to eighty thousand.'

'Oh,' Henry said, mollified only a little. 'That's still rather a lot.'

'Surely not for the princess?' Thomas said coaxingly. 'She is worth every ducat, I would say.'

Henry's top lip curled. 'I suppose so, but don't mention the dowry to the queen. She will say you shouldn't have made Charles come down.'

Thomas had no intention of speaking with the queen about the dowry, but nodded understandingly.

'So,' Henry said, 'when are we to go to war?'

'Not for some little time, Your Majesty,' Thomas said, and stifled a sigh as Henry's face fell once again. 'The emperor and I agreed two years hence.'

'Two years? But—'

'We are approaching the winter months,' Thomas interrupted before Henry could protest further, 'and as you know, winter is no time to start a war.'

'Yes, but—'

'And England is far from ready. Our fleet is depleted. We must build ships, and that cannot be accomplished in a matter of mere months.'

'Do you mean to say we have to wait two years before we can move against Francis?'

'I'm afraid so.'

Henry sighed but muttered, 'Very well,' and moved away to a table.

Thomas followed. 'How have things been while I was away? I trust all your nobles have been behaving?'

Henry nodded. 'Taking Buckingham's head has made them know their place.'

'That's good,' Thomas said, flinching at the lack of compassion in Henry's manner. 'I was worried there would be problems in my absence. But no more of that. Let us speak of you. You are the talk of both England and abroad.'

'What do you mean?' Henry asked sharply.

Thomas frowned. 'Defender of the Faith,' he explained. 'The title the pope gave you in recognition of your book.'

Henry relaxed. 'Oh, yes. That.'

But that's not what you thought I meant, Thomas mused, eyeing the king narrowly as Henry rambled on about his book. *So, just what have you been up to while I've been away?*

Thomas threw open his office door and strode in. 'Brian, tell me what has been going on with the king.'

Tuke jumped up as the door banged against the wall. 'The king, Your Eminence? What do you mean?'

Thomas pulled off his cap and tossed it onto the desk. 'He's been up to something, I can tell. I need to know what it is.'

'I really couldn't say, Your Eminence,' Tuke said stiffly. 'Gossip isn't within my remit.'

'Everything's within your remit, Brian,' Thomas growled. 'I told you, I wanted to know everything that was happening while I was away. I assumed you were keeping me reliably informed. Was I foolish to think that?'

'I told you everything I knew, Your Eminence,' Tuke

protested, 'but I do not receive information regarding the king's private activities.'

Thomas glared at him. 'Then bring me someone in my service who does.'

Tuke hurried from the room and Thomas opened the first document on the new pile of paperwork that littered his desk. He ran his eyes over it mechanically, registering only half of its contents, unable to concentrate. Damn Tuke. He had relied on him to tell him everything and the bloody fool had missed something.

It took almost half an hour for Tuke to return. He shuffled in, head down. 'I believe Master Cromwell might have the information you require, Your Eminence.'

Thomas tried to place the face of the short, stocky man Tuke waved into the office. It was a mean face, square, jaws losing their definition where the skin was sagging, and dark shifty eyes. It was a face that once seen should have been hard to forget, but yet Thomas struggled, even though the name Cromwell ran a faint bell. *By Christ, I must be getting old if I'm forgetting names and faces.*

'You have your ear to the ground in Greenwich?' Thomas asked.

'I keep both my eyes and ears open, Your Eminence,' Cromwell said. 'I find it pays to.'

'I'm glad someone in my service does.' Thomas shot a reproachful look at Tuke, who kept his head down and pretended to work. 'Tell me, what has the king been doing while I've been away? By which I mean, what has he been doing that he doesn't want me to know about?'

Cromwell put his hands behind his back and straightened. 'The king has a new mistress. Lady Carey.'

Thomas breathed a sigh of relief. Was that all it was? Henry had someone new warming his bed? Yes, that would explain his shifty manner, concerned the affair was common gossip. Henry had always been a prude when it came to carnal matters and done his best to keep his amours secret.

He searched his memory. Which one of the women at court was Lady Carey? She would be pretty, that was certain, for Henry liked pretty women, and she would be amenable, he had no doubt. Much like Bessie Blount had been. Carey, Carey. He drummed his fingers on the desk. Of course, William Carey's wife, one of Henry's Gentleman of the Privy Chamber. Thomas didn't mind Carey; he wasn't a bad influence upon Henry like Francis Bryan or William Compton. Did Carey know his wife was slipping into Henry's bed? Thomas thought it likely.

'Is this affair widely known?' he asked.

'Not at all,' Cromwell said. 'The king is being exceptionally discrete.'

'And the lady?'

'Won't be any trouble. Asks for nothing and keeps her mouth shut. She's very attentive to the queen, so I doubt if Katherine even suspects she's spreading her legs for the king.'

Thomas ignored the vulgarity, though he heard Tuke's loud, disapproving tut. 'If Katherine did suspect her, she wouldn't say. Is that all that's been going on?'

Cromwell nodded. 'There's nothing else worth mentioning.'

Thomas nodded, satisfied. 'Very well. Thank you, you can go.' As Cromwell headed for the door, he called after him. 'What is it you do for me, Master Cromwell?'

Cromwell turned back and met his eye. 'Whatever you need me to do, Your Eminence.' He left, leaving the door open.

Tuke got up to close it. 'He's a rough one, Your Eminence. Half the household are afraid of him.'

'Including you, Brian?' Thomas asked.

'He scares the shit out of me,' Tuke mumbled as he returned to his desk.

'Then I think he's just the sort of man I need,' Thomas said, smiling to himself as he picked up his quill.

CHAPTER EIGHT

'You had no right to take the Great Seal out of the country.'

Warham's grey face was turning purple as he blustered, and Thomas wondered if he let the old man go on, whether he would burst a blood vessel and perhaps die, and so put everyone out of their misery.

It was irritating, the way he had to put up with this kind of attack. If only he could do away with the Privy Council, or at least reduce the number of meetings he had to attend. The meetings were all for show, anyway, a sop to the councillors' pride to let them think they had a say in the way the country was run, when really all they were expected to do was agree with the decisions Thomas had already made.

Warham's cracked voice grew louder as he went on. 'You exceeded your authority, you hindered the running of the country, and…, and…' He was so angry, Warham could barely get the words out. 'The Great Seal is not your private property to do with as you please. Important business was held up while you kept it close in Calais.'

He broke off as the door opened and Henry entered. Every man quickly got to his feet.

'What is all this shouting?' Henry demanded, glaring at Warham. 'I can hear you all the way down the corridor.' He moved to take his seat at the head of the table. 'Archbishop, what the devil is the matter?'

The councillors resumed their seats. Warham remained standing, leaning on the table for support. 'I was informing His Eminence of the very great wrong he did in taking the Great Seal out of England, Your Majesty.'

'Did you, Thomas?' Henry asked in surprise.

'I did, Your Majesty,' Thomas said, determined not to apologise. 'I believed as your Lord Chancellor I had the right to do so.'

'You did not have the right,' Warham declared.

Thomas had had enough. He was a man who had kings and emperors deferring to him, and here was Warham, berating him like he was a schoolboy.

'The Seal was safest with me,' he yelled back, and all eyes turned on him, shocked by his outburst. Thomas put two fingers to his lips, regretting his loss of temper immediately.

Henry chuckled. 'Gentlemen, such wise heads as yours should not be brought to such petty squabbles as this.'

'But, Your Majesty—' Warham began.

Henry held up his hand. 'No more, archbishop. I trust Thomas with my life. I am sure we can trust him with the Great Seal.' He gestured for Warham to sit down, and the old man reluctantly obeyed. 'Now, have you done with the day's business?'

All the councillors looked to Thomas for an answer. 'We have nothing more to discuss,' Thomas said.

'Then if you would be so kind, gentlemen,' Henry said,

gesturing at the door, 'I would like a private word with His Eminence.'

The councillors rose and filed out of the room, Warham casting a sour look at Thomas as he went.

'Is something wrong, Your Majesty?' Thomas asked.

'Not at all,' Henry said, leaning back in the chair and drumming his fingers on the table. 'Sad news about the pope.'

'Indeed,' Thomas agreed.

In truth, he had been more than a little pleased to learn Pope Leo had died, the news of his death reaching England a day or two earlier. Thomas hoped Leo's death would put European affairs on hold for a little while, as the alliance the papacy had made with Spain might now mean nothing, and Charles would have to make fresh plans that would, inevitably, take time. Yes, Leo had died at a very good time, all things considered.

'Sad, but if we're honest,' Henry smiled a little slyly, 'his death presents us with an opportunity.'

'In what way?' Thomas asked, certain Henry wasn't thinking along the same lines as he.

'Well, a new pope is needed,' Henry said, his smile widening. 'And who better to lead the Church than you?'

Thomas's breath caught in his throat. 'I, Your Majesty?'

'Oh, Thomas,' Henry said reproachfully, 'no need for modesty. It sits most ill upon you.'

Thomas barely noticed the jibe. His mind was reeling. 'I have no desire to be pope, Your Majesty.'

Henry made a face. 'Now I know you're toying with me. Of course you want to be pope. More importantly, I want you to be pope.'

'You wish me to leave England?' Thomas asked, a lead weight landing in his stomach.

'Oh, I'm not saying it wouldn't be a great loss,' Henry said, putting his hand to his heart. 'But I cannot put my personal feelings above sound political sense.'

What sense is there is sending me away? Thomas wondered as he watched Henry play with the stem of a goblet, not realising the anguish he had caused in his chief minister. He wanted to shout at Henry that he wasn't play-acting, but that he really didn't want to be pope, that he had never wanted to be pope. But how could he make Henry understand he viewed wearing the papal crown as a curse, not a privilege?

'So, that's decided,' Henry said, and made to stand.

'Your Majesty,' Thomas halted him, 'I think you should know that I am unlikely to receive any votes.'

Henry made a face. 'Surely not? Your fellow cardinals all think you're a fine fellow, don't they?'

Are you quite serious? Thomas wanted to say. *Do you really have no idea how greatly disliked I am?* 'They think, quite rightly, that I am entirely your man.'

Henry's mouth puckered in amusement. 'Why do you think I want you sitting in St Peter's chair? Just think what you could do for me if you were pope, Thomas.'

'I am most content by your side, Your Majesty.'

The smile vanished from Henry's face. 'I want you to put your name forward, Thomas.'

Thomas could tell when Henry had made up his mind about something and would not be budged. There was no point in arguing. 'Then I shall, of course, Your Majesty, if you wish it,' he said.

And I will suffer the derision of all Christendom when I

fail to secure a single vote in conclave, he thought miserably as he watched Henry leave.

Despite Henry's optimism, despite the despatch of Richard Pace to plead his case, and despite the promise of money to anyone who would vote for him, only six votes were cast in favour of Thomas in conclave. Not enough, not nearly enough.

Thomas received the news that he had not been made pope in his office at York Place. Tuke had slid the letter from the Vatican under Thomas's nose without a word, not daring to speak of its contents, believing the news would anger his master.

But Thomas had read the letter without a word, and Tuke had retreated to his desk, a little bewildered by his master's lack of response. Thomas had simply set the letter aside, feeling a strange mixture of relief and disappointment. Although he had not wanted the job, it hurt his pride more than a little to have performed so badly, but at least he could tell the king his failure to be elected pope was not his fault.

A little while later, Cromwell came into the office, ignoring Tuke, who made a feeble protest at his unexpected entrance, and striding towards Thomas's desk. He held out a sheaf of papers.

'I think you should take a look at these.'

Frowning, Thomas took the papers and scanned the text. It took only a moment for him to realise what they were. 'So, John Skelton has been scribbling his verses again. What about this time?'

'You,' Cromwell said. 'You should read the one entitled *Speke Parrot.*'

Thomas rifled through the poems until he came to the one Cromwell mentioned. He was no judge of poetry – he had no idea whether Skelton's poem was well written or not – but there was no denying he had expressed his thoughts clearly and mercilessly. Skelton condemned the meeting in the Val d'Or as an exercise staged merely to flatter Thomas's vanity and which did neither the king nor England any good. It was mean of the man, but hardly original. Half the men at court had whispered the same thing.

Thomas tossed the page aside. 'I am not wounded by a poet's jibes, Master Cromwell.'

'But don't you want to stop him?' Cromwell demanded.

Thomas narrowed his eyes. 'Why should I want to do that?'

'Because you don't deserve to be talked about like this. He's defaming you and getting away with it.'

His concern touched Thomas. 'Where did you get these?' he asked, gesturing at the other pages Cromwell held.

'I found some courtiers reading them when I was at Greenwich this morning. They were passing them around and giggling.'

'It's annoying, I agree, but it's not the first time I've been defamed, and I'm certain it won't be the last.'

Cromwell leant on the desk. 'But if we allow rogues like Skelton to write this sort of thing about you... well, where will it end?'

'And if I do act against Skelton, and others like him, because there are plenty like him, Cromwell, do you know what will be said of me? People will say I act like a tyrant, that I will allow no criticism of myself, and I will be hated even more than I am already.'

'That may be—'

'Enough,' Thomas cut him short. 'I thank you for your concern, but I have far more important matters to occupy myself with than the ramblings of a second-rate poet.'

'You're not going to do anything about him?'

'No.'

'Do you want me to do something about him?'

Thomas looked up at Cromwell, wondering exactly what he meant by 'something'. He had the uneasy feeling Cromwell didn't mean having a friendly chat with Skelton and telling him to behave.

'Drop the matter,' Thomas said, and gestured Cromwell to the door.

Cromwell strode out of the room without another word.

'I don't like that man, Your Eminence,' Tuke said.

'I'd rather gathered that,' Thomas murmured, his attention already back on the papers he had been reading before Cromwell's entrance.

'I'm not the only one, you know? It's said you shouldn't have such a man in your service, that he does you no credit.'

Thomas signed his name at the bottom of a page and moved on to the next. 'Cromwell stays,' he said to Tuke, not even bothering to meet his secretary's eye.

CHAPTER NINE

1522-1523

William Cornish had excelled himself, Thomas thought as a pear hurtled towards the top table where he sat with Henry and Katherine. The pear landed on the table, almost knocking over his goblet, and Henry, laughing, grabbed it and threw it back into the crowd, where everyone tried to catch it.

As entertainments went, this had been one of the most successful, Thomas complimented himself. Master Cornish, the Master of the Revels, had constructed a miniature castle in York Place, and the great, green-painted edifice, named Chateau Verte, with its three towers, dominated the Great Hall. There had been nothing particularly original about the idea – ladies representing Virtues had been inside the wooden structure attempting to repel men laying siege to the castle – but this had been enacted with a great deal of enthusiasm which had spilt over to the audience. Even the Spanish ambassadors, for whom the entertainment had been staged, had shrugged off their usual reticence and joined in the fun. Only Katherine refused to show any pleasure in the spectacle, and Thomas wondered if it was because she knew one of the Virtues was the woman who had been warming Henry's bed for the past few months.

Thomas studied the women up in the towers. Which one was Mary Carey? Not the one with the sash labelled Constancy, surely? Her husband wouldn't agree, or was Master Cornish having a little jest of his own there? His eyes moved across. Pity, Bounty, Mercy, then? Surely, not Honour? That would be Master Cornish's sarcasm going a little too far. Thomas narrowed his eyes. No, from all he had heard of the lady, Mary Carey would be Kindness.

Their opposites, the Vices, suddenly burst out from behind the decorated screen that separated the Great Hall from the kitchens, and rushed to the front of the castle, accompanied by the sound of music from the minstrels' gallery. These ladies were dressed as Indians with black turbans, and their banners displayed names including Danger, Disdain, Jealousy, Scorn, Unkindness, Strangeness and Sharp Tongue. Thomas didn't bother to work out which women were beneath their disguises. Those labels could apply to just about almost any of the women at court.

Thomas jumped as Henry suddenly pushed back his chair and left the table, disappearing behind the screen. Casting a glance at Katherine, Thomas noted the tightening of her sagging jaw, the veins standing out in her neck. She knew where her husband had gone and why, he realised. Thomas guessed Henry was even now donning a costume to take part in the masque, and that he would inevitably seek out Mary Carey. It would look ill for Henry to consort with his mistress in front of his queen, and the Spanish ambassadors would waste no time informing the emperor that the English king had publicly dishonoured his aunt.

His fear was proved right a few moments later. Eight men burst into the hall to the sound of trumpets. They were spectacularly attired in hats made of cloth of gold and blue satin cloaks that swirled and shimmered in the candlelight. They too wore sashes across their chests emblazoned with words, this time Love, Nobleness, Devotion, Loyalty, Pleasure, Gentleness, Youth and Liberty. The only one of the men to stand at over six feet tall, Henry was easy to spot; he was Devotion.

Henry and his companions had got their hands on more fruit, and to Thomas's dismay, joined in the general fruit-throwing. *This is why the Spanish and even the French look down upon the English,* Thomas thought miserably, *because given half the chance, we behave like children.*

Fruit was flying through the air, and the aims were becoming less accurate as the masquers laughed louder. It didn't take long for the ladies in the castle to surrender, and they descended, slipping their hands into those of the waiting lords, curtseying and accepting kisses with giggles. A new tune struck up, and the masquers fell into step.

Thomas held out his cup for a refill and watched as the dancers threw off their masks and revealed themselves. He frowned. Henry, it seemed, hadn't sought out his mistress, after all. Mary Carey was dancing with Francis Bryan, casting anxious looks at Henry as he danced with a dark-haired wisp of a thing, slender like a boy, wearing a sash that bore the legend Perseverance.

Bryan swept Mary close to Henry, and at last, Henry caught his mistress's eye, caught the glint of reprimand. He politely disengaged himself from his dark-haired partner, handing her to Bryan, and took Mary's hand. She beamed with happiness, and as the pair moved as close as the dance allowed, Henry's previous partner was seemingly forgotten.

Thomas briefly wondered who the woman was who bore the mark of Perseverance.

CHAPTER TEN

Charles was coming to England to confirm the Treaty of Bruges, and Thomas was forced to return to matters of war. He had made one last attempt to forestall the seemingly inevitable conflict by inviting Francis to come to England at the same time as Charles, but Francis was no fool. The French king knew what Henry and Charles were up to and declined the offer in a letter to Thomas that, reading between the lines, implied Francis knew exactly what he had been about in Bruges.

If Francis was not prepared to bide his time any more than Charles or Henry, there was no point in further pretence and prevarication. Thomas was now resolved to do his king's bidding and make every effort towards war against France as Spain's ally. There was no sense, he reasoned, in trying to maintain an uneasy status quo.

So, Thomas had ridden to Dover to meet Charles as he stepped his leather-booted feet on an English shore for the second time. Unlike Charles's first visit, which had been made in relative secret, this visit was to be announced with all pomp. Spain was an ally of

England, not a guilty secret any longer, and Charles was determined to be seen, arriving with a huge entourage. Thomas escorted him to Dover Castle, along streets lined with brightly coloured banners and to the sound of trumpets blown in his honour. Charles was pleased, Thomas was pleased he was pleased, and saw him settled into his apartments before retiring to his own.

Cavendish eased off Thomas's right slipper and tipped it up. Sand came sprinkling out onto the floor. He did the same with the other slipper, then put a bowl of hot water scented with petals at Thomas's feet.

The sand had got everywhere, even managing to slip through his hose to wedge between his toes. Thomas wriggled them pleasurably in the water.

A cough made him open his eyes. 'Yes, George, what is it?'

'If I may, Your Eminence, I would like to go through some details with you.'

Thomas sighed. He would have liked to relax a little longer, but he knew Cavendish was right to carry on working. He nodded. 'Go on.'

Cavendish cleared his throat. 'We expect the king to arrive in approximately two hours' time. I am assured his apartments will be ready and that the kitchens are preparing the dishes you ordered.'

'Good, but tell me, is it still the king's wish that the emperor is not informed of his coming?'

'Yes,' Cavendish confirmed, pulling out a letter from the stack of papers in his folder. 'We had this letter from the king's secretary late last night stating that we are not to let the emperor know and to pretend we had no idea he was coming.'

Thomas rolled his eyes; Henry playing his games again. 'Go on.'

'The secretary writes that the king wishes to show the emperor the fleet. He means to take the emperor out to the *Henry Grace a Dieu*.'

Thomas groaned. 'Oh God, he doesn't want me with him for that, does he?'

Cavendish smiled and shook his head. 'There was no mention of your accompanying them.'

Thomas mouthed a silent prayer of thanks. He lifted his feet out of the water and gestured for his body servant to dry them with a towel. 'Is the itinerary settled, George?'

Cavendish consulted another piece of paper. 'Yes, we leave tomorrow for Canterbury, where we will stay with the archbishop at the palace, moving on to Rochester the following day, and from there on to Gravesend, where we will take barges up the Thames to Greenwich. We should arrive at the palace by late afternoon on that day.'

'The queen has been told of these arrangements?'

'Master Tuke wrote to her, and her secretary has confirmed that both she and the Princess Mary will be waiting to greet the emperor and the king when they step off the barges at Greenwich. Apparently, the princess intends to present the emperor with horses and hawks.'

'Does she mean to go hunting with him?' Thomas was surprised. The princess, like her mother, had little interest in the hunt.

'There was no mention of that, but the queen wants them to become better acquainted in view of their future marriage and is insisting that there be music after the banquet so the princess can dance with the emperor.'

That should be a sight to behold, the diminutive princess hand in hand with the gangly, big-chinned emperor. What a pair they will make. 'I have already allowed for dancing. You can write and tell her,' Thomas said.

Cavendish nodded. 'Your Eminence, I've been given notice of how the king intends to entertain the emperor during his stay here, and it is a very full schedule. It will leave you with very little time for an audience with the emperor.'

'The emperor is coming to see the king, George.' Thomas rose, wincing as the bones in his lower back protested. 'He's not coming to see me. I've already played my part and need do nothing but smile and nod until we get to Windsor and they sign the treaty. Then Charles can sail away again and we can all get back to normal.'

'Another treaty,' Cavendish smiled ruefully.

'Aye, another treaty,' Thomas nodded, 'and I expect this one will be worth as much as all the others over the past few years, which is to say, it will be worth nothing at all.'

'You sound annoyed, Your Eminence.'

'Not really, George,' Thomas sighed. 'It's just I can't help feeling that everything I do lately is a complete waste of time.'

'Well, that all went smoothly, wouldn't you say, Thomas?' Henry asked, leaning on the battlements of Dover Castle and squinting as the small boat carrying Charles drew alongside his anchored carrack.

'I would, Your Majesty,' Thomas said.

He supposed that as far as Henry was concerned,

Charles's visit to England could not have gone better. Henry had played the role of the perfect host and military ally, Katherine had simpered and fussed excessively over her nephew, and Charles had been courteous and gallant to his future bride, Princess Mary.

Henry turned to Thomas. 'So, what's the matter?'

Thomas shrugged. 'I fear it may be difficult to acquire the funding for this war.' *Especially when so much of England's wealth is currently floating away in the emperor's cargo hold,* he mused.

Henry had presented Charles with trunkloads of gold, a parting gift England could ill afford to a man who already had more riches than he knew what to do with, and was every day acquiring more as his subject, Cortes, went around Mexico seizing every treasure he could find.

'Oh, you'll find the money.' Henry patted Thomas's shoulder reassuringly.

'And then there is the earl of Sussex,' Thomas went on. 'Are we sure it is such a good idea to send him out with the emperor? Charles does not need an escort—'

'What are you worried about?' Henry asked.

'I am worried that the earl will not return as soon as his escort duties are over.'

Thomas looked at Henry expectantly, hoping the king would tell him what he and Sussex had discussed in the private meeting they had had and from which Thomas had been excluded. He suspected Henry had ordered Sussex to reconnoitre the French coast to establish what defences they had, which was reasonable enough. But Thomas also knew what a hothead Sussex was, and wouldn't put it past him to carry out raids on vulnerable French towns, with or without Henry's tacit permission. If so, it was a reckless decision, perhaps precipitating the war for which England was not at all prepared. But Henry only smiled at him and turned back to the sea.

Thomas sighed. 'To get the funds for this war, I will have to summon Parliament.'

'That's not a problem, is it?' Henry asked. 'When you make it clear to them why the money is needed, they'll agree, won't they?'

'I'm not sure they will. It took all my persuasion to make them grant the last subsidy you asked for.'

Henry glared at him. 'I am their king, Thomas. When I ask a thing, I do not expect to be told I cannot have it.'

Thomas's blood ran cold. Henry had never spoken so menacingly to him before. 'I will do all I can to persuade them, Your Majesty,' he promised.

Sir Thomas More, recently knighted by the king, examined the paper he had been given and shook his head. 'Your Eminence, really.'

Thomas held out his hands. 'It is the king's wish, Sir Thomas, not mine.'

'But this is a vast sum you're asking for.'

'I have faith in your ability to persuade the Members to agree to the subsidy.'

More made a face. 'Oh, I'm under no illusions why you appointed me Speaker of the House, but you must understand, I take my responsibility in Parliament seriously. The king does not have the right to order Members to agree, nor for you to instruct me to persuade them to anything. I can tell you now, I am not a man to do simply as I'm told.'

And don't I know it? Thomas thought grimly. 'I and the king simply ask you to do your duty as a subject, Sir

Thomas. The king cannot have his war if he doesn't have the money.'

'Perhaps it would be no bad thing if the subsidy was not granted,' More suggested, unknowingly echoing the thought going round in Thomas's brain. 'I am not personally in favour of war. I'm surprised you are.'

'I never said I was in favour.'

'Then why—'

'I serve the king, Sir Thomas. That is why I ask this of you.'

'Might you not consider that you may serve him better by persuading him against war?'

'Might not you?' Thomas bit back. 'He listens to all you have to say, so I'm always being told.'

'That's not a note of jealousy I hear in your voice, is it, Your Eminence?' More teased.

Thomas took a deep breath, unwilling to lose his temper. 'All I will say is, Sir Thomas, that if Parliament does not grant the subsidy for this war, I will leave it to you to tell the king so, and why.'

He turned on his heel and strode into the chamber. The Members got to their feet as he made for his chair, hearing More behind him calling out greetings. *Why do so many people like More and dislike me?* he wondered as he settled on the velvet cushion. *More is pedantic, argumentative, unbending and ferocious on matters of religion while I am always ready to listen and I persecute no one for what they choose to believe.* It really wasn't fair, but he had to acknowledge that if anyone could persuade the Members of Parliament to grant this subsidy, it was Sir Thomas More.

But even with More's power of oratory, Thomas knew it would not be easy, and he was soon proved right. More spoke well and at length. Hours passed, but still the subsidy had not been agreed.

Thomas needed to move. His calves were cramping, and he'd lost the feeling in his buttocks. A Member was replying to a question More had asked, and he broke off abruptly as Thomas got to his feet and stretched out his legs, one after the other.

'Gentlemen,' Thomas began, spreading his arms wide to acknowledge the entire chamber, 'I have been quietly listening these long hours to the words of Sir Thomas More and your responses, and to say I am appalled by your attitude would be to understate the matter. That you should all be unwilling to honour this perfectly reasonable request is beyond me. Have you no sense of loyalty, of duty, to your king? He does not ask for this subsidy for his personal profit but to protect England, to protect his subjects' livelihoods. And you would deny him?'

The Members were keeping quiet, though Thomas could feel resentment coming off them in waves. He had fudged the truth, he knew. War with France was Henry's passion; it had nothing to do with England's security or her economic stability. Henry wanted a glorious victory over his rival, King Francis, nothing more, nothing less.

'Will no one speak?' he cried. 'Will no one explain to me why you are so opposed to your king's request?'

More stepped up to him and put his mouth close to Thomas's ear. 'Your Eminence, you cannot ask this. It is not the custom in the House to debate with individuals.'

'Nonsense,' Thomas said, waving More back to his seat. More had had his chance to persuade. Now, it was Thomas's duty to instruct. He looked over the Members and recognised a face on the front bench. 'Master Darnell, what say you to my question? Why do you defy your king?'

But Darnell did not answer. Instead, the old man raised his chin and stared Thomas down. It was such an unusual occurrence that it quite unsettled Thomas. He looked away and sought another familiar face and asked him the same question, only to be met with another stony silence.

'Very well,' he said, his jaw tightening. 'I see you are all determined not to provide me with an answer. Then, allow me to give you some information that may change your minds. The Lords in the Upper House have already approved this loan, which you are so reluctant to concede, and a portion of the money raised will be put to repaying last year's loan.' *And by the time you realise that is a lie, it will be too late.*

Thomas fell silent, waiting for someone, anyone, to speak. The Members murmured amongst themselves for a long while. Thomas shifted from one foot to another, and glanced at More, who was watching the Members with unabashed curiosity, no doubt intrigued, perhaps amused, by such open defiance of the great cardinal.

Just as Thomas was despairing of anyone speaking, Darnell rose and addressed himself to More. Was that a deliberate slight, Thomas wondered, or just another example of House etiquette?

'The sum the king asks, eight hundred thousand pounds, is too great,' Darnell said. 'Could we agree on a lesser amount?'

More looked at Thomas. Thomas took a deep breath, doing all he could to control himself. He didn't want to lose his temper in front of all these men.

'You would ask the king to reconsider the amount of

money he is asking for? The Privy Council decided upon the sum after much debate and consideration. What right have you to demand those learned men say to the king he must ask for less? Do you claim to know better than the king's Council? I would not dare to question their wisdom. That you should do so is reprehensible. And let me tell you, I would rather have my tongue plucked out of my head with pincers than ask the king to take any less than the sum he has asked of you.'

Come on, you bastards, just agree. Out of the corner of his eye, Thomas saw More rise from his chair.

'Master Darnell,' More said with a sorrowful note to his voice. 'The king cannot accept a lesser sum. You must see that. To do so would demean him, and I am sure that is the last thing you want.'

Darnell cleared his throat. 'Of course not, Sir Thomas. We mean no disrespect to the king. Tis just that the king asks for so much and this request comes so soon after the sum we granted only last year—'

More held up his hands. 'Yes, yes, I know, but the king's needs are urgent and great.' He put a finger to his lips and frowned, considering. 'What say you to this? You grant the king the money he needs, but not to be given over all at once. It is to be spread over three or even four years, say.'

More glanced at Thomas for his approval to this suggestion. Thomas was about to object, to shout at More for his idea being a spineless compromise, but something made him hold his tongue. This might be a way to get Parliament to agree. Once he had their agreement and the first instalment, he could change the terms and there would be nothing they could do. He gave More the smallest of nods to continue. More ordered a vote, and Thomas held his breath as the Members stepped forward, mentally counting each Aye and Nay. He breathed again when all the votes had been counted and had it confirmed that the Ayes had considerably outweighed the Nays. The subsidy was granted. Henry could have his war.

'Thank you, gentlemen,' More said, and declared the House's business over for the day. 'Satisfied, Your Eminence?' he asked as the Members exited the chamber.

'I must thank you for your intervention and quick thinking, Sir Thomas.'

If More noticed the grudging note to Thomas's words, he did not show it. 'The amendment I suggested really was the only way to get their agreement. Without that compromise, I doubt they would have granted the subsidy.'

'You really think they would have denied the king?'

More shrugged. 'The English are a peculiar race. They will put up with a great deal, but ask for too much, push them too greatly, and they will push back.

Thomas nodded. 'You did well, Sir Thomas, and I shall see that your efforts will not go unrewarded. I shall have your salary as Speaker doubled for what you have done here today.'

More bowed his head and thanked him.

Not so saintly that you refuse more money, Thomas thought wryly as he watched More walk away. *And people claim I am greedy!*

Another night, another feast. An impromptu affair, this, for Henry wanted to celebrate the granting of his subsidy.

And spend yet more money he doesn't have, Thomas thought sulkily as he took a mouthful of his wine. He knew he was being a bore – Henry had already given up trying to engage him in conversation and had turned his back to talk to Bryan and Compton – but he couldn't summon up any enthusiasm for this so-called celebration. And if he was honest with himself, he was annoyed too, smarting that Thomas More had succeeded where he had failed. Time was when he had only to ask for a thing and everything would be granted. When did everything become so damned difficult?

Thomas let his gaze wander around the hall. Every table was filled, all the court present to help Henry celebrate and to take advantage of the king's generous bounty. Parasites, every one of them.

Thomas was suddenly aware of the noise in the hall getting louder. A ripple of conversation seemed to pass from table to table, growing in volume as it went, and now it was accompanied by laughs, guffaws and giggles and darted glances over shoulders towards the high table.

The courtiers were looking at him!

A sense of unease trickled down Thomas's spine. Something was amusing the courtiers greatly, and he had the uncomfortable feeling he was the butt of some joke.

A burst of laughter came from the far right table, so loud and jarring, it made Henry break off his conversation and look up.

'What the devil is going on?' he asked, his gaze on the source of the laughter. 'Francis, go and find out.'

Thomas watched Bryan push himself lazily out of his chair, adjusting the patch over his eye which had slipped a little, and saunter over to the table with the studied nonchalance that characterised all his movements. He put both hands on the shoulders of two courtiers who were blocking his view and pulled them apart.

The room had quietened as soon as the king had spoken and everyone's eyes were on Bryan now. Thomas saw Bryan hold out his hand and one of the courtiers put a sheaf of papers in it. Bryan rifled through them, a smile curving his fleshy lips. He cast a look back at Thomas and grinned. Thomas knew then he had been right; the laughter had been about him. His stomach clenched as Bryan made his way back to the table.

'Well, what is it?' Henry demanded.

'Poems, Your Majesty,' Bryan replied, holding up the papers. 'Written by your former tutor, John Skelton.'

'And they are amusing, are they?'

'Judge for yourself,' Bryan declared. 'I shall read a few lines if you wish.'

Don't let him, Thomas mentally begged Henry, but Henry nodded and bid Bryan to continue.

'This first one is called *Colin Clout*.' Bryan cleared his throat. '"You are so puffed up with pride that no man may abide your high and lordly looks." Mmm, I wonder who he can mean. Perhaps this will enlighten us. "Men say how you appal the noble blood royal." Still not clear? Then how about this? "But noble men borne.. blah blah blah... set nothing by politics. Therefore, you keep back and mock them to their face. This is a piteous case, when great lords must crouch and kneel."'

Bryan grinned broadly at Thomas and Thomas felt Henry turn his head towards him. Thomas kept his gaze fixed on Bryan, his jaw tightening as he read on.

'Ah, now,' Bryan said, tossing *Colin Clout* onto the table in front of Henry and selecting another page. 'This one is very good. It's called *Why Come Ye Not To Court?* "He is set so high in his hierarchy of frantic frenzy and foolish fantasy that in the Chamber of Stars all matters there he mars, clapping his rod on the board. No man dare speak a word, for he has all the saying without any reneging. He says, "How say you, my lords? Is not my reason good?"… blah, blah… "He ruleth all the roost with bragging and with boast, borne up on every side with pomp and with pride." Oh, and this bit is brilliant. "Why come ye not to court? To which court? To the king's court, or to Hampton Court? Nay, to the king's court. The king's court should have the excellence, but Hampton Court has the pre-eminence." Bryan threw back his head and laughed. 'Skelton has you there, Your Eminence,' he said, wagging a finger at Thomas.

Laughter was bubbling up from the tables again, restrained, unsure, but there all the same. Thomas risked a glance at Henry, and his insides shrivelled. Henry wasn't laughing.

'Well, Your Majesty,' Bryan cried, 'what think you of these poems?'

Henry's fingers drummed on the tabletop, the creases in his forehead deepening. He turned to Thomas. 'What does Skelton mean by this? That you hold a finer court than I?'

Thomas kept his eyes down, sliding his shaking hands into his lap. *How is this my fault?* he wondered resentfully. *Your bitter old tutor writes a poem making scurrilous accusations and I am the one who must answer for it?*

'Pay no heed to Skelton's scribblings, I beseech you, Your Majesty,' he said, feigning indifference. 'All the world knows you hold the finest court in Europe.'

'Then why does Skelton write so?' Henry demanded.

'He is a poet,' Thomas said with a smile. 'Such creatures exaggerate as easily as breathing. They will do anything to get attention.'

'Well, he certainly got yours,' Bryan smirked. 'You're a little red in the face, Your Eminence.'

'Aye, his face matches his robes,' Compton threw in.

Thomas kept the smile on his face as the laughter grew louder, not daring to catch Henry's eye again. He knew Henry was not laughing, nor even smiling, but watching him with a critical eye. His explanation that all poets were liars had not mollified Henry and that worried Thomas a great deal. The last thing he wanted was Henry brooding on Thomas's excessive wealth.

CHAPTER ELEVEN

Thomas received a message that Henry wanted to see him. It worried him.

It was unusual for Henry to summon him, their weekly meetings usually covering everything the two men had to say to each other, and as his barge ploughed through the water, he ran through all the subjects in his mind that might be troubling the king. Skelton's remarks? Entirely possible. Thomas had seen how irked Henry was by the suggestion his Lord Chancellor outshone him. The war with France? Again, entirely possible. It could be these matters on the king's mind, or it could be something entirely new, trivial, even. Thomas had no idea, and he hated this simple fact. He needed to know what he would be walking into when he came face to face with Henry.

Thomas found the king in his private apartments, sitting on a window ledge staring down into the gardens below. Thomas only saw the king's profile when he entered, but he could see the frown lines in the broad brow and the thrusting bottom lip. It was clear Henry was far from happy.

'Good morning, Your Majesty,' Thomas said hesitantly.

'Young people,' Henry sighed. 'Who do they think they are?'

Thomas was confused. What on earth was Henry talking about? 'Has a young person displeased you, Your Majesty?'

Henry's hand slammed down on the window ledge, making Thomas jump. 'When I was young, correct me if I'm wrong, Thomas, it was customary for children to be told who they would marry, not for them to decide for themselves.'

The Princess Mary? Thomas wondered. Is that who he means? But surely, her betrothal to the emperor pleases both her parents, and whatever pleases them, pleases Mary. And besides, she was too young to have any ideas of her own.

'You are quite right, Your Majesty,' Thomas said. 'Of whom do you speak?'

Henry slid off the window ledge and stepped towards Thomas. 'I have been told, and not by you, Thomas, that Henry Percy has pledged himself to Boleyn's youngest daughter.'

Thomas breathed again. It was not as bad as he feared. No diplomatic disaster, no personal animosity, just a boy whose brains were in his codpiece. But Henry was right; he should have known of it.

'Forgive me, Your Majesty, but this is news to me. They are betrothed, you say?'

'Betrothed and bedded, for all I know.'

'How do you know?'

Henry's face coloured. 'Lady Carey informed me,' he said, looking away.

Thomas nodded. Of course it came from Lady Carey. Who better placed to know what her sister was up to and to tell Henry all about it? Thomas could just imagine the pillow talk. 'Oh, my lord, you'll never guess. My sister has gone fishing and caught herself an earl. What fun! Isn't she clever? Don't you think so, Your Majesty?'

'The sister's name is…?' he asked.

'Anne.' Henry put his hands on his hips. 'I danced with her briefly at the masque.'

Thomas searched his memory of that evening. Yes, he could picture her. A dark-haired, willowy girl with sallow skin, wearing a silk sash bearing the word Perseverance. Henry had danced with her to Lady Carey's consternation. That slip of a thing had caught Percy's eye?

'God blind me,' Henry shook his head, 'a knight's daughter betrothed to an earl.'

Thomas recalled a vital piece of information. 'The Lady Anne is to marry into the Butler family. In Ireland.'

'You don't have to tell me, Thomas,' Henry declared angrily. 'Her marriage was to settle the land disputes there.'

'And it still can,' Thomas said, eager to calm Henry. 'Betrothals can be broken, Your Majesty. It can be as if they never were.'

'And if they have bedded? Or if they've declared themselves before witnesses?' Henry asked. 'They are as good as married in the sight of God, Thomas. No man can undo that.'

I can undo anything, Thomas wanted to say, but Henry was pacing.

'This is your fault,' he cried, pointing at Thomas. 'Young Percy serves in your household. He must have met with her when you've come to court. Sneaking around all this time when he should have been under your eye. Did you never notice he wasn't around?'

Thomas was minded to remind him that there were over four hundred people in his household and not all of them were within sight at all times, but he realised it wouldn't be a good idea to contradict Henry and Thomas bit down on the inside of his cheek to stop himself.

'If I have been remiss, Your Majesty, then I apologise. I have been rather busy, working on the plans for war with France, as you know.'

'Don't talk to me about France,' Henry said. 'That's where she's been, the Lady Anne. She's been in French households, learning God only knows what. You know what the French are like. I daresay that's where she's got the idea she can pledge herself to one of my nobles without my consent. I won't have it, I tell you.'

'Of course not, Your Majesty. As I said before, this situation can be rectified.'

Henry took a deep breath. 'Then do so. I don't care how, just part Percy and this girl.'

Thomas assured Henry he would see to it, bowed and began to back out of the room. He was almost out, almost safe, when Henry called out, 'Thomas!'

'Yes, Your Majesty?' he asked nervously.

'Don't let this sort of thing happen again. I may not be so forgiving a second time.'

Thomas strode into his office at York Place, his robes billowing in his wake. His secretaries and clerks sunk lower behind their desks, keen not to attract Thomas's eye and so escape the rough edge of his tongue, which they knew from experience could be very rough indeed.

Thomas reached his desk and snatched off his cap. He glared at the silk fabric scrunched up in his fist, then threw it against the wall. It made the barest of sounds as it hit the wood panelling and fell to the floor.

'Did you know, Brian?' Thomas demanded, rounding on Tuke who was watching him warily.

'Know what, Your Eminence?' Tuke asked, his eyes widening with worry.

'About Percy and this girl he's betrothed himself to?'

'I know of no girl, Your Eminence.'

'Get Cromwell in here,' Thomas ordered, moving to his desk and dragging his heavy chair out, wincing as it scraped on the floorboards. He flopped into the chair, trying to catch his breath, impatiently drumming his fingers on his desk.

'Henry Percy,' Thomas said when Cromwell entered the office. 'What do you know?'

Cromwell shrugged. 'He's a tosspot.'

Thomas stared at him, astonished by this answer. For a commoner to speak so of a noble, it was disrespectful, it was rude, it was... so very Cromwell. Thomas threw back his head and laughed, the tension he had been feeling ever since receiving the king's summons ebbing away.

'Oh, Master Cromwell, what a rascal you are. Sit down.' He looked across to the astonished Tuke and decided he didn't want him there. 'Leave us, Brian.'

Tuke stomped out of the office, letting the door slam as much as he dared. Cromwell picked up a stool, placed it before Thomas's desk and sat down.

'Did the king have something to say about Percy?' he asked.

'Oh yes, he had something to say,' Thomas nodded.

'But first, you tell me what else you know about the boy. There must be more. You miss nothing.'

Cromwell's mouth turned up in an ugly smile. 'He's been mooning over Sir Thomas Boleyn's youngest girl ever since the revels here. He must have a taste for flat chests and goggle eyes.'

'Is the girl not considered a beauty then?'

'She doesn't tickle my fancy, but some of the lads think she shows promise. I've heard Henry Wyatt has an eye for her.'

'And does she indulge Wyatt?'

'She doesn't discourage him, from all I've heard. Whether he's had her, I can't say, but if you ask me, it's likely. The girl's spent a lot of time in France, after all.'

'And Percy?'

Cromwell shrugged again. 'If he has, he's being discrete about it.'

'What? No boasting of a conquest?'

'Not a word. If you ask me, I suspect it's all very chaste on his side. He's that kind of boy.'

'But not on hers?'

'I reckon she'll try to get him any way she can. He's the sort who would do the honourable thing if he got her with child. Of course, he'd have to wed her in secret. I doubt the father would want his heir marrying a knight's daughter.'

'Never mind the father. The king will not allow such a marriage. He has come to hear of their betrothal and is greatly displeased.' Thomas frowned. 'Tell me, is there a lot of this going on in my household? These young men seeking out ladies?'

Cromwell laughed. 'Why do you think they're all so eager to go with you to court? While you're in the Council chamber or with the king, they're sneaking off to the queen's apartments to dally with her ladies.'

'You find that funny, Master Cromwell?'

Cromwell shrugged. 'It's just boys and girls doing what they've always done.'

'I won't have it,' Thomas said. 'Not in my household.'

'Won't have what, Your Eminence?'

'My gentlemen gallivanting so. They must be taught a lesson.' Thomas pointed Cromwell to the door. 'Summon Henry Percy to the Long Gallery. There should be plenty of idlers there who will make a willing and attentive audience.'

Thomas waited half an hour before making his way to the Long Gallery. He wanted to make the young man sweat, and to allow time for word to get around so that there were as many spectators as possible to see him give Henry Percy a dressing-down.

Cromwell was waiting for him at the door. 'He's in there,' he said, 'pissing himself.'

'What did you tell him?'

'Nothing. Just that you wanted to see him. He knows you've been with the king today.'

Thomas nodded, satisfied, and gestured for Cromwell to open the door. The chatter in the Long Gallery fell silent with flattering immediacy as Thomas entered. Henry Percy was standing in the middle of the room with a group of acquaintances who hastened away at Thomas's approach. Percy was a long-nosed youth, wide-mouthed and rather stupid looking, and Thomas doubted the Boleyn girl wanted him for his looks.

'You, sir,' Thomas said, coming to a stop before Percy,

'will explain to me why I am summoned into the king's presence to be told you've made a foolish alliance with a girl not fit to clean your boots.'

Percy's mouth fell open. There were a few sniggers from the spectators.

'Well?' Thomas demanded.

'Anne is not of my rank, admittedly,' Percy began, his cheeks reddening, 'but—'

'No, my lord, there is no but. If a girl is not of your rank, there is an end to it. You cannot have her for a wife. You will also explain how you believe you have the freedom to consort with this girl. In case you have forgotten, you serve me. When I go to court, which is where, I understand, you had your assignations with this girl, you are to remain on hand should I require you. If you are skulking around the queen's apartments, you are not where you should be.'

'It was only a few times,' Percy protested.

'I don't care if it was once or a hundred. Such lapses in your duty will not be excused and will not go unpunished. And that goes for anyone else thinking of paddling palms with the queen's ladies or any other lady at court.' He glared at the young men who all dropped their gazes to the floor. 'So, you will break off all intercourse with the Boleyn girl. That is my command and that is the king's command.'

Thomas turned to go, when to his surprise, Percy called out, 'Your Eminence, please, wait. I fear you do not understand all. You see, Anne and I have made promises before witnesses to wed. Indeed, we are as good as wed already.' He broke off, turning an even deeper red.

'Do you mean to say you've bedded with this girl? Well? Speak up, my lord.'

'Your Eminence,' Percy whispered, glancing around. 'I will not dishonour her in so public a manner.'

'Dishonour her? My lord Percy, the girl has been in France for years. I doubt her maidenhead survived as long as six months.'

Percy's eyes widened. 'Your Eminence, I must protest—'

But Thomas was in no mood for indignant expostulations. He held up his hand to silence the young man. 'You will not marry the girl. Is that clear?'

Percy straightened and raised his chin. 'I must marry her, Your Eminence. I've made a promise.'

'Are you defying me?' Thomas was astonished.

Percy swallowed. 'I am, Your Eminence.'

'Just who do you think you are?' Thomas roared, and Percy took a few steps back in fright. 'Have you no conception of your standing in this world? When your father dies, you will be in possession of the one of the greatest earldoms in the land. It is your duty therefore to consult with others more wise than yourself regarding your future wife. But to carry on in this sly fashion, to meet with this mere chit of a lass in secret, behind my back while you are in my service, shows not only the greatest folly but an appalling lack of respect for your betters. You have offended your father, and, more importantly, you have offended the king by this dalliance. I will send for your father to talk some sense into you, and be assured, my lord, he will not suffer your insolence. He will have this so-called betrothal with the Boleyn girl broken off before you can click your fingers.'

Percy held out both his hands beseechingly. 'Your Eminence, I had no notion the king would be so mightily offended. I am of age, however, and think I am more than capable of deciding on a wife for myself. You are wrong about Anne. Yes, she is the daughter of a mere knight, but her mother has Howard blood and the blood of the Ormonds also runs in her veins. I do truly believe Anne to be more than a suitable match for one such as I. I humbly beg you to intercede on my behalf with the king and beg his leave to wed the lady.'

Thomas's fists clenched. When he spoke, his voice was deceptively calm. 'Who do you think you are that you should ask such a boon of me and the king? You are a boy, and this girl a mere chit with an eye for a gullible young man with rank and fortune. Your marriage to Mary Talbot has been arranged, as has the Boleyn girl's into the Butlers. You are forbidden from communicating further with Anne Boleyn. You will not see her, you will not write to her, nor shall you receive letters from her. Your liaison, boy, is at an end.' He stepped up to Percy and looked the young man dead in the eye. 'Do I make myself clear?'

Percy paled. 'Yes, Your Eminence,' he said after a long moment.

Thomas turned on his heel and strode out of the Long Gallery, satisfied by the whispers that followed him out of the door.

Anne Boleyn slammed her bedchamber door and ripped off her headdress, hurling it across the room. Throwing herself down on her bed, she buried her face in the pillow and willed herself to cry.

No tears came, and that made her even angrier. She wanted to cry. She felt she would explode if she didn't. Sent back to Hever in disgrace where she had to endure the recriminations of her mother, as if she had done something wrong.

She heard the door open. 'Go away,' she groaned.

'Anne?' Her sister's voice was like treacle. 'Please talk to me.'

Anne sat up. 'There's nothing to talk about. What are you doing here, anyway? Shouldn't you be at court waiting for the king to summon you to his bed?'

'Why must you be so horrid?' Mary said, hurt. 'You know my going to the king's bed wasn't of my making.'

'You should have said you wouldn't do it.'

'I wasn't allowed to say no.'

'You never even tried. I would have refused.'

Mary opened her mouth to reply when there came a knock on the door. A maid came in holding a letter. Anne, her black eyes noting the Percy seal, snatched it from her hand and tore it open.

'What does it say?' Mary asked quietly as her sister's expression darkened.

'Percy is abandoning me,' Anne said, her voice breaking. She thrust the letter at her sister.

Mary took it and read. Percy wrote of how he was sorry but that he had been told he could not marry Anne as he had promised, that he had been shouted at by the cardinal before all his friends and told he was a foolish boy for wanting to marry a knight's daughter. He went into detail of his encounter with the cardinal and Mary bit her lip as she read, her heart breaking for the boy who was so obviously in love with her sister.

'Oh, Anne,' she sighed, 'I am so sorry.'

'Are you?'

'Of course I am.'

'Sorry enough to help me?'

116

'Help, how?'

'Write to Percy for me. My letters will be opened and he'll never get any I send. Tell him we must marry in secret, and then you must help me arrange it.'

Mary shook her head. 'No, I won't do that, Anne. You're in enough trouble already. To sneak off and marry?' She shook her head. 'Think what that would do to Father.'

'I don't care about Father,' Anne said through gritted teeth.

Mary's frown was disapproving. 'Yes, you do.'

'Oh, God, then speak to the king for me,' Anne said, banging her fists on the bed. 'Tell him I love Percy and he must give us permission to marry.'

'I can't do that either, Anne.'

'Of course you can. When you're alone with him, just tell him what Percy means to me. He understands about love, doesn't he? Well, then he'll tell the cardinal we are to wed and he must do nothing to stop us.'

'I'm so sorry, but you don't understand. For one thing, it's not my place to ask for favours from the king.'

'Then what is your place?' Anne cried. 'On your back with your legs spread? Is that all you're good for?'

'Anne, please, don't be crude. I cannot ask such a favour of the king for a very good reason. He doesn't want you to marry Percy. It was he who told the cardinal to part you.'

Anne stared at her. Her black eyes narrowed. 'The king—'

'He wants the Butler marriage, Anne,' Mary nodded. 'Don't ask me why. I don't understand politics. But he was furious when he learnt of you and Percy.'

'I don't believe you. You're just saying that so you don't have to talk to him.'

'I'm not, Anne, I swear it.'

'It was the cardinal. Wolsey's to blame.'

'You're wrong, Anne. It was the king.'

Anne lay back on the bed and fixed her eyes on the tester above. 'It was Wolsey,' she said. 'I shall never forgive him for what he's done to me.'

CHAPTER TWELVE

Thomas had the money Henry needed to go to war with France. The Church had contributed more than fifty-five thousand pounds, with over two-hundred thousand pounds coming from the king's subjects in taxes. With the subsidy from Parliament, Henry would have more than four-hundred thousand pounds in his war coffers. It was a great deal of money, but Thomas knew how quickly that would be spent and hoped the war would not go on too long. To ensure it would be over as quickly as possible, he decided the best person to organise the campaign was himself. But when he said so to Henry, the king was incredulous.

'You?' Henry cried.

'It is mostly administration, Your Majesty,' Thomas protested, a little put out by Henry's reaction. 'And if you'll forgive my immodesty, I am rather good at administration.'

'I'm not denying that, but this is a military matter. You're no soldier. Do you really think you are the right man?'

'I can manage,' Thomas insisted, and Henry had rather reluctantly agreed.

But he soon discovered that, in this case, Henry was right.

From the very beginning, indeed, from the very moment he had left Henry that day and returned to York Place to begin work on the campaign, he had made mistakes. Somehow, he had miscalculated and under-victualled the army. If soldiers had nothing to eat and drink, they would be unable to march, let alone fight. Every day, he received letters from irate commanders complaining there wasn't enough meat and beer for the soldiers and demanding he do something about it. Thomas had been despatching commissioners all over the country to butchers and brewers, desperately trying to make up the shortfall.

There were other problems, too; problems with weaponry, problems with communications, and problems with commanders who had ideas of their own how to fight a war. Thomas found himself overwhelmed by everything that was going wrong. But what was most galling was a problem beyond his control. England's allies in this war against France, the emperor and the duke of Bourbon, were not playing their parts and cooperating with the English commanders. The plan had been for Charles Brandon as head of the English army to invade France from Calais, while Charles led his army from the south and Bourbon from the east. In this way, Francis would have been cornered with nowhere to flee. But Charles decided that Boulogne, which lay in the army's path, was impregnable, and appealed to Henry to divert Brandon's attack towards Paris.

'He wants us to do what?' Henry cried when Thomas told him what Charles was asking.

Thomas held up his hands. When he had first received the letter from Charles putting forward the idea of an attack on Paris, he had reacted very like Henry. But then he had considered the idea. He knew it was a bold move, but if he could make Paris happen, it would shut up all his naysayers, all those men who said he should never have been given control of the war. A big success such as the capture of the French capital would force Skelton to write something in praise of him for a change and make all the men in Parliament show him the respect he deserved. If only he could make Paris happen.

'I know it sounds a little foolhardy—'

'A little?'

'But I am certain Paris can be taken. After all, if we are going to war, why not try for the greatest prize of all? Why not try for the capital?'

Henry ran his fingers through his thinning red hair. 'Are you sure, Thomas? Paris is deep within France and will be exceptionally well defended. Winter is approaching.' He shook his head. 'And I'm not at all convinced we can trust Bourbon to do what he says he will. You know, I wouldn't put it past him to march only so far and no further, and allow our English soldiers to take all the risks.'

Thomas couldn't argue with any of these points, but if he wanted to restore his reputation, he knew he had to be brave. 'I'm certain we can take Paris, Your Majesty,' he said.

Henry wasn't convinced, Thomas could tell, but he shrugged and said, 'Very well. If you and Charles are so sure it is the best course…'

And so Thomas had written to Brandon and given him his new instructions.

It was a dreadful mistake.

Brandon had started well, despite the supply problems, despite the fact his soldiers hadn't been paid and their morale was low, and had marched to within fifty miles of Paris. There he had set up camp, expecting, hoping, for the armies of Charles and Bourbon to join him. He waited in vain until September, when it became clear they were not coming. As the weather turned colder, Brandon was forced to march his army away from Paris to Flanders, and from there, he wrote to the Privy Council of mutinous soldiers, freezing temperatures, dwindling supplies and mud that stopped the army in its tracks. And in every letter, there was one person he blamed: Thomas Wolsey.

'How has this happened?' Henry asked when the other councillors had left the Council chamber.

Thomas was grateful Henry had dismissed them before asking him this question. The shame he felt at the mess he had made of the French campaign was like nothing he had ever known, and he dreaded being reprimanded in public. But it seemed Henry was going to spare him that indignity.

He swallowed. 'I'm afraid the duke of Bourbon acted as you so wisely predicted, Your Majesty. He has disbanded his army.'

Henry's face darkened. 'So, he intends to play no further part in this campaign. And I have had news that Charles has conquered all the towns he planned to and which benefit him, but refuses to move on Guienne as we had agreed.'

'The emperor has indeed dismissed his army and

returned home. But,' Thomas hurried on, 'I am sure his disbandment is only a temporary measure, occasioned by the onset of winter. Come the spring, he shall be mobilising again.'

'Oh, you think so, do you?'

Thomas hung his head. 'I wish there was better news. I am sorry.'

Should he say what he was sorry for? For assuring Henry he wouldn't make a pig's ear of the management of the army? For not foreseeing that their allies would serve their own ends and renege on their agreements? For making Henry look like a gullible fool? He was guilty of all of them, and Henry had the perfect right to punish him if he so chose. Thomas prepared himself for the worst.

Henry chewed on his bottom lip. 'Brandon could have done better, too. He's claiming he can't keep the army during the winter. Do you think he's right?'

Thomas's stomach gave a little flip. Henry actually wanted his opinion and was ready to blame his brother-in-law rather than him! Or was Henry tricking him into blaming Brandon?

'He could be,' he said carefully. 'The duke has martial experience and knows what he is doing.'

'I suppose so,' Henry sighed unhappily. 'Well, write to Brandon and tell him to bring the army home, but that he is not to come to court. I won't have him here reminding me of his failure.'

'At once, Your Majesty,' Thomas said, gathering up his things and getting to his feet.

'But I was right, wasn't I?' Henry said as Thomas made for the door. 'We should have kept to Boulogne and not tried for Paris.'

'Yes, you were right,' Thomas said, bowing his head, 'and I was wrong. I should have listened to you.'

Henry got to his feet, his huge body blocking out the light coming in through the window. 'This is the third time you've let me down in a military matter. You'd think I would have learnt my lesson after the last time, but…' he shook his head sadly. 'I won't make that mistake again, Thomas. From now on, you keep to the administration of my realm and keep your nose out of my battles. Yes?'

Thomas felt his cheeks flush with heat. 'Yes, Your Majesty. You were very kind to place so much faith in me. I'm only sorry that your faith was so sorely misplaced.'

Henry nodded. 'Then we'll say no more about it. Good day to you, Thomas.'

'Good day, Your Majesty,' Thomas said, and hurried out of the chamber.

CHAPTER THIRTEEN

1524-1525

It was all change at the Vatican again. The pope died in December, and Henry once again pressed Thomas to stand for election.

Thomas's feelings towards the papal throne hadn't changed. He didn't want to be pope, and was even more certain that none of his fellow cardinals wanted him to be either. But Henry insisted Thomas try again, and despatched Master Pace to Rome to drum up support. All to no avail. Pace arrived too late; most of the cardinals had already decided who they would vote for, helped along with bribes from interested parties, and no amount of money promised by Pace could sway them. Cardinal Giulio de Medici became Pope Clement VII and Pace returned to England to face Henry's disapproval at a job badly done.

Thomas did his best to appear disappointed, but he was already thinking ahead. Charles had fallen very ill and had no thought of going to war at present. Francis, sensing an opportunity to move against Spain, had marched into Italy to recover lost French territories. Francis had enjoyed an initial success by retaking the Spanish-held Milan, but then his army had succumbed to the plague, and an attempt to take Pavia failed, forcing him to besiege the city instead. But it was the wrong time of year to be stuck on the outside of a city. Francis's soldiers froze in their tents and their bellies went empty as meat supplies dwindled.

By the end of February, Francis was desperate, and charged his army at the Spanish incumbents, who, by now, were starving, and in desperation had opened Pavia's gates and rushed out to meet the besiegers head on. Their bold offensive move worked. The French army was brutally chopped down, Francis and his personal bodyguard surrounded, and the king declared the prisoner of the Emperor Charles.

When the news of Francis's defeat reached England, Henry was beside himself with glee.

'Isn't this wonderful news?' he cried when Thomas arrived in the privy chamber for their weekly meeting. 'Francis is a prisoner of the emperor!'

'Is it wonderful, Your Majesty?' Thomas asked. 'For a king to be made prisoner?'

The smile dropped off of Henry's face. 'Of course it is. For heaven's sake, Thomas, what's the matter with you? Don't you see? With Francis out of the way, his country is mine for the taking.'

Thomas swallowed down a groan. As soon as he heard of Francis's capture, he had wondered how long it would take Henry to contemplate another French invasion.

'Kate is pleased,' Henry went on. 'She says it's the perfect opportunity for me and Charles.'

'You and the emperor? Another alliance?' Henry

seemed to have forgotten how Charles had let him down before.

If Henry noticed Thomas's tone, he chose to ignore it. 'We will march into Paris together, and I will be crowned at Notre Dame. Once that's done, the Princess Mary will travel to Paris and wed Charles.'

'Have you corresponded with the emperor about this?' Thomas asked, hoping the answer was no.

'Not yet. Kate wanted to write to him at once, but I told her it must come from my Council.'

Thomas noted Henry wasn't asking for his advice or his opinion on whether this was a good idea. *Those days are gone*, he thought wistfully. He knew Henry didn't entirely trust his judgement anymore, and in a way, Thomas didn't blame him. But if Henry had asked Thomas what he thought of the idea, Thomas would have suggested that Charles neither wanted nor needed English aid in taking French territory, or in any other matter. And as for the marriage with the princess... Thomas doubted Charles even gave Henry's daughter a second thought. And yet, Thomas had no doubt that when asked, Charles would agree with everything Henry proposed, not hesitating to go back on his word when it suited him.

'I've already discussed it with Bryan and Compton,' Henry went on. 'And Norfolk, as he was here, too. They all think it is a splendid idea.'

I bet they do, Thomas thought. 'But if your Council disagrees?'

Henry's eyes bored into him. 'I leave it to you to ensure they do not, Thomas.'

Thomas smiled and nodded. 'I will see to it, Your Majesty,' he promised, wondering where the money for another French campaign would come from this time.

. . .

'I'm not going through all that again,' Thomas yelled at More across the Council table. 'Parliament will not grant another subsidy to the king, and I will not demean myself by asking.'

'But more money?' More cried. 'After all you've already been given?'

'It is the king's wish—'

'To have another pointless war? After the last debacle?'

Thomas's fists curled. 'We are not here to debate the sense of it.'

'Then what are we here for?'

'To do what the king wants, that's what.'

'Indeed?' More's eyebrows rose. 'And I thought we were here to advise him. To guide him towards what's best for England.'

'The king knows what is best for England,' Thomas said, his jaw tightening as he tried to control his temper, 'and that is him being crowned king of France.'

'Oh, that is a fantasy,' More scoffed, and gestured at the men around the table. 'We all know it.'

'Then, please, Sir Thomas, do feel at liberty to tell the king so,' Thomas shot back. 'I shall not stop you.'

In fact, I shall look on with pleasure as Henry orders your head from your shoulders for your impudence. Aye, that's shut you up, Thomas thought smugly as More sank back into his chair without another word.

Sir Henry Dagnall coughed politely. 'Forgive me, Your Eminence, but if you do not mean to appeal to Parliament for the money, then how do you hope to raise funds for this war?'

'Finally,' Thomas said, glaring at More, 'a sensible question. By going directly to the people, Sir Henry. I shall send out commissioners to every parish, every borough, and the people shall give the money to them.'

'You're not serious,' More said. 'Surely, you don't mean to tax the people in this way?'

'If you want to call it a tax, Sir Thomas,' Thomas shrugged. 'I prefer to think of it as a loan. We shall call it the Amicable Grant. The people will be happy to give money to their king if it means he can take his rightful place as ruler of France.'

More laughed unpleasantly. 'And you honestly believe the people will willingly hand over their money? They're taxed enough already. Do you plan to bleed them dry, Your Eminence?'

Thomas got up from the table, tugging his robes straight. 'You have my decision, gentlemen. This matter is not open for further discussion.'

He stormed out, leaving the councillors muttering amongst themselves, not caring what they thought of his idea or of him. It wasn't going to be easy, he knew that, but he had to get this money. If he didn't, Henry might turn his back on him for good.

Thomas's commissioners were sent out to collect the Amicable Grant, and the people refused to give it. As More had pointed out, the people had been taxed so many times over the last few years, they had no more to give. They didn't care about the king's desire for war; all they cared about was whether they had enough food to feed their children.

But they had to pay up, they simply had to. Henry must

have the money for his war or Thomas's career, perhaps even his life – there was no telling with Henry these days, not after Buckingham – was over. 'Get the money,' he had ordered the commissioners. 'I don't care how.'

It had been the wrong action to take. He remembered something More had said to him once, about the English taking only so much pushing before they pushed back, and it seemed Thomas had brought them to that point. In the taverns and inns, in the shops and guild halls, Wolsey was being branded a tyrant. Wolsey, the tax collector, Wolsey, the bleeder of men's souls.

Rebellion broke out, and Thomas had to despatch Thomas Howard and Charles Brandon to quell the uprisings. They met with little success; some pockets of feeble resistance were put down, but there were too many others and they were growing. Thomas had letters daily from the dukes, asking for help and more men, and he didn't know what to do.

And then a summons came from the king in the middle of the night, and Thomas had to dress quickly and have his barge rowed down the Thames in the inky blackness to Greenwich.

How much did Henry know about the rebellions? he wondered as the oars slipped through the water. Thomas had admitted to the king that there had been some resistance amongst the people, but not that the commissioners had been attacked or what was being said about him.

The doors swung open to admit him as he approached the privy chamber. Henry was standing by the window in his nightgown and dressing gown, his cap on his head. He turned as Thomas entered.

'Rebellion,' Henry roared, coming towards him and

brandishing a letter. It took all Thomas's nerve to stand his ground and not run back out into the corridor. 'My own subjects are rebelling against me.'

'What news have you had, Your Majesty?' Thomas asked, staring at the letter in Henry's hand.

Henry thrust it at Thomas, and he took it, smoothing out the creases the king's angry hand had made. Thomas glanced down at the signature before reading any of the text, and his heart sank. The writer was Howard and he didn't need to read the letter. He already knew Howard would lay the blame for the rebellion on him in every line.

'Why have you not told me of this?' Henry demanded. 'Why is the first I hear of this from Howard?'

'I had thought to spare Your Majesty—' Thomas began.

'You mean you wanted to keep me in the dark.'

'No, Your Majesty,' Thomas protested. 'Never that. You will remember I informed you there was some resistance to the Amicable Grant.'

'Do not equivocate with me,' Henry wagged a finger in his face. 'You told me your commissioners had run into a few problems, not that my people were rebelling.'

'It is but a few pockets of resistance—'

'Pockets!' Henry cried incredulously. 'By God's Blood, I'd hate to know what you call a full-blown rebellion. Howard writes he cannot put these rebels down.'

'I am sure the duke exaggerates—'

'You're sure, are you? Yet, Brandon says the same. Are they both exaggerating?'

'No, Your Majesty,' Thomas admitted miserably.

Henry moved back to the window. He thumped the side of the wall, and the glass trembled. 'How will this make me look?' he said after a moment. 'What will Charles say when he gets to hear about this? I'll tell you what he'll say. He'll say that I hold no authority in my own kingdom, that my subjects rule me. That they can do whatever they like and suffer no retribution.'

Retribution? Thomas's pulse quickened. Dear God, was Henry thinking what he thought he was thinking? 'I would counsel against using force,' Thomas said carefully. 'So far, the dukes have tried reason and persuasion, I admit, to little avail, but they have not used force for a very good reason.'

'And that reason is?'

'That pitting Englishman against Englishman rarely ends well.'

Henry thrust out his bottom lip. 'I would never wish for that. Is there any hope the people will come around?'

Thomas shook his head. 'I fear such a hope may be unrealistic, Your Majesty. As Sir Thomas More pointed out to me' – *aye, I'll get More into this, let Henry blame him too* – 'we must appreciate, we have asked a great deal of your subjects in recent years. There is only so much they have to give, even to you.'

'I am their king, Thomas.'

I am Thomas again, he thought, taking a deep breath of relief. 'Indeed, Your Majesty.' An idea occurred to him. 'I would like to make a suggestion. In truth, it is I, not you, who is being blamed for the Amicable Grant. Quite rightly blamed, as it was my idea. We should make it known, to our allies and to the people, that you have rebuked me for sending out the commissioners, that it was without your authority, and that you have issued an order recalling them. We will then issue a proclamation stating your people can make whatever contribution to your war chest they can afford. We can call it a Benevolence. Once they realise you have been more than generous, I feel certain they will pay, if not all, then at least some of the money we need. However,' he paused and swallowed a few times to moisten his throat, 'I think we may have to put off war for this year.'

Henry stared out of the window. It had started to rain. 'It will not make me look weak?'

'Indeed, no,' Thomas assured him with enthusiasm. 'You will appear merciful, a true prince.'

'Very well,' Henry said after a long moment. 'See it done. But I am very disappointed, Thomas. I had thought you served me better than this.'

Tears pricked at the back of his eyes as Thomas offered his deepest apologies, bowed and backed out of the room. The doors closed upon Henry as he watched the rain come down, and Thomas turned on his heel and hurried away, wanting no one to see the tears falling down his cheeks.

It had been a while since he'd been to the Guild Hall. It was smaller than Thomas remembered, or maybe that was because it was more full than last time. All the benches were filled; those men who hadn't been in time to get seats were having to stand. They all gave him wary looks as they settled, and Thomas set his jaw defiantly. He had told the king he would take the blame for the failure of the Amicable Grant, but he wasn't ready to give up on it just yet.

The hall quietened as Thomas rose from his chair.

'Gentlemen, I thank you for gathering here today. I come to tell you, the king, in his great wisdom and mercy, has decided to terminate the Amicable Grant. He has become aware of the people's feelings about the grant and has instructed me we are not to tax the people to hand over money they can ill afford. Let me say here, the recent rebellions have been entirely my fault. It was my error to demand the citizens of this kingdom give over their money when I should have appealed instead to the undoubted love they have for their sovereign. I am here today to rectify that error by asking instead for a Benevolence.'

He resumed his seat. It was sophistry, he knew. Amicable Grant, Benevolence, different words for the same thing, but a request sounded better than a demand. He folded his hands over his stomach and waited for his audience's agreement.

The men in the Guild Hall looked at one another, frown lines corrugating their foreheads. Then they fell to muttering amongst themselves, and Thomas grew annoyed. Their agreement should have been given at once, not all this conferring and thinking about it. Damn them! He'd apologised. What more did they want from him?

The chatter which had been steadily rising in the chamber suddenly hushed. Someone was standing up in the second row of benches. Thomas's eyes fixed on the man.

'Your Eminence,' the man said in a loud voice, and Thomas knew he was determined everyone in the hall heard him. This was no shrinking violet. 'You have no right to come here and demand a Benevolence of us. And I shall tell you why. In the time of King Richard the Third, a statute was set down that such Benevolences were illegal.'

What was the idiot saying? Talking about King Richard and illegalities. Thomas got to his feet.

'I marvel you speak of King Richard, a man who usurped the throne and murdered his own nephews. You speak of legality enacted during the reign of such a man, yet how can anything that such a man proclaimed be legal, just and right? Sit down, man, and speak to me no more of Richard. Not one of that man's acts was honourable.'

'I will not sit down,' the man cried. 'This is a free country, is it not?' he appealed to his audience and received cheers of agreement. 'As you say, Your Eminence, King Richard committed illegal and dishonourable acts, yet during his time, many good acts were made law, only it was not he who made them. They were made by Parliament, which you sought to bypass, firstly with your Amicable Grant and now with this so-called request for a Benevolence. A tax by any other name.'

Thomas fumbled for an answer, but the ache in his head was making it hard to think. A slow clapping filled the hall, growing louder and louder, faster and faster. This man had the entire hall on his side – even the mayor of London was clapping – and Thomas stood alone.

Thomas raised his hands and patted the air. *Please stop*, he mentally begged, and slowly, the clapping ceased. He took a deep breath.

'I can see you are all of one mind and will not consent to grant your king a Benevolence,' he said, ignoring the growls of disapproval his words provoked. 'I will merely therefore ask that each of you consider your duty and loyalty to the king and give whatever you think appropriate privately.'

Thomas didn't wait for their answer, not this time. He strode out of the hall, head held high but his stomach turning somersaults.

Cavendish was waiting for him outside the chamber. 'How did it go, Your Eminence?' he asked with a smile, which dropped off his face as he registered Thomas's expression. 'Not well?'

'No,' Thomas said, 'not well at all.'

'What happened?'

Thomas glanced back at the closed doors of the hall. 'I've lost their respect, George. That's what happened.'

CHAPTER FOURTEEN

1526

Thomas hurried along the corridor, courtiers scattering before him, and waved impatiently for the guards to open the doors to the privy apartments.

'Your Majesty,' he panted, 'I just heard what happened. Are you hurt?'

Henry was in his chair, one leg outstretched on a foot-stool. 'Stop to catch your breath, Thomas. A fuss over nothing. You should not have been bothered.'

Henry was embarrassed, Thomas realised as he stood there, his body heaving with the unaccustomed exertion. Not an hour earlier, a page in Thomas's household had burst into the clerk's outer office and delivered the news that the king had had an accident and almost died. Thomas had heard the page, and had rushed out from his office demanding to know more, his heart beating fast at the thought of Henry dying.

Henry had been out hawking and slipped down into a muddy ditch. It had been raining hard for days, and the mud, though it looked reasonably solid to the eye, had the substance of quicksand, and Henry toppled and fell head-first into the ditch. The mud pulled and sucked, and Henry, unable to get a grip, had floundered, his mouth filling with mud. His companions had looked on aghast, stunned into inaction, and it was a page who had saved Henry from suffocation. The page grabbed his king by the ankles and tugged and tugged until he pulled Henry free.

'Of course I should have bothered,' Thomas protested. 'Your safety is my paramount concern.'

'Well, I shall not deny it shook me. After what happened with Brandon…' Henry shrugged and turned his gaze to the window.

Thomas knew what Henry was thinking. Not long before, he had been jousting against Brandon, and had neglected to pull down his visor before making the charge. Brandon's lance had struck Henry's shield and shattered into a thousand pieces. Many of the splinters had flown into Henry's unguarded face, and it was a miracle he had suffered no serious damage, only a few scratches that had already healed. But Thomas had been with Henry in the tent afterwards and had seen how unsettled the king was by his brush with death. Perhaps now was a good time to suggest the king give up jousting?

'I should like to know the name of the page who saved your life, Your Majesty,' he said. 'He must be rewarded. I dread to think what would have happened if he had not acted so quickly.'

'There's no need. I have already rewarded him,' Henry said. 'But what happened today, it has made me think, Thomas. If I had died—'

'God forbid, Your Majesty.'

'If I had,' Henry continued a little testily at the interruption, 'my daughter Mary would inherit my throne. A

138

nine-year-old girl, Thomas. but by God's Blood, she's all I have.'

'It is unfortunate God has not blessed you with a son,' Thomas agreed.

'Not by my queen, no,' Henry said, a crease deepening between his eyes, 'but I do have a son by another.'

'You speak of Fitzroy, Your Majesty. But he is a bastard and cannot ascend the throne.'

'Yes, I know,' Henry said impatiently, 'but—'

'And we must not give up hope that the queen will bear you a son.'

Henry made a noise of impatience. 'Kate no longer bleeds, and in truth, I lack any desire to lie with her again.'

'But you visited her chambers only last week,' Thomas protested. He knew because his spies had told him so.

'For form's sake, Thomas,' Henry said, his cheeks reddening. 'I would not have her dishonoured, but I cannot…' He made a gesture at his crotch, and Thomas understood.

'Does this happen only with the queen?' he asked.

'Yes,' Henry cried, outraged at the suggestion. 'With other women, I am…' he floundered again.

'Capable?' Thomas suggested.

'Exactly,' Henry said. 'It is Kate's fault; she is no longer bonny. But to return to my son. Bastards can be legitimised, can they not?'

'They can,' Thomas said carefully, 'but it is never ideal.'

'Nor is having a girl inherit,' Henry countered, and Thomas could not disagree.

'And yet, I am sure the Princess Mary will not be a girl when the time comes. She will be a woman.'

'Aye, a woman married to a foreign prince who will

become king of England. My realm will become a mere territory of the Spanish, not a proud country in its own right.'

It was true, Thomas reasoned. A legitimate son would be best, but if the queen no longer bled…

'Katherine will not like it, of course,' Henry said, breaking into Thomas's thoughts.

'Forgive me, Your Majesty,' Thomas said, struggling to follow, 'the queen will not like what?'

'Why, me raising up Fitzroy. But I must not be selfish and put her feelings before what is best for my kingdom.'

'Raising up Fitzroy?' Thomas repeated blankly.

'God's Blood, Thomas, what's the matter with you? Why are you so slow today? I will have Fitzroy made duke of Richmond. It was my father's title before he became king. It's fitting my son has it now.'

'So, you mean to disinherit the Princess Mary?'

Henry shrugged. 'If that's what will ensue. I cannot concern myself with her in this matter.'

'And yet, the princess is betrothed to the emperor, who expects her to inherit the throne,' Thomas reminded him. And she will lose all her value if she doesn't have that to offer him, he wanted to add, but didn't dare.

Henry waved dismissively. 'The dowry is more than generous. And what need does Charles have of England when he has so much already?' There was a note of bitterness in his voice. 'No, that consideration will not sway me. I want Fitzroy raised up and I mean to have it so.'

'If that is your wish, then I shall make the necessary arrangements,' Thomas said. 'I shall leave you if you're sure you are quite recovered.'

'Oh, there is nothing wrong with me that a little food

and wine will not put right.' Henry smiled as the door behind Thomas opened. 'And a little female company.'

Henry rose, gingerly testing his leg, and Thomas turned to see William Carey enter, followed by his wife. Henry acknowledged Carey with the briefest of greetings before taking Lady Carey's hand and pressing his lips to her slender fingers.

Thomas excused himself from the chamber, his exit barely noticed.

It was hot and stuffy in the Great Hall of Bridewell Palace. Sunlight streamed in through the windows and pierced Thomas's eyes. Needle-like pain stabbed, and he closed them, willing the pain away. The pain receded a little, and he shifted to the right, out of the sunlight, and brushed elbows with Charles Brandon. Brandon glared at him, offended by the contact, and stepped pointedly away. Thomas pretended not to notice.

There were four of them standing beneath the canopy of estate: the king, Howard, Brandon and Thomas, leaving no room for all the other nobles present, and these formed an ugly, straggling group on both sides. Thomas scanned the faces, trying to work out what they were thinking. Were they pleased at this turn of events? Or were they all outraged that a bastard boy was about to be made greater than them?

Trumpets sounded, and all attention was on the doors at the far end of the hall. They opened and Henry Fitzroy was ushered into the hall by the women who looked after him. The little boy looked all around with large, bright blue eyes. There was bewilderment and not a little fear in them. Thomas felt sorry for him. Had anyone bothered to explain what was happening, he wondered, or had the poor boy just been bundled into his finest clothes and told to behave? It suddenly occurred to Thomas that as the boy's godfather, he should have explained, told him not to worry, that all he had to do was stand in front of his father and do as he was told.

Thomas glanced at Henry. The king hadn't seen the boy for some time and he wondered what the king thought of his bastard son. The boy was a pretty thing, though not too pretty, and seemed strong. Thomas expected to see love, perhaps pride, on Henry's face, but what he saw shocked him. There was no love or pride there, only judgement.

Henry was looking at his son through narrowed eyes, his head cocked to one side, the same way Thomas had seen him looking at his horses or considering the craftsmanship of a suit of armour. What did he think? Thomas didn't know. Perhaps Henry was looking at the boy and wondering why such a fine specimen could not have been got legitimately on his queen.

The boy came to a stop at the edge of the dais and looked up. Henry in full regalia was a sight to intimidate anyone, but he made no attempt to put the boy at his ease. There were no smiles for the young Fitzroy, no wink of reassurance. This was a solemn, important event for the king, and there was no room for his customary bonhomie. The ceremony began, and the boy was manoeuvred into position, told when to kneel, when to respond.

The boy did well, despite the length of the ceremony. Henry was pleased, and there were smiles aplenty now it was all over. Henry was accepting congratulations from all his friends and nobles, and Fitzroy was left standing alone, seemingly forgotten.

Thomas stepped up to the boy, whose shoulders had drooped and whose eyes were closing in tiredness.

'My dear lord,' he said, bending down to eye level, 'how proud your father is of you.'

'Is he, godfather?' the boy squeaked, looking around Thomas to Henry, who was laughing at some comment of Brandon's.

'Of course he is,' Thomas assured him. 'I wonder if you understand what this ceremony has meant.'

'My nurse told me it means I will be king one day. Is that true?'

Thomas nodded. 'But not for some time yet. You will be a man when the time comes.'

'When the king dies?'

'Yes, when your father dies,' Thomas said, and an icy chill ran down his spine as he looked back at Henry. A memory came back to him, a conversation he and Cromwell had had when Cromwell had said all the new men at court, those that didn't have bloodlines that could be traced back to the Conquest, owed everything they had to Henry. Had Cromwell realised Thomas was one of those new men and that when Henry died, he might be one of those thrown to the wolves?

He made a fervent, silent prayer. *Please God, do not let that day be soon.*

Thomas had not been back at York Place for an hour when a summons arrived from the queen. Wondering what on earth the queen wanted to see him about, Thomas clambered back into his barge and made his way to Greenwich.

Lady Willoughby met him at the river steps.

'What is this about, my lady?' Thomas asked as he stepped onto the slippery stones.

'She's very upset, Your Eminence,' Lady Willoughby said, leading Thomas towards the palace. 'She has heard about the ceremony this morning at Bridewell.'

'You mean to say she didn't know the king was ennobling the boy?' Surely, she had been told, he thought, horrified.

'Oh, yes, she knew of it weeks ago, but she thought the king wouldn't go ahead with it. We told her he meant to, but the queen was sure he wouldn't publicly humiliate her so.'

'Did she speak to the king?'

'She's hardly seen him to talk to. And besides, the queen would never demean herself to beg him not to do it. You know how she is.'

'Perhaps it would have been better if she had,' Thomas replied grimly. 'What does she want to see me for?'

'I'm sorry, Your Eminence,' Lady Willoughby said in answer.

'Sorry for what?'

She must have detected the impatience in his voice. 'I'm afraid she rather blames you for it all.'

Thomas groaned. Lady Willoughby hurried on ahead to the queen's privy apartments, Thomas following at almost a gallop. He took a deep breath as he entered the chamber.

'This is your doing,' Katherine declared before he'd even started his bow, 'making that bastard boy duke of Richmond.'

'The boy has been raised to the degree the king thought proper, my lady,' Thomas said.

'And who helped him make that decision?'

'The king is quite capable of making his own decisions. He spoke to me of the matter, not the other way around.'

Katherine stared at him, her eyes narrowing. 'What a liar you are.'

'Lady,' Thomas said, tightening his jaw to stop himself from making a tart rejoinder, 'I beg you, do not call me so. I am not lying. This decision was the king's, and his alone.'

Katherine rose and paced the room, her heavy skirts making a loud, rustling sound. 'Why has that bastard been raised so high?'

'He is the king's son. It's right his status reflects that.'

'But what's behind it? There must be a reason. Something planned. Tell me what it is.'

'There is no reason other than what I have already said, my lady,' Thomas lied.

He wasn't about to tell Katherine the truth why Fitzroy had been raised to the dukedom, that her husband, the king, intended to set aside their daughter and make his illegitimate son his successor. That was something she should hear from Henry, if ever he decided to tell her.

'Do you know what you've done?' Katherine said, and there was a catch in her throat as her voice rose. 'You have declared to the world that I have no place at my husband's side. When you raised his bastard—'

'I did not, my lady. I merely carried out the king's wishes.'

'The entire world knows the power you have, Your Eminence. My lord does nothing without asking you first.'

Perhaps once, Thomas wanted to say, but not any more.

'And I suppose that is why you have dismissed my most faithful Spanish ladies. To diminish me.'

'Those ladies who were dismissed have all been replaced. Your state remains the same as ever it was. How then can you claim to have been diminished?'

'Because their replacements are not of my choosing,' Katherine cried through gritted teeth.

'No, my lady, they are of mine,' he admitted. 'I shall be frank with you, as you have been so frank with me. Those ladies who were dismissed were spies for foreign kings. They conveyed private information to people who had no business knowing that information.'

'You had no right.'

'I have every right, madam. The security of the kingdom was being compromised, and I will not allow that to happen.'

'You accuse me of allowing my husband's realm to be endangered?' Katherine cried.

'I make no claim you knew of your ladies' disloyalty. But their disloyalty is a fact, and there is nothing more to be said about the matter.'

'Is there not?' she snarled.

Thomas sighed loudly. 'As I am here, my lady, there is a matter I would like to speak with you about. The king has instructed me he wishes the Princess Mary to have her own household. She is to be removed from the palace and placed at Ludlow Castle by the end of the week.'

The blood drained from Katherine's face, and she took a step towards him. Her foot caught in her skirts and she stumbled, her knees hitting the floor hard. 'No,' she cried.

Two of her ladies rushed to her aid. They put their hands beneath her armpits and hauled her to her feet.

'Sit her down,' Thomas instructed, and the ladies guided Katherine to her chair.

As he looked upon Katherine, the anguish in her expression, Thomas felt ashamed of the pleasure he had taken in telling her of the arrangements for the princess. He knew Katherine loved her daughter dearly and that it would be a wrench to have her live elsewhere, but she must have known such a day would come, just as the day would come when the princess married and left England for another country altogether. Perhaps, Thomas wondered, Henry had been too kind in not removing Mary to her own household sooner. Their proximity had allowed mother and daughter to become far too attached.

Eager to depart and leave Katherine to the care of her ladies, Thomas took his leave. As the doors closed upon him, he heard Katherine whimpering, 'Don't let him take her from me.'

CHAPTER FIFTEEN

The plague was back in town and the king had removed to Eltham Palace, taking with him only a skeleton staff and planning to keep a quiet Christmas.

But the last thing Thomas wanted was a quiet Christmas, and he moved to Hampton Court where he announced the gates would remain open and anyone who wanted could come and be fed and entertained.

Thomas could hear the pleasure he was affording others, even from his office. He had arranged for a play to be put on and he would have liked to see it himself, but he couldn't leave his work. What he was working on was too important, and besides, Henry wanted it before the week was out.

He'd thought it ironic, when Henry had said he felt the time had come to impose some order upon the court and cut out waste and idleness. Hadn't Thomas attempted to do that more than five years ago, when he had convinced Henry to dismiss those of his Gentlemen who were nothing but parasites on the royal purse? How long had that purge lasted? Not more than a few months. Henry had brought his friends back one by one, giving Thomas a sheepish smile each time.

What had brought about this change of heart? Thomas wondered. Had Henry at last realised the dire state of the Treasury? Had he realised that his coffers were not bottomless? Whatever the reason, Thomas was glad. Not only was it a desire that was entirely in keeping with his own, but it was a scheme he could execute with skill. This was what he was made for, planning for efficiencies, not campaigning for war funds and being branded a tyrant.

Tuke had brought him the royal household account ledgers, and as Thomas worked through them, he was appalled by the wastage he encountered on each page. No wonder Henry had no money; it was all being spent on filling the bellies of his courtiers. So much food was being produced at mealtimes that the broken meats bowls were overflowing. Thomas had no desire to do the poor people who gathered at the palace gates out of their scraps, but the king simply could not afford to provide so much food that not even his greedy courtiers could consume it all.

Fires were being lit in rooms where no people gathered, and the finest beeswax candles used in chambers of lesser courtiers when they should have no better illumination than that afforded by tallow. And it was clear there were too many servants at court. Thomas estimated there were two servants for every courtier. He would dismiss at least a third, and the Yeoman Warders would not escape either. He would halve their number and those that remained would share their duties with the Gentlemen Pensioners. Just those measures alone would save thousands of pounds.

Thomas chided himself for allowing the household to come to this pass. He'd lost sight of his priorities, he realised. Instead of chasing foreign alliances that always ended in failure, he should have been keeping an eye on the king and reining in his spending.

This thought brought him to the last point on his list of urgent and necessary reforms, one he hoped Henry would endorse wholeheartedly, though he had his doubts. Henry was still surrounded by his friends, men who played cards with him and beat him more often than not, seizing the king's gold coins with undisguised pleasure, who went hunting and chased women with him; in short, men who encouraged all Henry's vices and none of his virtues. It would be a pleasure to point out his friends' faults and convince the king he would be better off without them. And now that Henry had matured and asked him to make such changes, Thomas felt sure there would be no argument. How satisfying it would be to say to Bryan, Compton, and Carew, 'Be gone. Your presence is no longer required.' They would protest and appeal to Henry, but to no avail, because it would be what Henry wanted. And when they were gone, Thomas would replace them with men he could trust, men loyal to him. Sir John Russell, for one, to counter the influence of Exeter, who Thomas knew the king would not part with. He would replace Compton with Henry Norris, a refined and charming man who did not indulge in puerile pastimes but could be relied upon to elevate the atmosphere of the privy chamber and show the king more sophisticated pursuits than practical jokes upon innocent bystanders and indiscriminate womanising.

But maybe, Thomas considered, he shouldn't attempt to throw out the king's friends. That was where he had gone wrong before. Perhaps he could just remove them from their paid positions? They'd still be around, of course, but he would have his own men about the king to counter their influence. Yes, he would give that some thought.

But he would replace Richard Pace. Thomas had heard worrying reports of the king's secretary behaving oddly, and Cromwell had told him rumour had it Pace was losing his wits; he certainly had failed Thomas rather too often of late for him not to take the rumour seriously. And if the poor man really was sick in the head, it would only be cruel to keep him in such a position with so much responsibility. No, far better for Pace, far better for Thomas, if he was replaced. William Knight would suit the position of king's secretary, a man who knew exactly what Thomas would expect of him.

A peal of laughter broke into his thoughts, and he looked up, wondering if he should allow himself a brief respite and go down and join in with the merry-making. He cast a look back down at his papers, considered a moment, then put his pen back to the page. This, he decided, was much more fun.

Thomas heard the shouting even before he reached the queen's privy apartments. He hurried along the corridor, drawn by the loud roar of Henry's voice, and flicked his hand angrily at the Yeoman Warders to open the doors.

Henry was standing over Katherine, his mouth mere inches away from her gable hood as he shouted at her. Katherine was cowering in her chair, one hand over her face, whimpering noises coming from between her fingers.

Henry turned at Thomas's entrance. 'Thomas,' he roared, 'what say you to this?'

To what? Thomas wondered desperately. Henry could be referring to so many things. The morning's reports had informed him of disputes in the City, smuggling in the West Country, gossip at the court of France. Henry's anger could be caused by any of those or none of them.

Thomas evidently took too long to reply, for Henry spoke again, providing the answer to Thomas's unspoken question. 'Don't tell me you haven't heard, man. That devil Charles has insulted me and dishonoured my daughter.'

Thomas winced. 'Yes, Your Majesty. I am aware he has married—'

'Isabella of Portugal,' Henry cried, and a fresh wave of crying erupted from Katherine. 'Well may you weep, madam. This is your nephew of whom I speak, that young man you so fawned and fussed over when I graciously invited him to visit us, who has done nothing but lied to me and taken me for a fool. Your blood, madam, not mine.' Henry turned to Thomas. 'I should never have trusted that young man. Never.'

'He has deceived Your Majesty most grievously,' Thomas agreed.

'Why?' Henry asked, and Thomas sensed his blustering rage was nearly spent. 'Why has he married Isabella when he could have had my daughter?'

Thomas hesitated. He could have told Henry exactly why. Firstly, that Isabella was of marriageable age whereas Mary was still a child, not fit to be wed for another six years or more. Secondly, Charles's nobles had never wanted him to marry an English princess. In their opinion, England was too insignificant and the princess unworthy of marriage to the emperor. In fact, so keen had Charles's nobles been that he should not marry Mary that they had actually paid him to look elsewhere. Thirdly, and most importantly, Isabella had come with a dowry of a million ducats, a sum worth twice as much as the eighty thousand pounds Thomas had negotiated for Mary's hand.

Charles had managed it well, Thomas couldn't deny that. The emperor had set out his conditions the month before in a letter to the Privy Council, insisting Mary be sent to Spain without delay so she could learn the language and manners of the country that would become her home. In an almost careless aside, Charles had also asked that Henry send four-hundred thousand pounds with Mary to aid him in his invasion of France, an invasion Thomas knew Charles had no intention of launching. The Privy Council had refused the conditions with Henry's indignant agreement – England didn't have that kind of money; she was in need of funds herself – and Charles had taken that refusal as justification to look elsewhere for a bride. He had sent another letter, apologising for his marriage but hoping, trusting, that Henry understood. There was no mention of the money Henry had loaned Charles on his last visit to England, and Thomas knew it would never be paid back. If the whole affair hadn't angered Henry so much, Thomas would have admired Charles's duplicity.

Instead of saying all this, Thomas lied. 'I cannot say, Your Majesty.'

Henry shook his head in disgust, and his hands went to his hips in a gesture that was becoming very familiar. 'Well, I am done with Spain and their so-called emperor. I'll have no more of him.' He glared down at Katherine, who was crying silently, and narrowed his eyes. 'Thomas, I understand Louise de Savoie is begging us to help her free King Francis from the emperor's captivity.'

'That is correct,' Thomas said eagerly, hope reviving in his heart. Some good might come out of this sorry affair after all.

'Then we must help the lady,' Henry said. 'Write to her, Thomas, and begin negotiations for a renewed peace with France.'

Katherine's cries ceased as she stared up at her husband with red, wet eyes. Henry didn't deign to give her another look.

An alliance with France. Thomas's heart leapt with pleasure. 'At once, Your Majesty,' he said.

Thomas scanned the despatch he had received from the English ambassador in France. 'King Francis has put his name to the emperor's Treaty of Madrid and has been released from captivity. Louise de Savoie sends her thanks for our support in petitioning for her son's release and also sends the first instalment of monies, which we named as condition for our help.' He picked up another page. 'The terms of the Treaty of Madrid are as follows. King Francis has sworn to surrender the territory of Burgundy to the emperor, to renounce any claim to Milan, Genoa and Naples, and to marry the emperor's sister, Eleanor, dowager queen of Portugal.' Thomas flicked a glance at Henry to see how he took this news. Henry's expression gave nothing away, so he continued. 'The emperor insisted on King Francis sending him his two sons as hostages to secure the terms of the treaty.'

There was a muttering of disapproval from the councillors around the table at this last.

Thomas set down the papers. 'I doubt if King Francis will hold true to the terms of the treaty. It was made under duress.'

'But he has sent his sons to Spain,' Warham pointed out.

Thomas nodded. 'He has, but he knows they will at least be treated fairly, if not well. The emperor will ensure no harm comes to them.'

Warham nodded and turned his face towards Henry. 'You are very quiet, Your Majesty,' he observed.

Henry was scowling and quietly drumming his fingers on the tapestry cloth that covered the Council table. 'I do not care for how King Francis has been treated by the emperor. For one sovereign to demean another so.' He shook his head. 'All I can say is I am glad we are no longer allied to that perfidious young man.'

I share that sentiment, Thomas thought ruefully. *Please God, do not change your mind again and turn against the French once more.* But as he studied Henry, he thought that was unlikely. Henry's mind seemed to be on other matters. He had not spoken of war for some time. He no longer pestered Thomas about the state of his fleet, or how much it would cost to equip an army for an invasion. Indeed, Thomas's spies informed him the king did not even speak of war in his privy chamber with his friends. There, the chatter was all about hunting and dancing, women and music, and an occasional remark that signalled displeasure with his Spanish queen. Well, that suited Thomas. Anything that reduced Katherine's influence over Henry could only be considered a good thing.

'So, we should wait and see what happens across the Narrow Sea between the emperor and King Francis,' Warham said, 'before proceeding with a new treaty with France.'

Henry sighed. 'In truth, I am sick of treaties, gentlemen. How many have there been over the last few years? I've lost count.'

'We must have alliances, Your Majesty,' Warham said.

'Must we?' Henry said, raising his eyebrows at the aged archbishop. 'I wonder if they do not do more harm than good. I sometimes think the only trustworthy man is an Englishman.'

Thomas frowned. Henry was unhappy, and Thomas felt a small stab of guilt for being pleased the alliance with Spain had fallen apart. He should have realised how Henry must be feeling, no doubt imagining all of Europe was laughing at him for having been fool enough to trust Charles.

I will take his mind off state affairs, Thomas decided. Henry needed to be distracted, and Thomas knew how to do that. He would put on feasts and masques, dances and revels, and Henry would enjoy himself again. He would not give Henry any reason to brood on his misfortunes.

The French envoys, in England to deliver the latest instalment from King Francis, seemed to be enjoying themselves. There they were, taking the hands of as many of the English women as they could, not distinguishing between wives and maids, keen to show the English how wooing should be done. If only they knew what the English really thought of them, Thomas mused. Or perhaps they did and didn't care. After all, the Frenchmen usually ended up with women in their beds while the Englishmen were left to drink themselves into oblivion.

All a lot of fuss over nothing, Thomas thought as he picked up his wine cup and took a sip. He smacked his lips in pleasure. The wine was his favourite, the Burgundy. How much of it did he have left? Not enough, probably, after all the entertaining he had been doing lately. He would get Cromwell to order some more from his supplier in Calais. Cromwell had got a very good price last time; managed to get it down by at least seven per cent. What a useful fellow Cromwell had proved to be.

Thomas scanned the room. There was one Frenchman

leaning into a woman, the feather in his cap tickling her cheek. Thomas couldn't see his hand, but he wouldn't have been surprised if it was disappearing up the woman's skirt, judging by the look on her face. He shook his head in disapproval. There was such wantonness in the young these days. He had never been so profligate with his emotions. He had loved deeply once, Alice... he frowned, trying to remember her name. Frost? No, that wasn't it. Frank? No. Finch! That was it. Alice Finch. He shook his head and laughed to himself. He hadn't thought of her in years, and wondered what had made her suddenly pop into his head. Loveplay, he supposed, that had done it. He looked back at the Frenchman and his lady, and felt a slight twinge of envy.

Joan! He said her name silently, drawing it out, letting it linger. God, he missed her. But there was no point thinking of Joan, he chided himself. She'd made it very clear in her reply to the letter he'd written while sad and lonely in Calais that while she would always love him, she could never return to the life they had had together. He'd appreciated her honesty, and had written back saying he understood and that if she ever wanted to marry, he had just the man for her, a George Legh, who he considered a fine fellow in need of a wife just like Joan. Joan had taken him up on his offer, and her last letter informed him she was expecting George's child. There was joy in her words, and though she hadn't written so, Thomas had sensed a silent rebuke of 'And this one I'm going to be allowed to keep' in her words. He felt a little jealous of her new husband, but it soon passed as he acknowledged the life she had now, while it pleased her greatly, could never satisfy him. But still, it would be pleasant to have someone lying in bed beside him of a night, to put out a hand and feel flesh receptive to his touch. He knew he could find another woman to warm his bed, but that was all she would do; another woman would never love him as Joan had done. Another woman would only be interested in being his mistress for what she could get out of him.

Still, I'm not alone in that. Thomas looked at Henry seated next to him, and wondered if a king could ever be loved for himself. Certainly, Katherine loved Henry, Thomas would swear to that, but then she had had good reason to love him. Henry had saved her from the poverty and obscurity his father had forced her into, sweeping down and carrying her off like the gallant knights of King Arthur's time he so loved to read about.

But what of Henry's other women? Bessie Blount. Had she loved him? Had Mary Carey? By all accounts, she had been a sweet creature but she had been more forced than persuaded to service Henry, and could a woman ever love a man for that? She'd lasted longer than most of Henry's amours, it was true, but even she had gone now, her purpose served. Had the king grown tired of her or she of him? Had she been sent away to give Henry the freedom to chase after her sister who had caught his eye? That must have been galling for Mary if it was true. To be supplanted by her sister. But this Anne was an ambitious creature, he mused, nodding to himself. She'd once aimed for an earl, Henry Percy, and been deprived of that particular catch. Now she was angling for a king, and not even spreading her legs to catch him, if what Cromwell told him was true. The artful little bitch. That was probably a trick she'd learnt in France, how to lead a man on without giving too much away. Had Anne told Henry she loved him? Henry was a fool if he believed her.

A high trill of laughter broke into his thoughts and

Thomas glanced to his right to see the Boleyn chit surrounded by men. The Frenchified flirt, he renamed her with a smile. Aye, there she was, chatting away with her admirers, but always looking over her shoulder to make sure the king was watching. Thomas flicked his gaze to Henry and he saw the pouty mouth and piggy eyes narrowing. Oh yes, he was caught. What had Henry let himself in for with this Anne?

'Thomas,' Henry cried, dragging his gaze away from Anne, 'a fine feast, this. We show these Frenchies a thing or two, don't we? We know how to put on a good show.'

Thomas hid his wince with a smile. Henry's voice was too loud; the French might hear. 'I like to think I set a fine table.'

'Oh, you do, you do,' Henry declared, waving his arm wide and knocking over a goblet. A servant hurried to clean up, and Thomas wondered if it was such a good idea to let the king drink so much of his finest wine. 'But let's be honest, everything you do is fine.'

There was something in the way Henry said those words that made Thomas a little uneasy. 'I'm not sure I understand you, Your Majesty.'

'Well, just look at this place,' Henry said, gesturing at the hall. 'What a palace you have made here.'

Thomas smiled. Yes, he had. Hampton Court, his dream of the perfect residence for a man such as himself, had become a reality. He had created a true Renaissance palace in England, the only one of its kind, and one that was being talked about throughout Europe with admiration and envy. He was proud of what he had built, far more than he could ever put into words.

Henry leant in closer, his wet lips at Thomas's ear. 'You know, Thomas, there are some who say you shouldn't be allowed to have such a place, that's it far too good for someone like you.'

Someone like me. Thomas's top lip curled. 'What people, Your Majesty?'

'Some of my friends. No.' He laughed and thumped the table. 'All of them, actually. And others.' Henry flicked a glance at Anne.

So, the black-eyed chit had been talking about him to the king, had she? The impudent bitch.

'I mean,' Henry continued, 'this place, this Hampton Court Palace, is far grander than anything I own, and I'm king, Thomas. Do you think that's right?'

Thomas felt suddenly sick. He should have known this day would come. Ever since Skelton had circulated those damned poems of his criticising Thomas for being so grand, there would have been talk of this kind. And Henry would have thought about it and brooded on it, and would only need someone to suggest that it wasn't right for him to agree.

He cleared his throat. 'I have long been of the opinion that it only enhances your reputation for you to have subjects able to build such homes as this. After all, it demonstrates the wealth of your kingdom and your great generosity, Your Majesty, in allowing your subjects to enjoy so much. No other king would allow their subjects such liberty. They would be tyrants, demanding that only they should enjoy such luxury.'

Henry considered this. 'There is some truth in that. I am no tyrant, Thomas.' He fell silent for a long moment, and Thomas's heart thudded against his ribcage as he saw the good humour leave the king's face. 'And yet, there are others who feel I'm wrong to allow such liberties.'

Do something, Thomas told himself, *before Henry humiliates you in front of everyone.*

'If Hampton Court is magnificent,' Thomas said, putting on a smile that showed nothing of the anxiety he was feeling, 'then I say it is magnificent only for your benefit, so that when you come to stay here, you feel comfortable.' Anne was sidling up to Henry, and he clutched at a sudden idea. 'I shall go further. If you like Hampton Court so much, I insist you have it for your own.'

Henry's eyes widened, the little mouth fell open. *Here it comes*, Thomas thought, *the refusal, the assurance that Henry would never dream of taking a man's home away from him.*

'Accepted,' Henry cried, grabbing Thomas's hand and wringing it. 'Nan,' he said, turning to Anne, 'did you hear? Thomas has given me Hampton Court.'

Anne's black eyes settled on Thomas. The thin lips pressed together and curved in a sly smile. 'How generous of His Eminence,' she purred, pressing her stomach against Henry's shoulder. 'I imagine that will be a loss His Eminence will feel keenly.'

'Not at all,' Thomas said, his shaking hand reaching for his wine cup. His throat was dry and he downed the entire cup. 'I have many places to call home, my lady. Any one of them will do for me.'

'And of course this will be much more convenient for His Majesty,' Anne said, gracing Henry with a glance. 'He has need of a residence outside of London that matches his estate, and this is far too grand for a prince of the Church, far more than any man save the king needs.'

'As you say, Nan,' Henry said, beaming up at her. He reached up to caress her neck, but she pushed his hand

162

away irritably. Henry's expression swiftly changed from one of pleasure to one that was apologetic and disappointed.

You bitch, Thomas thought as he smiled at Anne. *You cunning little bitch.*

CHAPTER SEVENTEEN

Henry had summoned him to Greenwich.

What else will I have to hand over to appease the king's vanity? he wondered bitterly as he clambered into his barge. Losing Hampton Court had left a physical pain, even though Henry had generously insisted Thomas retain a suite of rooms there for his private use, and he was hoping Anne Boleyn wouldn't encourage the king to help himself to any more of Thomas's treasures.

When he arrived in the privy chamber, Thomas found Henry slumped in his chair, contemplating the flickering fire.

'I am here, Your Majesty,' Thomas announced himself quietly when Henry didn't seem to notice.

Henry didn't reply at once. His small eyes slowly moved to Thomas, and studied him closely, taking in his scarlet robes and glistening gold cross.

'Do you remember, Thomas, some years ago, before I married the queen, there was some concern amongst my Council as to whether such a marriage would be lawful?'

'I remember.' Thomas gestured at a chair and Henry

nodded. 'I remember Archbishop Warham voiced an objection to you marrying your brother's widow, but the pope gave a dispensation and any obstacles were therefore removed.'

Henry tutted. 'Dispensation or not, I still married a woman who had been my brother's wife.'

'Arthur's wife only in name, Your Majesty. The marriage was never consummated.'

'So Katherine claimed.'

'You did not doubt her word at the time,' Thomas reminded him carefully.

'Oh, Thomas, what did I know of women then?' Henry cried. 'I was but a boy. I knew nothing. My father saw to that, keeping me close confined as if I were a girl.'

'Are you saying you now believe Katherine lied?'

Henry made a face. 'Not deliberately, no. She was a green girl, Thomas, and perhaps she wasn't aware of the… the…' He coloured and looked down at his fidgeting hands.

'The act of consummation, Your Majesty?' Thomas ventured.

'Exactly. For all I know, Kate might have thought becoming pregnant constituted consummation and not the first coupling.'

Henry was clutching at straws with this idea. Thomas doubted Katherine had been as ignorant as that. 'What exactly are you asking of me, Your Majesty?'

'This troubles me greatly, Thomas. I need the matter decided once and for all. My conscience cannot rest easy till it be so, one way or the other.'

'But, Your Majesty, how can the matter be resolved?' Thomas laughed. 'The queen is certainly no virgin now.'

'For God's sake, Thomas, this is not a laughing matter.'

Henry snatched up a Bible from the table beside his chair. It fell open at a particular page, evidence it had been scrutinised carefully. 'Here. Read that.'

Thomas took the Bible and bent his gaze to the passage beneath Henry's stabbing finger. *If a man should take his brother's wife, it is an unclean thing. He hath uncovered his brother's nakedness; they shall be childless.*

'Aye, Leviticus. I am familiar with this passage,' Thomas said, handing the Bible back to Henry, 'and admittedly it does give one pause. But I believe it is contradicted in Deuteronomy where it says a man has a duty to take his brother's widow to wife.'

'But why the contradiction, Thomas?' Henry cried. He pushed up from the chair and paced the room. 'They can't both be right, can they? The Bible only confuses matters, and I must have this matter resolved if I am to ever rest easy in my mind.'

'What do you want me to do, Your Majesty?' Thomas asked, watching Henry storm up and down.

Henry came to stand by Thomas's chair and clamped a heavy hand on his shoulder. 'I want you to discover whether my marriage to Katherine is lawful, or, God help me, I have been living in sin all these years. Will you do that for me, Thomas?'

Thomas took a deep breath. 'Of course I will, Your Majesty.'

'What did the king want?' Cromwell asked, not looking up from his books as Thomas entered the office.

Thomas threw his gloves on the windowsill. 'The king's conscience is troubling him. He's concerned his

166

marriage to the queen is…,' he threw up his hands and shook his head, 'oh, I don't know… cursed.'

Cromwell's eyebrow rose. 'Cursed?'

Thomas snorted a laugh as he fell down into his chair. 'I don't know if that's the right word for it. The king showed me a passage in Leviticus that says if a man takes his brother's wife to bed, he shall have no children by her.'

'Maybe he has a point,' Cromwell said, turning the page in his ledger and writing a note in the margin. 'I mean, there aren't any sons, are there?'

'He has a daughter,' Thomas pointed out.

'She doesn't count, though, does she? There's plenty of people think a woman can't rule, and plenty more who think they shouldn't.'

'It's not ideal for a woman to sit on the throne, certainly,' Thomas admitted, rubbing his chin. 'But you forget Richmond. The boy was ennobled precisely because of the lack of a legitimate heir. Therefore, it doesn't matter whether Henry and Katherine have a son. The throne of England will be occupied by a man with Tudor blood. The line will continue.'

'Come now, Your Eminence,' Cromwell said, taking out his penknife and trimming the nib of his quill. 'I distinctly remember you saying a bastard inheriting the throne is the worst of all possible scenarios.'

'I don't deny it, Cromwell.' Thomas slammed his hand down on the desk. 'But do you not see where Henry's conscience will lead him? If it transpires the dispensation should not have been given and that he has been living in incestuous sin all these years and that's why he has no legitimate male heir, then he will move heaven and earth to rid himself of Katherine.'

'Can he do that?'

'What? Get rid of a wife who is of no further use?' Thomas nodded. 'Oh yes. It's been done before.' He narrowed his eyes at Cromwell. 'What's that look on your face, Cromwell? What are you thinking?'

Cromwell shrugged. 'Would it be so very terrible if the king did get rid of her?'

Thomas drummed his fingers on the desk. 'Katherine is very popular, but…' he sighed heavily, 'I don't deny she's outlived her usefulness. She's failed to give the king a son, and she has an unfortunate tendency to involve herself in foreign affairs…'

'And?' Cromwell prompted.

'I suppose if Katherine were to be put away, it would leave Henry free to marry again. And a younger woman could give him the son he needs.'

'A French princess, even?' Cromwell suggested with a gleam in his eye.

Thomas couldn't help but smile back. Cromwell knew he had a preference for French alliances, and a marriage would be a perfect way to cement the friendship between England and France. Thomas tapped his finger against his lips. Maybe he could use Henry's troubled conscience to his own advantage.

'The king wants enquiries to be made into Katherine's alledged virginity at the time of their marriage,' he said.

Cromwell laughed as Thomas had done. 'And how the devil are you supposed to discover the truth of that matter after all this time?'

'I shall begin by interrogating the men who were present at the time. I'm sending you to Winchester, Cromwell. I want you to have a chat with Bishop Fox.'

. . .

Cromwell strode into Thomas's office and threw his leather satchel down on Tuke's desk. Tuke tutted loudly and moved the satchel aside.

'You stink of horse sweat, Master Cromwell,' Thomas said, noting Tuke didn't dare rebuke Cromwell for his impertinence.

'I can wash if you want,' Cromwell offered, 'or I can give you my report right now.'

Thomas looked up at him. Really, the cheek of the man. With anyone else, Thomas would have given a sharp answer.

'Very well. Give me your report.'

Cromwell snatched off his gloves and fell down into the chair by Thomas's desk. 'Bishop Fox cannot speak of his own knowledge regarding whether the marriage was consummated. He said he simply doesn't know the truth, but believed Katherine when she said it hadn't. He did recall a protest was made at the time, but by whom…,' Cromwell threw up his hands. 'He does, however, remember very clearly that the king insisted on marrying Katherine.'

'Was Fox lucid?'

'He rambled a bit, but he did seem sincere.'

'Or was he being clever?' Thomas asked. 'I mean, do you think he was avoiding giving you an answer one way or the other?'

Cromwell scratched his head. 'I wouldn't expect Bishop Fox to be anything other than clever, even in his dotage. He's near eighty years old, blind from cataracts, and I daresay he couldn't tell you what he had for supper last night, but to be fair to him, asking him to remember an incident from more than fifteen years ago is asking a lot. This doesn't help you, I know.'

'I'm sure you tried your best,' Thomas said unhappily. 'I've had a letter from the king this morning, imploring me to establish the truth at all costs. If Bishop Fox cannot, or will not, remember, then I must find others who do.'

'Or find others who will testify the way the king wants,' Cromwell said with a smile.

Thomas turned a stern look upon him. 'I give you a great deal of licence, Master Cromwell, but do not over-step the mark with me. The king has asked for the truth, not a version of the truth that suits him.'

'Are you sure that's what he's done?' Cromwell asked seriously. 'It seems to me the king wants to be rid of the queen regardless of the truth.'

'It seems to you, does it?' Thomas asked sarcastically. 'Forgive me, Master Cromwell, are you in daily confer-ence with the king and I not aware of this fact? Does he open his mind to you and tell you his innermost desires?'

'No, Your Eminence,' Cromwell admitted, chastened.

'No, I thought not. A word of advice. Never presume to know what the king wants until he has told you.'

A muffled snort of laughter came from Tuke's direc-tion. Cromwell turned his head and glared at the secretary. Tuke lowered his head and got on with his work.

'I shall remember, Your Eminence.' Cromwell got to his feet. 'What will you do now?'

'There is nothing else for it. I shall have to summon a legatine court to try this matter.'

'And what verdict will you be hoping for? That they are lawfully married or that they're not?'

Thomas looked up at him. 'I haven't decided yet, Cromwell.'

. . .

The legatine court was assembling in the Great Hall at York Place. Thomas watched the members enter from the upstairs gallery, out of sight and in shadow, courtesy of a velvet curtain that allowed him to see without being seen. He was not looking forward to the coming days. It gave him no pleasure to debate the matter of the king's marriage, not because he had sympathy for the people involved, but because he doubted whether a definitive answer could ever be reached, and if there was one thing Thomas liked it was being able to close the book on a matter. Oh, why could Katherine simply not die and spare him all this bother?

Thomas heard a shuffling behind and half-turned his head to see Archbishop Warham coming out of the private room he had been given to rest in.

'You are well, I trust, William?' Thomas asked, returning his gaze to the hall below.

'Well enough for this,' Warham said, joining Thomas at the rail. He sighed and shook his head. 'I said the marriage should never have taken place. All those years ago, I said it was wrong.'

'Yes, you did,' Thomas agreed sourly. 'But I trust you will weigh the arguments carefully when deciding on your verdict?'

Warham shot him an indignant look. 'Of course I shall. Just as I trust you will not presume to tell me what that verdict should be?'

Thomas turned to him with a smile. 'I would presume. No, William, you will hear the arguments and reach your decision and it will be accepted, whatever it may be.'

'The king wants the marriage to be found lawful, I take it?'

'The king wishes the correct verdict to be reached,' Thomas said carefully, his mind returning to the moment he told the king he had summoned the legatine court. Henry had been content until Thomas had told him he would need to appear to give testimony.

'Why must I appear?' Henry had demanded. 'Why cannot you and the others debate and decide on the matter themselves without involving me?'

'The hearing is dependant upon your testimony, I'm afraid. It must come, as it were, from the horse's mouth to have validity.'

'But I did not want to appear eager to have the matter debated,' Henry had said sulkily, and Thomas understood why. Henry wanted to appear guiltless of suggesting the marriage was invalid.

Thomas had held up his hands. 'I will order you to appear to defend your marriage. You will seem a reluctant defendant, nothing more.'

Henry had been satisfied with that.

'What does the queen think of all this?' Warham asked, gesturing at the scene below.

'The queen has no knowledge of this,' Thomas said. 'The king did not wish her to be told in case there is no need.'

'Of course there's a need,' Warham said, frowning. 'And how do you expect to keep this quiet? Secrets get out, Thomas, they always do.'

Thomas knew that, but he said nothing. That was the king's problem, he reasoned, not his.

'The queen shall not hear it from me. Not unless the king instructs me to tell her.' *And I hope to God he does not*, he added mentally. 'Time we were starting, William,' he said, and made his way down the stairs.

The first day proved tedious, just a deal of legal matters to be got through and the presentation of documents, the most important amongst these the original dispensation. The second day was little better, and Thomas had to stop himself from openly yawning. Only on the third day, when Henry was due to appear, was Thomas's interest roused.

Henry strode into the Great Hall, his long legs taking him swiftly to the chair with its canopy of estate set on Thomas's right. Henry nodded to Thomas, his eyes full of meaning, and Thomas stood up to begin.

'Your Majesty,' he said, 'you have been charged with having been living in sin with Katherine, former princess of Aragon, the lady being the widow of your late brother, Prince Arthur. As legate of the Holy See, it is my duty to see that the rites of marriage are not abused in any way. However, since I am not only a papal legate but your most devoted subject, I am firstly compelled to ask Your Majesty whether you will submit to these proceedings.'

Henry nodded, his brow furrowed. 'I most certainly do. This is a matter that has long troubled my conscience, and though it is my greatest hope that this legatine court finds me not guilty of corrupting the bonds of marriage with Katherine, I will submit to its ultimate verdict.'

Thomas thanked him and sat back down to examine the paper before him, a list of questions he and Henry had compiled that would be used in his questioning. Thomas had rehearsed Henry for hours, until he could answer without hesitation and without saying something he should not. They didn't want any surprises.

Over the next three hours, Thomas asked his questions and Henry gave his answers, growing fidgety with each passing minute. Recognising the signs of royal boredom,

Thomas decided to end the session, even though he hadn't got through half of what he had hoped. Realising too that Henry would not welcome another day or more answering questions, Thomas declared that in future sessions, the king would be represented by Dr Bell. Henry's face broke into a relieved grin, and he strode purposefully out.

CHAPTER EIGHTEEN

'Read that out again,' Thomas ordered Tuke quietly, not really believing what he had just heard.

Tuke cleared his throat and reread from the latest letter to arrive on his desk. '"The pope has been taken prisoner by Imperial troops following an attack of the greatest savagery upon Rome. The Imperial troops pillaged churches, destroying holy relics and shrines, raping any woman they encountered and butchering all the men. The pope, fearing for his very life, fled to the Castel Sant Angelo, where he was discovered and is now kept close confined."' Tuke refolded the letter. 'Is it possible?' The words shuddered out of him.

Thomas didn't answer. Like Tuke, he was shocked by this news, but his mind was also busy. What did this turn of events mean for the legatine court? The pope being a prisoner of the emperor surely meant that nothing could be officially decided or ratified, so any verdict reached would be useless.

'What can we do to help?' Tuke asked.

Thomas frowned. 'Help? Help whom?'

'The pope, Your Eminence,' Tuke said, a little bewildered by the question. 'Should we not try to free him?'

'Are you quite serious? What chance does England have against an Imperial army?'

'We have the best soldiers in the world,' Tuke declared defiantly.

Oh, you fool, Thomas thought, shaking his head at his secretary. Where did the English get the idea they were the best at everything, that God was always on their side?

'We are most certainly not going to declare war on the Spanish,' Thomas said, holding out his hand for the letter.

Tuke handed it to him. 'I doubt if the king will agree,' he muttered and returned to his desk.

Thomas watched him as he sat down and got on with his work. Tuke was right. This news was just the sort of thing that would spur Henry to take up arms, especially given the way he felt about the emperor. He rose, snatching up the letter and grabbed his gloves from the windowsill.

'Where are you going, Your Eminence?' Tuke asked.

'I'm going to the court,' Thomas said. 'I have to tell the king about this before anyone else does.'

Thomas found Henry in the gardens at Greenwich.

'Imperial forces have sacked Rome?' he said, sinking onto a stone bench and reading the letter Thomas had given him again. 'It says here Charles employed mercenaries to fight for him.' Henry made a face of disgust. 'Well, what can you expect of such a man? He has done nothing but deceive me since we met, and I am mightily glad we are no longer allied to him. I could never stand shoulder to shoulder with a man who hires mercenaries to fight his battles for him and then stands back and allows them to commit such atrocities.'

'Indeed not, Your Majesty,' Thomas agreed, watching Henry's face for signs of intent. 'But this does have unfortunate consequences for us.'

Henry was still reading the letter. 'How do you mean?' he asked distractedly.

'Regarding the legatine court. You see, without the pope, any verdict it reaches cannot now be ratified.' Thomas shrugged. 'There is no point in continuing.'

Henry jumped up from the bench. 'Do you mean to say this matter of my marriage cannot be resolved?'

Thomas took a step back, wary of the vehemence in Henry's manner. 'I fear not, Your Majesty.'

'But I must have it so.' Henry's voice had risen dramatically, and Thomas was aware of courtiers staring. 'I cannot have it delayed.' He took a deep breath and lowered his voice. 'My conscience cannot bear a delay, Thomas.'

Thomas smiled uneasily as Henry picked at a sprig sticking out of a hedge. Why, he wondered, the fervour about his conscience? Henry had had this little niggle plaguing him for years, but had never given it much heed. Why was Henry so concerned about his marriage now?

'I've been thinking I should tell Kate,' Henry said.

'No,' Thomas said before he could stop himself. He could just imagine what Katherine would do if she knew of Henry's troubled conscience. There would be letters smuggled out of England and winging their way to her nephew before Henry could blink. 'I mean, I don't think that would be wise. There's no need to upset her now, not with the legatine court ending in this way.'

'She'll have to know sometime, Thomas. I cannot bear all this pretending we are man and wife, all this…' Henry

177

shook his head and turned away. 'Very well. I shall say nothing at present. I understand King Francis has invited you to his court?'

'Yes,' Thomas said, surprised by the change in subject. 'The king has issued an invitation to celebrate the alliance between our two countries, but I will, of course, decline in view of the—'

'Nonsense,' Henry cut him off. 'You must go. If King Francis sees fit to invite you, you should not refuse. It would be very rude.'

Thomas stared at Henry. 'You wish me to go?'

Yes,' Henry said. 'If nothing else, it will show Charles how close we are to France. How soon can you leave?'

Thomas sighed. 'I can be ready to sail in a month.'

'Good. Excellent.'

'You really wish me to go?' *Please, say this is a jest.*

'Yes, yes, of course I do,' Henry said, and made a shooing gesture. 'Send me daily reports. I want to know exactly what you're doing and what's happening over there.'

A trickle of unease ran down Thomas's spine. Henry had never asked to be kept informed before. *I want to know exactly what you're doing*, Henry had said, as if he suspected Thomas would be up to no good in France. Thomas bowed and was walking away when Henry called out.

'And, Thomas?'

'Yes, Your Majesty?'

'Don't go making any arrangements without consulting me first.'

Thomas frowned. 'I go to feast the alliance, Your Majesty, that's all, so, forgive me, but what sort of arrangements do you mean?'

Henry shrugged. 'Marriages, alliances, that sort of thing. Don't commit me to anything. You understand?'

No, I don't understand, Thomas thought, but he nodded and said, 'Of course, Your Majesty.'

Henry broke his promise only a few days later and told Katherine he believed their marriage to be a sin.

When one of his spies in the queen's bedchamber came to tell him of this, Thomas silently cursed the king and cursed himself for overestimating his powers of persuasion. He had believed Henry when he had agreed not to tell the queen of his troubled conscience. What a fool he was to have done so.

'The queen was crying so loudly, Your Eminence,' his informant said, helping herself to another cake. Crumbs tumbled from her mouth as she spoke and Thomas wished she would either eat or talk, not do both at the same time. 'We could hear her from out in the corridor.'

'Did you hear what the king said to her?' Thomas asked.

She looked away, embarrassed. 'Well, we couldn't help but hear. It's not as if we were listening at the door.'

Thomas smiled understandingly, knowing that that was exactly what she and her friends had done. 'What did he say?' he pressed.

The lady put the remains of her cake on the dish and rested her hands in her lap. 'He said that although it pained him deeply, he had no choice but to admit their marriage was not lawful, that they had been living in sin and therefore they had to divorce.'

'Did the queen understand?'

She frowned. 'Did she understand that it pained him?'

Thomas did his best to hide his impatience. 'Did she understand their marriage had never been valid?'

'She was crying, Your Eminence.'

'Yes, because it was a great shock to discover she had been living in sin with the king all these years. But did she agree with him?'

'I don't know, Your Eminence. She was crying so greatly, I'm not sure she even spoke to the king.'

'Did she say nothing to you or the other ladies after the king had left?'

The lady shook her head. 'The queen could barely speak, she was so distressed. Oh, no, I forgot. She did say something. She said she would never enter a nunnery.'

'I see,' Thomas said with a smile, though his heart was sinking. 'Well, thank you for bringing me this information.'

The lady looked disappointed she wasn't to be allowed to finish her biscuit and wine. Tuke showed her out as Thomas returned to his desk. His mind was reeling. It was clear to him now that Henry had never intended waiting for the legatine court's judgement. That was just a formality he felt he had had to endure, and now that had become pointless, he had taken the next step and told his wife of his conscience.

But what is driving him? Thomas wondered. Was it simply the desire for a legitimate male heir? Thomas knew Katherine no longer bled, so even if Henry was still visiting her bed, he would never get a child on her again.

Thomas sighed. So, the king wanted a divorce. Then he would have to ensure he got one. He would help the king get rid of Katherine as quickly as possible, but it wouldn't be easy. Katherine had already said she would not go quietly – no nunnery for her – and Thomas believed her.

Her love for Henry was very strong. Even if Henry no longer wanted her, Thomas suspected Katherine would do all she could to keep hold of him.

But if she was going to fight for her marriage, then she would need help. No doubt she would contact her nephew, but Thomas couldn't concern himself with that young man just yet. A message to Charles would take weeks to arrive and more weeks to reply. In the meantime, Katherine would undoubtedly seek advice and help within England. And Thomas believed he knew who she would turn to first.

Thomas found Bishop Fisher, despite the warmth of the day, wrapped up in a blanket in his privy chamber. The old man gave him the thinnest of smiles, the yellow-tinted eyes watching him warily as Thomas took a seat opposite and gave the red velvet cushion a good plumping.

'A personal visit from His Eminence,' Fisher smiled. 'I am honoured.'

'I'm on my way to France, to Amiens,' Thomas said.

'Ah, that would explain the look of unease on your face. I shall pray you have an easy crossing.'

'I'd be grateful. For myself, I'd rather not go, but…' Thomas sighed, 'the king insists.'

'You should have sent me word. I would have had rooms made ready for you to rest overnight.'

'Thank you, but there's no need. I'm not stopping. I come here on the king's business.'

'My dear Thomas, when did you ever come on anything else?'

'Well, that is to say, he hasn't sent me, but I wish to ask you something regarding the king. Him and the queen.'

Fisher spread his hands, gesturing Thomas to continue.

'Has the queen written to you,' Thomas asked, 'or sent a message via one of her people?'

The old man drew in a raggedy breath and set his eyes on Thomas's silk covered knees.

'Has she?' Thomas asked impatiently.

Fisher raised his gaze to Thomas. 'The queen has sent to me, just a few days ago, in fact. A man came here and said there were certain matters that had arisen between herself and the king and upon which she would value my counsel.'

'Nothing more than that?'

Fisher shook his head.

'And your reply?'

'I sent a message back saying I would be pleased to offer my advice to the queen but only with the king's approval and permission.'

Thomas let out a silent breath of relief. Katherine would get no help from Bishop Fisher. 'Did she explain what the certain matters were?'

'She did not. But I believe I can work them out. The king has some concern over the validity of his marriage. Am I right?'

Thomas nodded. 'You are correct. The king is concerned that the dispensation issued by the pope to allow him to marry his brother's widow was not lawful, that it should not have been given.'

'Which explains you holding a legatine court.'

Thomas could not help but smile. 'That was supposed to be a secret.'

'It's hard to keep a secret amongst the clergy, you know that. I assume you've had to disband the court in light of what has happened to the pope?'

'Yes,' Thomas said gloomily, 'and as you can imagine, the king was less than pleased.'

Fisher made a face that suggested he could imagine well enough. 'And your trip to France?'

Thomas shook his head. 'Unrelated. I go to celebrate the treaty we have just signed.'

Fisher frowned. 'You came to see me just to find out if the queen has been in touch?'

'No.' Thomas ran a hand over his face, feeling the stubble prickle against his palm. 'I shall be frank, John. The king is not merely worried about whether his marriage to Katherine is a sin or not. He wants a divorce.'

Fisher shook his head sadly. 'The marriage was lawful, Thomas. I agree, the dispensation was controversial at the time, but after all these years....' He sighed. 'The king cannot just say it is not so. Does he wish to marry another woman?'

'No. But obviously, if he was free, it would make sense for him to remarry.'

'A French princess, perhaps?' Fisher suggested with a smile.

'I do not deny the thought had occurred,' Thomas said, a little embarrassed to have been read so easily. 'But there are many hurdles to overcome before we reach that point.'

'Indeed,' Fisher agreed. 'Only the pope can grant the king a divorce, and the pope is not currently in an position to do that.'

Thomas edged closer. 'That is the real reason I'm here. I have an idea, and I wanted your opinion on whether it is feasible or not.'

'I'm intrigued.'

'The king is eager for this matter to be resolved as soon as possible. As you say, the pope's imprisonment inevitably means a delay, perhaps a very long delay. But if an interim pope, say, were to be appointed…'

'You?'

Thomas didn't like Fisher's derisory tone. 'Why not?'

'No reason,' Fisher said, his bushy eyebrows rising. 'It is an unusual situation, but presumably the process remains the same. You would need to be elected by the College of Cardinals. Aren't some imprisoned with the pope in the Castel Sant Angelo?'

'Some, not all. And yes, they would need to elect me.' Thomas took a deep breath. 'I'm thinking of writing to those that are free and asking them to meet me in Avignon.'

'Will you tell them why?'

Thomas shrugged. 'To discuss how the Church can function with the pope in captivity.'

'And then you will suggest it can best function with you at its temporary head.'

'You have it. What do you think?'

Fisher drew in a deep breath. 'Audacious, even for you. But if anyone can do it…' He laughed. 'I wish you luck. I hope for your sake you succeed.'

'Why for my sake?'

'I fear the king has changed, Thomas, and not entirely for the better. He seems less…' Fisher searched for the word he wanted, 'reasonable than he used to be. I see him growing more like his father, which admittedly is no bad thing, but he has much of his grandfather in him too, more perhaps than is good for him. Or for anyone else, come to that.'

Thomas stared at the old man. 'You fear for me?'

'You're very useful to the king, Thomas, and long may you always be so. But his father was not sentimental, and

184

as I say, Henry is becoming more and more like him.' Fisher clapped his hands. 'But I must not keep you. You are on your way to France.'

'Indeed,' Thomas nodded and rose.

'Kings, queens, emperors.' Fisher shook his head with a smile. 'I remember you all those years ago when you first came to court as old King Henry's almoner. Who would have thought then you would rise so high?'

Thomas stared down at him. 'I would have thought it, bishop.'

'Yes,' Fisher said, his eyes full of understanding. 'I suppose you would.'

CHAPTER NINETEEN

Bishop Fisher's prayers seemed to have worked. The crossing to Calais was mostly uneventful, Thomas feeling only a little seasick, and he made his way to Amiens with, if not pleasure, then at least content in the knowledge he would be treated well by the French king, something he felt had been lacking at the English court of late.

And he needed treating well. The Narrow Sea journey had been bearable enough, but ever since setting foot on French soil, Thomas had been beset by trial after trial. He had almost broken his neck in Boulogne when the cannon firing to greet his arrival caused his mule to rear and nearly throw him, and walls near his private apartments had been covered in graffiti of the most base and insulting kind, including a depiction of a cardinal's hat with a gallows looming over it etched into the stone windowsill of his privy chamber. Then there had been the repeated thefts of his private property; silverware and personal items had gone missing and were never recovered. And to top it all, one member of his personal band of musicians had died, it seemed, from sheer exhaustion. Thomas thought he could be forgiven for wondering if this journey was ill-fated.

And then Thomas had received word that King Francis had been in a riding accident and had badly injured his leg. The news worried him more than all the other calamities put together. Would Francis put off their meeting, or worse, decide he was too incommoded to meet with Thomas at all?

So it was a relief when Pequigny Castle came into view and Thomas saw the gates open and the king riding out to greet him. Thomas kicked his mule's sides and galloped to meet him halfway.

'I am glad to see you able to ride your horse again, Your Majesty,' Thomas called as they both reined in their mounts. 'I heard of your accident.'

King Francis nodded. 'Aye, I had a bad fall. But I am better, if not fully recovered. Well enough to do this, at least. I could not let you enter Amiens without greeting you personally.'

'You do me too much honour, Your Majesty.'

'Impossible. Not for the man who did so much to secure my freedom from the emperor.'

Thomas almost reddened with shame. It was true that he had written to Charles to plead for Francis's release, but that had been one letter, one measly little letter written so Thomas could say he had done something. There had been so much more he could have done had he had a mind to.

'Come,' Francis said. 'Let me show you to your lodging. I doubt you will find it as comfortable as your famous Hampton Court, but I hope it will do well enough.'

The mention of Hampton Court irked him, but Thomas forced a smile onto his face. 'I would bear any discomfort to be a guest of yours, Your Majesty, but I am sure the lodgings are splendid, far too good for one such as I. Please, lead the way.'

The festivities had come to an end. The Treaty of Windsor had been celebrated, copies made, signed and sealed, the public banquet completed. Now, Thomas could afford to relax a little, as least as much as a private meeting with the king and his mother would allow.

Louise de Savoie fingered the stem of her goblet and looked at Thomas shrewdly. 'We have had a letter from the emperor. He has heard from his aunt, Queen Katherine, who is most unhappy. It seems there is a question over her marriage to your king, Your Eminence.'

So, Katherine had managed to get a message to Charles, Thomas thought in dismay. If Francis and his mother knew of the trouble in England, how many other European sovereigns knew of it too? So much for hoping the troubled marriage could be kept a secret.

'The question of the validity of the original dispensation has been raised by some in England,' Thomas said, careful not to let them know it had been Henry who had raised the question. 'It may be that the marriage between my king and Katherine was not lawful.'

'To have been living in sin all these years?' Louise flicked a glance at her son. 'Poor Katherine must be stricken with shame.'

'I fear Katherine does not see it that way,' Thomas said, knowing Louise had no sympathy at all for Katherine. It had been no secret that Louise had found Katherine's company tedious when they had met at the Val d'Or. 'But as you have raised the subject, I wonder if I might ask you a hypothetical question?'

'Please do,' Francis said.

Thomas took a gulp of his wine, dabbing his lips with a napkin before continuing. He wanted to phrase this question just right. 'If King Henry were free to marry again, would a French princess be considered as a possible bride?'

Francis looked at his mother, who gave him an almost imperceptible nod in reply. 'There is a girl who would do for your king,' he said.

'Tell us,' Louise said, tapping the table to get his attention. 'Has King Henry asked you to ask us this?'

Thomas smiled. 'I think we had better leave the matter there, lady.'

Louise nodded, understanding his reluctance to give her an answer. 'He would need to be free first, of course, and he isn't.'

'Nor likely to be,' Francis added, popping a grape into his mouth. 'Charles will not allow his aunt to be so disgraced, and he has the pope under his thumb. He will instruct Clement not to rescind the dispensation. Henry is stuck with his queen, I fear.'

'But, my darling,' Louise said, her eyes twinkling, 'His Eminence has a plan to circumvent that particular problem, do you not?'

Thomas stared at her. How did she know?

'A plan?' Francis said. 'What plan?'

'I had hoped,' Thomas said, a little shyly, 'my fellow cardinals would realise that a pope in captivity is unable to lead the Church and that a temporary head be appointed. In short, I suggested I be that temporary head.'

'Have the cardinals you wrote to responded?' Louise asked.

His cheeks grew hot. 'Only six replied, and none of

them agreed to meet with me in Avignon. It seems they would rather halt all Church business until the emperor lets the pope go free.'

'You have my sympathy, Your Eminence,' Francis said. 'One tries to do one's best, and one's fellows let one down.'

'Indeed,' Thomas agreed, hoping he hadn't shown how truly disappointed he was.

He had never wanted to be pope. Whenever Henry had made him put his name forward before, he had always been glad when another was elected. But now, he needed the power that went with being the leader of the Church. If he were pope, even temporarily, Thomas could declare the original dispensation invalid, annul the marriage and arrange another to a French princess, thereby creating a dynastic alliance that not even Henry would sever without acknowledging there would be severe repercussions.

As he gulped down his wine, accepting a plate of sweetmeats from Louise, Thomas realised with dismay that he was no nearer giving Henry what he wanted than he had been when he left England.

'I think you should have told Wolsey what you intend,' Anne said, rubbing her fingers along the back of Henry's chair.

Henry shook his head. 'Thomas doesn't need to know just yet, my love.'

'You mean if he knows, he will do all he can to thwart us.'

'Now, now, Nan,' Henry said, taking hold of her hand and shaking it gently, 'Thomas works hard for me always.' Anne gave him a look that suggested otherwise and he thrust out his bottom lip sulkily. 'Why do you not think so?'

Anne shrugged and looked across the room to her uncle, who read the meaning in her eyes and nodded. 'My niece has a point,' Howard said. 'After all, Your Majesty, just think back over the last few years. Wolsey failed to get the funding for your war with France and caused your subjects to revolt. The alliance with Spain was beset by problems from the very beginning, and he allowed the emperor to deceive you with promises, and I don't know what else. And yet, still he prospers. Tell me, Anne. How much money do you think the cardinal has?'

'Why, Uncle,' Anne said on cue, 'I cannot begin to guess, but it must be a great deal. Any man who can build such residences as Hampton Court...' She glanced at Henry to see his reaction. 'But at least that palace is now in the hands of a man who deserves it.'

Henry grinned. He was indeed very pleased to be the owner of that particular palace and was already working on how he could make his own improvements.

Anne tutted, annoyed that her words had not provoked more of a reaction from Henry. 'And what is he doing in France?' she cried, throwing up her hands in exasperation.

'Well, we don't know,' Howard replied.

'No, we don't know, Uncle,' Anne agreed vehemently. 'Feathering his own nest, no doubt.'

'He's gone to ratify the treaty,' Henry protested, a trifle impatiently.

'But what else?' Anne said.

'Nothing else. I explicitly told him he was to make no arrangements for me.'

'Such as?'

'Well,' Henry looked away, 'marriages, that sort of thing.'

'Because you haven't told him about us,' Anne said with a note of triumph. 'I suppose he's over there arranging a marriage with a French princess. You'll be betrothed before you know it, Wolsey's pockets a little more full, and I'll be dismissed from the court.'

'Nan, please,' Henry pleaded, growing a little tired of being harangued in this way.

'He needs to know, my lord,' Anne insisted, and cast a glance at her uncle, asking permission to continue. Howard nodded. 'After all, we will need a dispensation to wed.'

Henry looked up at her, his brow creasing. 'Why so?'

'Because of Mary,' Anne said, and was pleased to see Henry's face colour. 'You bedded her. If you bed me, you shall be committing incest, and that will be as bad as marrying your brother's wife.'

'I wish I had never laid eyes on your sister,' Henry said vehemently, kissing both of Anne's hands.

'Wishing a thing will not make it so,' she said sourly, drawing them away.

'You know, Anne,' Howard interrupted, 'perhaps it's best Wolsey doesn't know a dispensation will be needed. He's bound to stall if he knew about it. After all, he won't want the king to marry you. Perhaps it's best if we bypass him altogether.'

'How do you mean?' Henry asked.

'You can send direct to the pope in Rome.'

'The pope is a prisoner of the emperor,' Henry pointed out.

'But he must be allowed visitors,' Howard said. 'He is still the pope, Your Majesty, and Charles must respect that.

He must allow the Defender of the Faith to communicate with Clement.'

Henry's chest swelled with pride at the mention of his title. But then he frowned. 'Wolsey's always been my intermediary with Rome. How do I get in touch with Clement? Will he see anyone not sent by a cardinal?'

'Of course he will,' Howard assured him. 'All you have to do is choose a faithful man who will do as you tell him and who won't go blabbing. One of your secretaries will do. Just choose the one you trust most.'

'Aye,' Henry nodded, 'I will send William Knight.'

'There, you see, you have the answer,' Howard cried happily. He winked at Anne. 'What need you have of Wolsey?'

Anne smiled smugly back.

Cromwell coughed from the doorway. 'Forgive me for disturbing you, Your Eminence, I know you're resting, but I think you'll want to see the man I have here.'

Thomas, enjoying a rare moment to himself, closed his book reluctantly and nodded, knowing that if Cromwell said he should see his unexpected visitor, then he most definitely should. A moment later, Cromwell returned, followed by William Knight.

'Master Knight,' Thomas said, surprised and gesturing the old man to a chair, 'what do you do here in France?'

'The king sent me,' Knight said, sinking into the chair opposite Thomas gratefully. He gave a deep sigh of relief. 'That is, the king has sent me to Rome, but I felt I simply couldn't go there without seeing you first.'

Thomas's nerves began to tingle. What was the king doing, sending envoys to the pope without telling him? He jerked his head at Cromwell to stay in the room and close the door.

'Why is the king sending you to Rome?' he asked Knight.

'Cup of wine?' Cromwell offered, and put a cup into Knight's hand before he could answer.

'Oh, thank you, Master Cromwell,' Knight said, taking a gulp.

'Secret mission, is it?' Cromwell asked.

Knight looked up at him, then across to Thomas, his gaze asking why His Eminence was allowing Cromwell to talk to him so impudently. Thomas didn't care if Knight was affronted; he wanted an answer.

'Well?' Cromwell pushed.

'Yes, it is.' Knight directed his answer to Thomas. 'Why it should be so, I have no idea, though I suspect he is being advised by certain people.'

Cromwell turned to Thomas. 'The Howards.'

'Why have you been sent?' Thomas asked again.

'The king wants me to ask the pope to issue a dispensation on the grounds of consanguinity.'

Thomas glanced at Cromwell, who gave an equally confused glance back. 'You've lost me, Master Knight. Why would he need such a dispensation?'

'Well, because of Lady Carey having been his mistress,' Knight shrugged, taking another gulp of wine.

'What the devil are you talking about?' Thomas cried, his patience wearing thin.

Knight was taken aback and stared, a little wary, from Thomas to Cromwell and back again. 'Lady Anne Boleyn being Lady Carey's sister,' he said, frowning.

'Yes, I know. So what? He doesn't need a dispensation to take her as a mistress.'

'But he will need one to marry her,' Knight said.

'Marry her?' Thomas cried, rising from his seat and towering over Knight.

'Are you saying the king intends to marry Lady Anne?' Cromwell asked.

'Well, yes,' Knight replied. 'That's why he wants a divorce. Did you not know, Your Eminence?'

Thomas fell back into his chair, stunned. He heard Cromwell pull Knight to his feet and show him out of the office.

'Your Eminence?' Cromwell said. 'Are you all right?'

'Yes, Cromwell,' Thomas said after a moment. 'Quite all right.

'You didn't know what the king intended?'

'No, I didn't. Did you?'

'I heard rumours, but that's all they were. I didn't think even the Howards were that ambitious.'

'You should have told me. I rely on you to keep me informed.'

'I'm sorry. I should have done, I realise that now.'

'Why?' Thomas wondered. 'Why does he want to marry her? I can get him a French princess.'

'I suppose she's convinced him he's in love with her,' Cromwell shrugged. 'Although what he sees in her, I don't know.'

'Oh, but it makes sense now,' Thomas cried, slapping his forehead at his stupidity. 'The king told me not to make any arrangements for him while I'm here in France. No marriages, he said. Well, now I know why, don't I?'

Cromwell seated himself in the chair vacated by Knight. 'Why didn't the king tell you what he intended?'

Thomas's jaw set hard. 'I don't know. Maybe he thought I would try and talk him out of it.'

'And would you?'

'Of course I would,' Thomas snapped. 'Why marry the Boleyn girl? She's nothing. So, she refuses to spread her legs for him. Is that reason enough to marry her?' He wiped his hand over his face. 'It's just like his grandfather when he married the Woodville wench. She refused to go to his bed, and so to get her into it, he promised her marriage and so ruined all the work Warwick had done to get him a foreign bride.'

'Have you spoken to King Francis of a marriage for a French princess?'

Thomas shook his head. 'I raised the possibility, that's all. I've committed the king to nothing, thank God.'

'So, what will you do now? Will you let Master Knight continue on to Rome?'

'I can't stop him. How would that look to the king? No, I must let him carry on.' Thomas sighed. 'See that Knight is taken care of tonight, Cromwell. He is a good man. He did well to let me know of this, especially as it was against the king's instructions.'

'I'll see he's all right,' Cromwell promised. He studied Thomas. 'Are you all right?'

'In truth, I don't know, Cromwell. The king has never treated me like this before, and I don't know why he should. What have I ever done but for his good? When have I ever put another's wishes before his? Never, I tell you, and this is how I am rewarded.'

'Women,' Cromwell said wryly.

'Aye,' Thomas agreed. 'Women.'

CHAPTER TWENTY

Thomas returned to England and made it his first duty to see the king.

Henry was at Richmond, and Thomas sent word on ahead that he was coming. In his letter he asked in which private place the king would like to meet with him, it being the custom between them to speak alone together before they gave audience to the rest of the Privy Council. When he arrived, Thomas was dismayed when a page brought a message, not from the king but from Lady Anne, stating he was to come to the privy chamber where they both currently were. Thomas nodded at the page, trying to hide his dismay that his meeting was not to be with Henry alone but with the Night Crow, as Anne was being called, as well.

Thomas passed through the doors of the privy chamber, and saw Anne standing by Henry's chair, her hand draped over his shoulder, his fingers playing with hers. Thomas forced a smile.

'So you're back,' Henry said without rising, taking in

his presence with the briefest of glances before returning his gaze to Anne. 'How did it go in France?'

'The treaty is signed,' Thomas said, 'and King Francis wished me to remind you of his great love and friendship. To demonstrate his love, he has sent several gifts for you. A golden chalice and patten, gold and silk altar cloths for your chapels and several exquisite tapestries.'

'Excellent,' Henry said carelessly.

Are you not even going to ask to see them? Thomas wondered. 'On other matters, I fear we have been less than successful.' He glanced at Anne. What was that he saw in her eyes? Pleasure at his failure, or something else entirely? 'You remember, I wrote to you of my idea to form a temporary Church authority while Clement is a prisoner of the emperor. I thought it might aid Your Majesty's secret matter. Unfortunately, my suggestions met with little enthusiasm from my brother cardinals.'

'How is that possible, Your Eminence?' Lady Anne asked. Was she so at ease that not only would she address him directly but without obtaining the king's permission to do so first? 'I thought a request from you was as good as a command.'

'Would that were so, lady,' Thomas said, 'but alas, it seems not. I understand Clement himself forbade any of the cardinals from meeting with me, I suspect, following pressure from the emperor, who it seems, has discovered your secret matter.'

Henry's frown deepened. 'How did he find out?'

Thomas shrugged. 'I am afraid that rumours were already spreading before I left for France. And it seems the queen was able to get a message to him after you told her of your troubled conscience.'

Had he been too sarcastic with that last comment? The

look Anne gave him suggested he had, but Henry seemed not to have noticed.

'Of course she told him,' Anne said. 'She would do anything to thwart us.'

Henry looked up at her adoringly. 'I am sorry, my love. Would that I could silence her.'

'Permanently?' Anne suggested with a raise of a dark eyebrow.

Henry's mouth twitched in amusement and he reached up to stroke the top of the breast that was peeking above Anne's bodice.

Thomas stared, wondering what on earth had happened to Henry. There had been a time when he would never have acted so licentiously before another person. Had his presence been forgotten already? He coughed delicately to remind the king he was there.

Henry snatched his hand away and Thomas saw the pink in his cheeks deepen. 'But the treaty, Thomas?' Henry said, not meeting his eyes. 'That has been a success?'

'A great success,' Thomas confirmed. 'It was all we could have hoped for.'

'Well, that is something,' Henry said. 'That seems to be everything. You may go, Thomas. We'll speak further tomorrow.'

Dismissed? Just like that, after no more than a quarter of an hour audience? He had not even been offered a cup of wine. Thomas felt his own face reddening. He thanked the king and retreated, angry as the doors closed behind him.

This was not the kind of welcome he had expected or was used to.

. . .

'Joan?' Thomas cried in delighted surprise as he entered his private office back at York Place. 'What are you doing here?'

He moved forward to embrace her, holding her a little tighter and a little longer than was appropriate, he realised. He stepped back, embarrassed.

'Well, I know I should have made an appointment,' Joan joked.

'You never have to,' he assured her, holding both her hands and kissing them lightly. 'Have my lazy servants looked after you?'

'Very well,' she said, sitting down in the chair he guided her towards. 'That young man of yours…'

'Which young man? Oh, you mean George Cavendish.'

'Cavendish, yes, that was his name. Said he would not allow me to wait, but that he would see me here himself. It was very kind of him, considering I'm only a—'

'You are never 'only' anything, Joan,' Thomas said, mentally thanking Cavendish for his kind treatment of Joan.

Joan smiled, dimples appearing in her cheeks, and he resisted the urge to put his arms around her and hold her. She looked into his face.

'You look tired, Tom.'

He sank into his chair opposite. 'Oh, a little, my dear. I've only just returned from France and I went directly to see the king, so I haven't had a chance to rest.'

'You should make time,' she scolded kindly. 'You're no use to anyone if you make yourself ill.'

He waved her concern away. 'Tell me, how is your family?'

'All hail and hearty. My husband sends his regards.

And I had a letter from our son.' She leaned forward and took hold of his hand. 'You should have told me what you were going to do for him.'

Thomas smiled. He had arranged for their son to become the dean of Wells, an entirely nepotistic appointment that had caused more than a few fellow Churchmen to curse Thomas and whisper behind their hands. 'It was the least I could do.'

'Well, he's very grateful,' Joan said. 'And so am I.'

He shook his head; he didn't need Joan to be grateful. It was enough she was pleased. 'And what of Dorothy?' he asked. 'I've not heard from her lately.'

'Our daughter's fine, too. We're all well, Tom, which is more than I can say of you.'

'It's just weariness,' he protested, growing a little annoyed at her persistence.

'It's more than that,' she said shrewdly. 'We hear the rumours, even in Norfolk.' She got up and moved to the small table by the window to pour them both a cup of wine. She pressed one cup into his hand. 'I know you've lost Hampton Court.'

Thomas swallowed down a mouthful of the wine. 'I didn't lose it, Joan. I gave it to the king.'

Joan fell back into the chair. 'For God's sake, why? You've put your heart and soul into that place, Tom, as well as God knows how much money. Why give it to the king? Has he not enough houses of his own?'

'I didn't want to,' Thomas admitted bitterly. 'I had no choice if I didn't want to incur his disfavour.' He gave Joan a sad smile. 'It is too grand, it seems, for the likes of me.'

'What do you mean for the likes of you?' Joan cried,

and Thomas's heart swelled to hear her so indignant on his behalf.

'I am a self-made man, Joan,' he explained, 'and I have made enemies.'

'You mean the nobility.'

'Yes, them, but not just them. Many people hate me. It doesn't matter,' he said, holding up his hands as Joan was about to protest, 'I can bear their dislike. I cannot bear the king's. And the king was not happy about me having so grand a home.'

'Was he unhappy, or was that woman jealous?' Joan asked sharply.

'What woman?'

'Nan Bullen, isn't that her name? The king's new bedwarmer, that's what we've heard.'

Thomas shook his head. 'Then you've heard wrong, my dear. Lady Anne does not warm his bed. At least, not yet.'

'But everyone says she's his mistress.'

'She holds herself very dear and will not submit.'

'The clever bitch. Well, don't you see?' she added at Thomas's quizzical expression. 'Men like the chase, do they not? Give the king what he wants as soon as he wants it, and he will quickly tire of her. If she holds out, his passion is stoked.'

'Do all women think so strategically?' Thomas laughed.

Joan's mouth twisted in a reluctant smile. 'Not all women have the means.' She gestured at her plump body as if it were poor goods.

Thomas wasn't having that. Joan was beautiful, to him, at least. 'I have no idea what the king sees in her, and I know I am not alone. She is skinny and small, her skin is sallow, her hair too dark, and has no breasts to speak of.'

'It takes all sorts, Tom.'

'That must be true.' He rubbed his chin. 'But whatever she has to attract him, it has changed the king. He is not as he once was.'

'How do you mean?'

Thomas considered. 'He is impatient and suspicious. I think the Howards and the Boleyns are constantly pouring poison in his ear. The reports I get say they are very often in his company, even to the exclusion of his friends, and the Howards do not care for me. I shudder to think what they say of me to the king.'

Joan frowned. 'You're not in any danger, are you, Tom?'

He shook his head. 'I am fine, Joan. Whatever may be said of me, the king knows he needs me.'

'He needs you?' Joan cried. 'Is that all?'

'No, that's not all,' he said, annoyed by his choice of words. 'The king loves me. He and I have been friends for far too long for any slip of a girl to change that.' Now it was his turn to lean forward and take her hand. He kissed her fat fingers. 'You must not worry about me, Joan.'

'I cannot help but worry about you,' she said, smiling.

Shall I ask her to come back to me again? he wondered. This felt so good, to be sitting with her, telling his worries and having her worry about him, just like the old days. He opened his mouth to speak.

'I can only stay a few days, Tom,' Joan said, sliding her hand from his. 'George needs me.'

Thomas sank back in his chair, hoping the growing darkness in the room hid his disappointment.

CHAPTER TWENTY-ONE

Clement had escaped from the Castel Sant Angelo.

Thomas suspected the emperor had grown tired of being called a tyrant throughout Europe for imprisoning the pope and arranged for his captive to find a way out of the fortress. With Clement now free and able to receive visitors, Thomas decided to send a request that the king's divorce from Katherine be granted.

Thomas had recently appointed a new secretary. He'd grown a little tired of Brian Tuke's complaining and sent him away to serve a new master. His replacement was Stephen Gardiner, a very different type of man, and Thomas was not entirely sure he had made a good choice. Gardiner was waiting, a trifle impatiently, at his desk, quill pen poised to write the letter Thomas was forming in his mind.

It was proving a little tricky. Thomas was used to writing diplomatically worded letters, couching his requests and orders in flowery language, but he felt that the time for such missives had passed. Henry was, like Gardiner, growing impatient. His separation from

Katherine was taking too long. Although he was still courteous in public, in private Henry railed against his wife, accusing her of stirring up foreign opinion against him through her nephew, and declaring that if it hadn't been for her meddling, they would be divorced by now. So annoyed was he that Henry wasn't even pretending that his conscience troubled him still. He no longer cared whether Katherine had slept with his brother or not. Henry didn't want her as his wife, he wanted his Anne, and he would do anything to get her. Or rather, he would make Thomas do anything to make it so.

Thomas wondered a little resentfully if Henry realised just how difficult a task he had given him. The king could not just demand a divorce and expect it to be granted. He especially could not expect it when his wife was the aunt of the most powerful man in Europe and the man who had the pope under his thumb. Clement might be physically free, but in every other way, he was entirely bound to Charles.

But Thomas knew he must try, else Henry would never be satisfied. He needed a very special emissary, a man who had cunning and persistence, who would do all he could to get an audience with the pope. Inspiration came to Thomas in the middle of the night. He had sat up in bed and declared to the darkness, 'Sir Gregory di Casale. He's the very man.'

Thomas nodded at Gardiner that he was ready to begin dictating his letter to di Casale. He began by stating that to avoid him being turned away at the gate as an obvious envoy from Wolsey, he was to dress in the manner of a servant of the duke of Ferrara, a person Thomas knew was accustomed to always being granted an audience by Clement. Once he was in front of the pope, di Casale could admit the truth, that he carried a message from England, and explain how important it was that Clement grant the king's divorce. After all, he was to say, Henry had always been a faithful and dependable son of the Church, and would do all he could to defend the Church against her enemies, whosoever and wherever they might be. Once that had been said, di Casale was to impress upon the pope just how greatly the people of England wanted their king to have a son to succeed to the throne after him. If Henry were to die without a male heir, di Casale must say, Cardinal Wolsey foresaw a terrible civil war would ensue, which it was the pope's duty, as the father of Christendom, to avoid if at all possible. And avoidance was possible as long as Henry was free to marry again.

'Is that all, Your Eminence?' Gardiner asked, flexing his fingers against cramp.

'Just one more paragraph,' Thomas replied and nodded for Gardiner to pick up his quill again. '"I am sending ten thousand ducats to your bank in Venice. You must use this money to persuade the cardinals still in Rome to support you in this commission. Do not assume they will all require the same amount. Some may be more cheaply bought than others, so start low and let them negotiate you upwards."' He broke off and Gardiner, convinced Thomas had finished this time, reached for the sand shaker to dry the ink.

'Actually, Stephen,' Thomas halted him, 'there are two other points I wish to mention. Take this down. "I wish you to make it clear to the pope that if he refuses to grant King Henry the right to have his marriage tried in England, or if he agrees to a trial but it doesn't give the king the verdict he desires, that I will find it difficult, if not impossible, to serve any future interests the pope or his successors might have, as the authority and judgement of the Church will be seriously undermined. Inform the pope that there are other, secret reasons I will not commit to paper as to why the king must be granted a divorce from Queen Katherine. Imply, but do not state directly, that these reasons relate to the state of her body and that there is no remedy for them. He should be able to determine what we are getting at by those words." There, I have finished now. You can sign and seal it, Stephen, and have it despatched at once.'

As Gardiner headed out the door with the letter, Thomas breathed a sigh of relief that he had done all that he could, his only desire now that he could be sure his stratagem would prove successful. He had covered every point, every difficulty he could foresee, but even so, there was no guarantee di Casale would be admitted into Clement's presence. And what then? Failure to get an audience would be bad enough, but what if di Casale spoke with the pope and Clement still refused to accede to his demands? Henry would not be merely angry but furious with Thomas for his failure, and he had the unpleasant feeling that such a failure would not be forgiven, not with the Boleyns and Howards egging him on. Thomas knew his very life was in danger if he did not get the king his divorce.

Clement scowled as his secretary closed the door upon his visitor. Had he escaped the prison of the Castel Sant Angelo only to be confronted by a ruffian in the disguise of a gentleman? And not even a ruffian come on his own business, but a proxy for that scoundrel Wolsey.

'I am sorry, Your Holiness,' the secretary said, scuttling

back to Clement's desk, 'but I thought he was one of the duke of Ferrara's men.'

'That's what you were supposed to think. Typical of Wolsey to employ deception,' Clement said grimly.

The secretary shook his head. 'I would not have thought a man of the Church would stoop so low.'

'Wolsey doesn't need to stoop,' Clement muttered and reached for the notes the secretary had taken during di Casale's visit. 'Look at this. Everything that man said is Wolsey making threats.'

'Are you sure? I thought the cardinal is merely anxious for his king's marriage to be annulled.'

Clement tutted impatiently. 'And how can I give him that annulment when the king's wife is the emperor's aunt?'

'But if the marriage was invalid—'

'Who says so? King Henry? Cardinal Wolsey?' Clement scoffed. 'My predecessor issued a dispensation. The marriage was valid then and it must be valid now. The king must not be allowed to dispose of the queen simply because he wants to marry his whore.'

The secretary winced at the use of the word. 'Wolsey must have an answer.'

'Yes, I know,' Clement said reluctantly. 'Otherwise I might find an assassin in my bedchamber.'

The secretary chuckled at his master's joke, then realised his master wasn't smiling. 'Shall I write to the cardinal, Your Holiness?'

Clement nodded, his brow crinkling as he considered his response. 'Perhaps there is a diplomatic way out of this,' he said. 'Yes, I think I shall ignore this latest entreaty from Cardinal Wolsey and answer instead the message Master Knight brought.'

The secretary sorted through his pile of papers, finding the page he sought. 'Master Knight. That would be the request for a dispensation allowing the king of England to marry the sister of a former mistress.'

'Yes. That is one dispensation I am willing to sign.' He smiled at his secretary's astonished face and shrugged. 'What does it cost me to allow the king to marry another woman? By issuing the dispensation, I appease the king so he ceases to pester me while not upsetting the emperor who has forbidden me to annul his aunt's marriage. King Henry cannot marry another woman while he is married to Katherine, so the dispensation will be useless.' He gestured for his secretary to write. The secretary snatched up his quill and dipped it in the ink pot.

'Will not the cardinal be displeased that you grant this dispensation and not the one he asks for?' he asked.

'I daresay he will,' Clement said with a sigh, 'but I imagine I will bear Wolsey's displeasure well enough.'

Thomas drummed his fingers on the pommel of his chair as he stared into the fire. He had received news from Italy, and it was not what he hoped. Clement had not agreed to annul the marriage, though he had signed a dispensation allowing Henry to marry Anne. But what use was that? Without an annulment, without a divorce, Henry wasn't free to marry anybody.

And now, Thomas had to tell Henry he had failed. He felt sick at the very thought.

It was all that woman's fault, he thought savagely, kicking at the footstool by his feet. The Night Crow. If it hadn't been for her…

Thomas shook his head, unwilling to get worked up

over something he couldn't control. He reached for the pile of papers by the side of his chair, snatching off the topmost page, and scanned the letter. The abbess of Wilton had died, it told him, and a new abbess needed to be appointed. The writer recommended that an Isabel Jordan be given the post and expressed concern that other women were being recommended by those who had influence at court who were not fit for such an important position. Frowning, Thomas wondered who the writer could mean by influential people, then turned over the page to see that Gardiner had written a note to Thomas. It read: 'The Lady Anne wishes Dame Eleanor Carey to be appointed abbess of Wilton.'

Thomas screwed up the letter, clenching it in his fist. That bloody woman was sticking her nose into Church matters now. Just who did she think she was? He knew of Eleanor Carey; the woman was notorious. Though unmarried, Dame Eleanor had already had two children by two different men, and so rumour had it, was conducting a love affair with a third. And the Night Crow wanted this wanton woman to be made abbess!

Thomas snatched up his quill and dipped it in the ink pot. Flattening out the letter, he rested it on his writing slope. 'Stephen,' he wrote, 'Dame Isabel Jordan is to be made abbess of Wilton. I will consider no other lady!' He signed it, *Thomas Cardinalis*.

And let the Night Crow do her worst, he thought as he threw his quill aside.

CHAPTER TWENTY-TWO
1528

Thomas squeezed his eyes shut, hoping it would help ease the pain in his head. It didn't, and he opened them again with a sigh. God, he felt terrible. His entire body ached, and he couldn't get warm, no matter how many blankets Cavendish laid on top of him.

The plague had returned to London and was sweeping through the narrow streets, killing indiscriminately. How many times had he caught the plague now? Twice? Three times? Surviving when others, younger and healthier than he, had died. But not this time, he feared. No, this time, he was not going to escape. He could feel it. And besides, he had no reason to live anymore, not now he had lost the king's love.

Before he had fallen ill, a letter had arrived from Greenwich bearing the king's seal. It was not the kind of letter Thomas was used to receiving from the king. This letter was full of anger and condemnation.

'The Lady Anne was most aggrieved to learn of your involvement in the abbess of Wilton matter,' Henry wrote. 'She has had to explain to her brother-in-law why his sister's appointment, which she had promised would be unopposed, has met with resistance from a quarter such as yourself.'

So, the Night Crow has been made to look a fool, has she? Thomas had thought with pleasure. But his happiness faded as he continued to read Henry's words. 'It is not your place to interfere in such matters. The appointment of the abbess of Wilton was not your concern, and I am sore displeased that I must remind you of this.'

He had set Henry's letter aside, deeply hurt by its contents, and wondering if he had acted foolishly by letting his personal feelings influence him, making him careless of incurring Henry's displeasure.

Cavendish came into the room. He peered at Thomas. 'How are you feeling, Your Eminence?'

'Terrible,' Thomas croaked, closing his eyes. 'You shouldn't come too near, George. I don't want you to catch this.'

'In truth, Your Eminence, I doubt if I could avoid it even if I wanted to. Three men in the kitchens have taken to their beds, and two of your secretaries, too.'

'You should get yourself to the country.' Thomas heard a crackle of paper and opened his eyes. 'What's that you have there?'

'A letter from Mistress Legh,' Cavendish said.

'I cannot read it now.'

'It's not for you, Your Eminence. It was addressed to me.'

'To you?' Why was Joan writing to George?

'Mistress Legh has instructions for me,' Cavendish said, and Thomas could have sworn he saw amusement on the young man's face. 'She writes that she has heard the plague is in town and that you are not well, and that I am to make you leave for Hampton Court immediately.'

Thomas managed a smile. 'She is very kind to think of me. But how can I leave? I can barely get out of bed.'

'Your barge can be made very comfortable,' Cavendish said, 'and I will easily find strong men to carry you down to the river steps. I have sent a messenger to Hampton Court to expect us and to make your rooms ready.'

'Hampton Court is no longer mine, George.'

'And I know that the king has kept a set of rooms for your personal use,' Cavendish said in a distinctly mothering tone. 'You are free to use them at any time and this is that time, Your Eminence. You are not allowed to refuse. Mistress Legh threatens me with terrible tortures if you attempt to.'

'I shall do as you order me, George,' Thomas said, more than a little pleased to have Cavendish take charge in this way. 'But I wish to dictate a letter before you make the arrangements.'

'Of course, Your Eminence,' Cavendish said, and gathered his writing materials. 'Ready.'

'To the king,' Thomas said. 'Write, "I am most distressed to have displeased you and the Lady Anne in the matter of the abbess of Wilton Abbey. I assure you that was not my intention. Had I known of the Lady Anne's, and indeed, your own preference for Dame Eleanor Carey, I would, of course, never have presumed to recommend Dame Isabel Jordan. If I could turn back time and undo that recommendation, I would. If it is any consolation to you, I believe I shall not trouble you for much longer. I am sick with the plague and do not think to last the week. I am being moved to Hampton Court, which by your great kindness, you allow me to enter, and it is a great solace to me that I will end my days in the place I put so much of myself into for your great glory. Your most beloved servant, Thomas Cardinalis." Send that at once, George.'

'I will, Your Eminence,' Cavendish said. 'But you're not dying, you know? You will be well again, I am sure of it.'

'You may be sure of it, George, but I am not. And that reminds me. Before we leave, tell Cromwell he is to hurry the workmen along on my tomb. They are moving too slow and I will have need of it soon.'

'Your Eminence, I will not listen to you talking like this,' Cavendish said sternly, and started for the door.

'But you will tell Cromwell, George? You'll do that for me?'

Cavendish had his hand on the handle. 'Yes, even though you will not be needing your tomb for some time.'

He went out, closing the door quietly behind him. George was very kind, and Thomas made a mental note to make a provision for him in his will as soon as he got to Hampton Court. The young man deserved something for such devoted service.

If only there were more men like him, he mused, as the room darkened and he fell into a deep sleep.

Thomas did not die.

Only a few days after arriving at Hampton Court, he began to feel better, and a few days after that, he discovered he had an appetite and called for a supper of pork pie with syllabub to follow. Once he was strong enough to leave his bed, he took Cavendish's arm and visited the chapel, sinking creakily to his knees to thank God for his deliverance. To have survived the sweat yet again could only mean God had need of Thomas Wolsey still.

When Thomas felt strong enough to walk unaided, he ordered Cavendish to organise a litter to take him to Windsor Castle to pay a visit to the king. When he arrived in the privy chamber, Henry looked at him warily from the far side of the room.

'You are quite well?' he asked apprehensively.

'I am fully recovered, Your Majesty,' Thomas assured Henry.

Henry nodded and took a few careful steps closer. 'I prayed for you. God heard me. He always does.'

'I thank you for your prayers.'

'And now I'm praying for the Lady Anne,' Henry said, snatching up a Bible. 'She has the sweat. I had to send her back to Hever.'

Was that really love? Thomas wondered as he watched Henry open the Bible. To send the woman he wanted to marry out of his sight when she might be dying? Why, if Joan had still been with him and she had come down with the sweat, Thomas would never have left her side until she was well again.

'And how is the Lady Anne faring?' Thomas asked.

Henry shut the Bible with a sigh. 'I sent Dr Butts to tend on her. She is suffering, he writes, but that she is strong and he has hopes of her recovering. You must pray for her, too, Thomas.'

'I certainly shall,' Thomas lied. *Oh God, let the bitch die. If only she were dead, my life could return to some semblance of normality. Henry and I would be friends again.* He studied Henry, sitting there in his chair, dejected. Now was the time to make a personal apology, while Anne was away. 'I am glad you agreed to see me,

Your Majesty. I had thought my temerity in the matter of Wilton Abbey had set you quite against me.'

Henry frowned at him. 'Wilton Abbey? Oh, that. Yes, I was angry with you, wasn't I? But the truth is I didn't know of the Carey woman's notoriety when I wrote to you. I found out later of her lack of chastity. Nan only told me of her good points. No, you were quite right not to recommend her, quite right.'

Thomas's heart swelled with joy at this admission. This was how he and the king were when no one was else was around to stir up trouble.

'I hear Bishop Fox is dying,' Henry said, abruptly changing the subject. 'Not from the sweat, though. Old age. Pity. He's been a good servant to me.'

'Indeed, yes,' Thomas agreed, glad Henry had mentioned Fox's imminent death. The matter had been occupying his own thoughts for some days now. 'If I may take this moment to broach an uncomfortable subject, Your Majesty, you are aware the bishopric of Winchester is in your gift. When Bishop Fox dies and it becomes vacant, I wonder if you might consider appointing me?'

A smile tugged at Henry's lips. 'You want another bishopric, Thomas? Don't you have enough? You were but recently appointed bishop of Durham, weren't you?'

'I was, Your Majesty,' Thomas said, 'but if you were to give me Winchester, I would resign Durham and request that it be given to another.'

'To whom?'

'Thomas Wynter.'

Henry snorted. 'You want me to give Durham to your son? Oh, forgive me.' He put fingers to his lips, making himself look like a naughty schoolboy. 'I'm not sure I'm supposed to know who his father is.'

'He is my son, yes,' Thomas acknowledged, refusing to let Henry embarrass him. 'And as his father, I naturally want what I can for him. But if you think me impertinent for asking—'

'If I did think you impertinent, I wouldn't be the only one, would I? But still...' Henry tapped his fingers on the pommel of his chair and narrowed his eyes at Thomas. 'Aye, you can have Winchester when Fox dies. But I want to think about Durham.'

What's there to think about? Thomas wanted to ask. Instead, he said, 'You have another man who might suit in mind?'

'Maybe,' Henry said, looking away, leaving Thomas wondering who the king wanted to bribe with the bishopric of Durham and to what end.

CHAPTER TWENTY-THREE

Campeggio hated England. He had hated it the last time he was here, back in 1518, when Pope Leo had sent him to get England's support for one of his many treaties. That had been a farce, as this trip was doubtless going to be too. Just another sop to the king of England to convince him Rome was on his side and doing all she could to help him resolve the matter of his troubled marriage. Campeggio was firmly convinced Clement had just grown tired of being badgered by English envoys and arranged for the marriage to be tried to stop them coming.

Campeggio was worried, though, about Wolsey. No doubt Wolsey would be expecting him to do something, without realising that the pope wanted him to do precisely nothing.

'Why send me?' Campeggio had griped when Clement gave him his instructions. Clement knew he was a martyr to gout and that the journey into such a cold, damp climate would exacerbate the problem, but oh no, go he must. There were times when Campeggio wished he had never entered the priesthood. It had been a late decision in his life, after having a wife and children. He had been looking for a little peace, he seemed to remember. So much for that. What chance had he ever had of peace as the pope's right-hand man, when the rulers of Europe were constantly at odds and one must needs pacify first one king, then another, changing allegiances, making enemies, remaking friends?

Oh, why me? he mentally repeated as his litter entered beneath the gate of Brandon's house on the Strand and smiled bravely at the party waiting to greet him. He was taken through to a suite of rooms that were to be his for the duration of his stay in London. The duke kept a fine house, Campeggio thought as he lowered himself onto the bed, not as fine as Wolsey admittedly, but he would at least be comfortable while he was forced to remain in this Godforsaken hole.

Francis Bryan breezed into the privy chamber, untied his cloak and threw it over the back of the nearest chair. He helped himself to wine and a chunk of cheese before acknowledging the other men in the room.

'God, what a journey!' he moaned as he chewed on the cheese.

Henry glared at him. 'How is Cardinal Campeggio?'

Bryan flopped down in an empty chair. 'Complaining about his gout. I've seen him settled at Brandon's place. He'll be all right.'

'But did he say anything? Anything about my divorce?'

Bryan shook his head. 'Wouldn't say a word. I think the pope's given him orders to keep his mouth shut.'

'I'll bet he'll talk to Wolsey before he talks to you,

Your Majesty,' Nicholas Carew said sourly, refilling Henry's cup, and moving to Bryan to do the same for his. He leaned close and whispered, 'He's had a quarrel with the Lady Anne.'

Now Bryan understood the gloomy aspect of Henry's face. Never one to sulk himself, he couldn't stand it in others. 'Nick tells me Anne's upset,' he said bluntly, ignoring Carew's disapproving glare.

Henry kicked his footstool across the room, where it crashed against the wall beneath the window.

Bryan chuckled. 'That bad, eh?'

'She accused me of not wanting to marry her,' Henry growled. 'Said I don't want the pope to invalidate my marriage to the queen, that I'm just delaying matters until she's so old, she'll have no option but to be my mistress because no other man will want her.'

'You should have told her it's not you who's delaying, but Wolsey,' Bryan said, taking a sip of his wine.

Henry's eyes slid towards him. 'What do you mean, Wolsey's delaying?'

'Well,' Bryan shrugged, 'it's obvious, isn't it? He doesn't want Katherine gone. Spain might be England's enemy, but she's not Wolsey's, not with all the money that comes his way in Spanish pensions. And I asked around in Rome while I was waiting for Campeggio to get himself ready to leave. Word is the cardinals think Wolsey's pleas to Clement were half-hearted at best. That he didn't really try to get him to move on the dispensation, let alone your divorce.' He felt Carew's eyes upon him and knew his friend was wondering how much of what he had just said was true. Some of it was true, the rest... well, who was to say he lied? He looked at Henry.

Henry was frowning. 'No, I can't believe Thomas

didn't try,' he said after a moment. 'Thomas never goes after anything half-heartedly.'

'Then why hasn't he managed to get your divorce?' Carew asked, hitching himself up on the windowsill. 'He's very good at getting himself bishoprics and benefices, building palaces that are too good for him, but when you ask him to do something for you…' He threw up his hands, letting his unspoken words infiltrate Henry's mind.

'We're not the only one's saying this, either,' Bryan pointed out. 'The Howards—'

'The Howards have always loathed Thomas,' Henry interrupted.

Bryan opened his mouth to speak, but a look from Carew made him shut it again. He understood. It was too much and too soon to criticise Wolsey. He would wait until tomorrow to have another go. That would have given Henry plenty of time to brood on his chief minister and realise he would be better off without him.

Thomas shooed his attendants out of the room, waiting until the door had closed before taking a seat beside Campeggio's bedside. 'How are you, Lorenzo?'

Campeggio gestured at his legs. His gout had worsened and he had kept to his room. 'As you see me, Thomas. I regret I am unable to leave my bed at present.'

Thomas's jaw tightened. What was the use of the old fool if he couldn't do anything? 'I am sorry to hear it,' he said. 'Thankfully, I see you are only ill in body and not in mind. We can talk, can we not?' He smiled encouragingly at Campeggio, who after a moment, nodded reluctantly. 'I realise His Holiness will have given you instructions as to how your time here in England is spent.

I would appreciate it if you would tell me what those instructions are.'

'My instructions are to hear the king's case,' Campeggio said.

'And what verdict have you been instructed to reach?'

'Thomas,' Campeggio gave a disapproving smile, 'I cannot reach a verdict until I have heard the arguments.'

'You know the arguments, Lorenzo,' Thomas snapped. 'The pope knows the arguments. This trial is a mere formality. I know it. You know it.'

Campeggio's face hardened. 'I know nothing of the sort.'

Thomas's hands curled into fists. 'The king must have the divorce. He must be free to marry the Lady Anne.'

'Yes, I have heard of this Anne Boleyn. She is a whore, is she not?'

Thomas looked warily around the room and lowered his voice when he answered. 'You must not call her such.'

Campeggio shrugged. 'It is what the pope calls her, what the emperor calls her. It is what she is being called throughout Europe. And her sister was the king's mistress before her. Wantoness must run in the Boleyn family.'

'The Lady Anne is not his mistress,' Thomas said, wondering if it was still true. 'The king has not bedded her.'

Campeggio frowned, looking doubtful. 'Indeed?'

'Indeed.'

'And you know that, how? Do you have spies in the lady's bedchamber as well as the king's?'

'There is no need to be crude,' Thomas muttered.

'Thomas, you know as well as I that there is more to consider about this matter than the satisfaction of a king's desire.'

Thomas chewed on his bottom lip and came to a decision. He would tell Campeggio the truth. 'Lorenzo, I will be plain with you in the hope you will be plain with me. I need this divorce. If the pope does not grant it, I fear for my very life.'

Campeggio's face fell. He leant forward and put his hand over Thomas's. 'How has it come to that, Thomas? You, who are so beloved of the king.'

'Was so beloved of the king,' Thomas corrected with a sad smile. 'No longer, I fear. The Lady Anne has…' he broke off as the words threatened to choke him. 'She and her family have persuaded the king that I serve my own interests rather than his.'

'That has never been true, Thomas,' Campeggio said. 'I know that is not.'

'It is not, and I thank you for saying so. I have always been the king's good servant. So what if I have done well for myself? I think I have earned the right.'

'I shall tell you what the pope instructed me.' Campeggio slid his hand away to lean back into his pillow with a sigh. 'He feels the best resolution to this matter would be if Katherine can be persuaded to enter a convent and thereby consent to a divorce. Do you think that is a possibility?'

Thomas shook his head. 'I doubt Katherine will agree to that.'

'Then can King Henry be persuaded to abandon the idea of divorce altogether, to accept the dispensation issued by the pope that allowed he and Katherine to marry was valid?'

'I do not think the king will even contemplate accepting that,' Thomas said sorrowfully. 'He is besotted with the Lady Anne.'

Campeggio shook his head as if he didn't understand how a man could be so very much in love that he would cause so much trouble. 'As we understand it, the king's motive in claiming the marriage is not valid is the lack of a male heir. The pope has a solution to this problem.'

Thomas was intrigued. 'Which is?'

'That he grants a dispensation allowing the Princess Mary to marry the duke of Richmond.'

Thomas's mouth fell open. 'To marry her half-brother?'

Campeggio held his hands up. 'I agree, it is distasteful, but it would ensure a man succeeds to the throne.'

Thomas put his head in his hands. 'Is this all you have for me? Options that neither party will accept and an incestuous marriage?' A sudden rage welled up in him. He got to his feet, knocking over his stool. 'My very life may be lost over this, Lorenzo. If I do not get the divorce for the king, he will never forgive me.'

Campeggio stared at him, open-mouthed. Just as quickly as it had arisen, Thomas's anger left him. 'I know it's not your fault,' he said, putting out his hand in apology. 'You have your orders, and,' he smiled ruefully, 'I have mine.' He took a deep breath and shrugged. 'Perhaps now Katherine has had time to think, she may reconsider a nunnery. Will you help me talk to her?'

'Of course,' Campeggio said quietly. 'Anything I can do.'

'Then I shall arrange a meeting,' Thomas said. 'Thank you. I will leave you now, Lorenzo, let you sleep.'

He yanked open the door and strode out, praying Katherine would listen to reason.

.   .   .

Katherine had not wanted to see Thomas and Campeggio. It had taken Campeggio informing one of her ladies, who had tried to turn them away at the door, that the pope specifically wanted his envoy to have an audience with the queen to gain them entrance to her privy chamber.

When they entered, Katherine was sitting in a chair by the window, a Bible in her lap, a rosary twined around the fingers of the hand draped over the chair's arm. She didn't look at them.

'I have no desire to see you, gentlemen,' she said. 'I have nothing to say.'

'Yet we must talk with you, my lady. To spare yourself from grief.' Campeggio nodded at Thomas and Thomas sank to his knees.

'Madam, I beg you, for the sake of the realm, do not contest the divorce. Go into a nunnery and live out the rest of your life in peace and quiet.'

Katherine finally turned her head and looked down her nose at him. 'You are unused to being on your knees, Your Eminence. Does it not hurt your bones to be so?'

'Madam, I will endure any discomfort in the pursuance of my king's wishes.'

'And there you have it,' she nodded, her lips turning up at the corners in a bitter smile. 'The king's wishes. Do you know, Your Eminence, he told me his conscience pricked him, and that was why he declared we were never married in the eyes of God? But that is not true. It was not his conscience that pricked him but the lusts of the flesh. That whore, Anne Boleyn, has bewitched him.'

Thomas glanced up at Campeggio, standing uncomfortably at his side. Campeggio had told him on the journey over to Katherine that he would go down on his knees too if he had to, but would prefer, in view of his gout, to stay on his feet.

'Madam,' Campeggio said, 'for you to enter a nunnery would be the easiest course.'

'For the king? For the whore? For you?' Katherine said, fixing him to the spot with a hard stare. 'And for you?' she turned on Thomas. 'Yes, that would be best for everyone but myself and my daughter.'

'Consider the king, madam,' Thomas said, knowing he had to appeal to her love for Henry if they were going to get anywhere. 'His concern is the security of his kingdom. If he has no son to succeed to the throne, the very safety of the realm will be at stake. The throne will be contested.'

'Our daughter will become queen.'

'The nobility will not accept a woman.'

'You cannot know that,' she retorted. 'You assume so. They may surprise you.'

'You know the English, madam,' Thomas said wearily. 'They are nothing if not predictable.'

Katherine raised her chin. 'I love the king, Your Eminence, and will not declare our marriage to have been a lie.'

'You worry that your life will be constrained if you enter a convent, madam,' Thomas said understandingly, 'but that is not so. I will petition the pope to allow you to do as you pleased. Your life will be as ever it was. The only sacrifice you will need to make is take a vow of chastity, but I know you will find that no hardship.'

'You know nothing,' Katherine spat.

'My lady,' Campeggio said, and Thomas heard the note of disbelief in his voice, 'surely a life of repose and reflection would be welcome at your age?'

'At my age?' Katherine queried. 'How old do you think I am?'

'You are in your fifth decade, are you not?' Campeggio queried, and Thomas winced.

'I am but two and forty,' Katherine cried indignantly.

Campeggio coloured at his error, though Thomas acknowledged it had been an easy mistake to make. Katherine looked much older than her forty-two years. She had grown very plump, especially in the last five years or so, and her face was jowly and double-chinned. The pretty young woman she had been when she married Henry was no longer discernible in the old woman seated before them.

From that moment on, Thomas knew their mission to Katherine was a lost cause, but he and Campeggio tried for a further hour to persuade her to enter a nunnery. Katherine steadfastly refused. Campeggio reached a point where he could no longer remain standing, and knowing Katherine would never allow either of them to sit in her presence, Thomas got unsteadily to his feet. His legs had pins and needles and he stretched out his feet, one by one, to get some feeling back into his calf muscles. He nodded to Campeggio that they were leaving.

'I am sorry you are so stubborn, lady,' he said to Katherine. 'You have displeased the king, whom you claim to love above all others.'

'Not above God, Your Eminence,' Katherine said. 'I love my husband the king, but I love God too and I will need to answer to him on the day of judgement.'

'We will all have to answer to God in the next world, lady.'

Unfortunately, he mentally added, *I have to answer to the king in this one first.*

CHAPTER TWENTY-FOUR

1529

Many months had passed, and Thomas was miserably aware he was no nearer giving his king what he wanted than when the idea of divorce had first been broached. Katherine had proved intractable. She would not enter a nunnery, she would not even consider that her marriage was no marriage at all. She was the queen, she was the king's wife, and she would die so.

'We need evidence,' Thomas had said to Henry when he demanded to know what progress had been made, 'that the marriage with your brother was consummated.'

'What evidence can there be?' Henry scoffed. 'God's Blood, Thomas, the bloody bedsheets will have been washed long ago.'

'Verbal testimony,' Thomas explained patiently. 'Witnesses who will swear that your brother and Katherine were put to bed and that intercourse took place.'

'Were there any witnesses?'

'I will find them,' Thomas promised. When he returned to York Place, he summoned Cromwell. 'Witnesses, Cromwell. I need you to find me some.'

Cromwell fell down into the chair by Thomas's desk. 'I've been making enquiries, and I've found someone who claims Prince Arthur spoke to him the morning after the wedding and made a joke about being in Spain all night and being parched.' He gave Thomas a pitiful look. 'A poor joke at the best of times.'

'Quite,' Thomas said, not caring a fig for the quality of the jest, 'but it is testimony, nonetheless. Anyone else?'

Cromwell shook his head. 'Not at the moment, but we're trying.'

'We need others to testify to the consummation, Cromwell.' He thought of what Henry had said. 'Any washerwomen still alive who might have handled the soiled sheets?'

Cromwell laughed. 'You really want me to go looking for washerwomen?'

'I don't appreciate your humour, Cromwell,' Thomas said sharply, wiping the smile off Cromwell's face. 'Especially not after the news I've had.'

'What news?' Cromwell asked.

Thomas gave a deep sigh. 'Regarding the original dispensation allowing King Henry to marry Katherine. The Spanish claim that the dispensation stated the marriage could go ahead regardless of whether Katherine was deflowered by Prince Arthur or not.'

'They're lying,' Cromwell said, shaking his head. 'The pope would never have equivocated in that way.'

'The Spanish say they have a copy of this alternative dispensation.'

'Then it's a forgery,' Cromwell shrugged. 'It's proof of nothing.'

'Unless it has the Vatican seal on it,' Thomas said.

'We have to see it, Cromwell said decisively. 'We shall

have to get the Spanish to send over their copy so we can have a look at it and determine its authenticity.'

'You really think they will send it?' Thomas raised a doubtful eyebrow.

Cromwell had an idea. 'We could get the queen to write to the emperor. After all, if what they claim is true, then it helps her case, doesn't it? If they don't send it, their side of the story can't be substantiated, and as evidence, it's useless. Oh, come, we have to try.'

Thomas nodded. 'Oh, yes, Cromwell, we have to try.'

Katherine sat up in bed, tears pricking at her eyes. She would not weep again; she needed to save her tears. Besides, weeping made her ill, made her unable to think, and she needed all her wits about her. Wolsey was too clever an enemy; she couldn't afford to give him anything he could use against her.

'Will you write the letter?' Lady Willoughby asked from her bedside.

'The king demands I do,' Katherine sniffed. 'Fetch pen, ink and paper, Maria. You shall write it for me.'

Lady Willoughby did as she was bid, and resettled herself on the stool, smoothing out the bedclothes to make a flat surface for the pen and paper. She dipped the quill in the ink pot and waited for her mistress to speak.

Katherine spoke briefly and to the point. She asked her nephew to forward the dispensation he had so her husband and his councillors could examine its authenticity and so produce it in evidence at the trial.

'Sign it, 'Katherine the Queen', but do not seal it,' Katherine said. 'Wolsey will want to read it first.'

'That is intolerable, madam,' Lady Willoughby said, horrified. 'He has no right to read your letters.'

'No, but he will do it anyway. He always has. Ready your pen, Maria. I want to send another letter.'

'To whom this time?'

'To my nephew again,' Katherine said, her jaw hardening. 'Write this: "To my dearest, most beloved nephew. You will receive another letter from me in which I ask you to forward the copy of the dispensation you have. I write here to implore you not to send it to my husband. While I do not doubt the motives of my dear lord, I have reason to doubt the motives of his councillors, and in particular, that fiend Cardinal Wolsey. I am sure that once the dispensation you possess is in his hands, he will destroy it, as it does not aid his cause in having me put away. I know it is his greatest desire to separate me from the king, and there is no low deed to which he will not stoop to achieve that end. Do this for me for the love I know you bear me. I remain your greatly afflicted but most loving aunt, Katherine, Queen of England."' She waited while Lady Willoughby finished scribbling, watching the words she had spoken take shape on the page.

'How will I despatch this letter without the cardinal seeing it, madam?' Lady Willoughby asked when she had sealed it.

'My chaplain will take care of that. I just have to hope it will reach my nephew. Put it in my chaplain's hand, Maria, and in no other. There are so few people I can trust in this place.'

Lady Willoughby assured her she would.

. . .

Thomas strode into the Council chamber in no mood for pleasantries. He looked around the table. 'What news from Rome?' he demanded. 'Has the pope made any improvement?'

More answered. 'Alas, no. His health has worsened considerably, and the word is that he will not recover. That he will, in fact, die soon.'

Thomas's heart beat faster. When he had heard of the pope's illness, he had hoped Clement would rally. Clement, though still under Charles's thumb, was at least prepared to play his part in the king's divorce and hold a trial, whereas a new pope might be even more beholden to the emperor and withdraw all support. If that were to happen, where would that leave Thomas Wolsey?

'I shall pray for His Holiness,' Thomas said, 'as we all must.'

The men nodded as one, all but Cromwell, who now always accompanied Thomas to Council meetings, where he had often proved invaluable. Cromwell was staring oddly at him. Thomas considered asking him why, but thought better of it. Cromwell would not share his thoughts with so many others present. If what was on his mind was of any importance to Thomas, Cromwell would seek him out privately.

'I understand we have received a copy of the Spanish dispensation,' Thomas said, and More said he had it.

Thomas clicked his fingers and it was passed along the table. He quickly scanned the Latin, and a small flicker of joy entered his heart. 'The date,' he said, a little breathlessly. 'It is dated the twenty-seventh day of December, 1503.'

More frowned. 'What of that, Your Eminence?'

'Well, don't you see? It's the wrong date. It isn't dated

with the ecclesiastical calendar it should have been when the new year begins on Christmas Day, but rather the first of January. If this was genuine, it would have been dated the same as the original bull, the twenty-seventh of December, 1504. It is a forgery. It must be.'

'May I see?' Cromwell asked, holding out his hand for the paper. Thomas gave it to him. He too scanned the Latin as Thomas has done. 'You're right, Your Eminence. And I see here other inaccuracies.' He grinned at Thomas. 'My lawyer's mind spots these kind of things.'

'I am glad of it, Master Cromwell,' Thomas grinned back. 'I shall tell the king the Spanish dispensation is a forgery and we must write to the emperor expressing our doubt it is genuine.'

'We should hold back some of the details,' Cromwell suggested. 'Let's not give them the means by which to produce another forgery that can explain them away.'

Thomas nodded. 'Excellent, Cromwell. Thank God I have someone here who has a brain in their head.'

He got on with the rest of the Council's business for that day and then brought the meeting to an end.

Cromwell lingered as the councillors trooped out. 'Thank you for saying that, Your Eminence.'

'No thanks needed,' Thomas said, waving away the gratitude, 'I meant it. If each of them had only half your brains, I wouldn't need to do everything myself. Was there something else?' he asked as Cromwell tapped his fingers on the table.

'This news about the pope,' Cromwell began. 'At first, I thought nothing of it, just another change of leader in the Vatican, another inadequate we would have to deal with, but now I'm not so sure.'

Thomas sank back in his chair, throwing his quill down. 'Explain.'

Cromwell nodded. 'I know you've always avoided it in the past, but consider this. Is now not the best time for you to try to become pope? Why not? If you were pope, you could give the king his divorce like that.' He clicked his fingers. 'But I don't really need to tell you this. You know it already. That's why you tried to become temporary pope during Clement's imprisonment.'

'It's no good me trying. I have no support.'

'You say that, but you don't know. Wave enough money before them and we might convince the cardinals to vote for you. And the cardinals may consider it a bonus that you're no friend to the emperor.'

There was silence for almost a minute as Thomas considered Cromwell's words. 'It would mean leaving England for good.'

'Why would it? The papal throne might be in Rome but the pope can live anywhere he chooses. And considering how dangerous life is for a pope on the Continent these days, it might be advantageous to have the Narrow Sea between you and the emperor.'

Thomas laughed. 'If I were pope—'

'If you were pope, there'd be no need for a trial, no need to concern yourself with the emperor or try to reason with Katherine. You could give the king exactly what he wants.'

Thomas's heart beat faster. There would be an end to this awful matter. Cromwell was right. To be pope was to be able to make Henry's dream of divorcing Katherine and marrying Anne come true. And how grateful Henry would be then! He would love him once again, even more than before.

'Has there ever been an English pope?'

'Pope Adrian the fourth,' Cromwell answered promptly. 'Wore the papal crown from 1154 to 1159.'

'What facts you have in your head, Cromwell,' Thomas said, impressed.

'I think another English pope is long overdue, Your Eminence,' Cromwell grinned. 'Don't you?'

Thomas hid his smile behind his fingers and mentally agreed that it was.

But all this talk came to nothing, for within a week or so, Clement rallied and was restored to health. The papal throne would not be empty, and Thomas had to forget any idea of becoming pope.

A legatine trial was now inevitable. The king's secret matter would be tried, and tried in public. Thomas could hardly believe it had come to this. The king and queen of England forced to appear in a public court like common people to have their past lives, their most intimate affairs, discussed and debated by clergymen and lawyers.

Thomas set a date for the trial. On Friday the eighteenth of June, at Blackfriars, Thomas and Campeggio would preside over the trial of the king's marriage.

CHAPTER TWENTY-FIVE

An immense crowd had gathered outside Blackfriars priory, and they booed and hissed as Thomas and Campeggio passed before them and went inside. Thomas, having become used to such receptions of late, ignored their hostility, but Campeggio tugged at his arm anxiously.

'The people are with the queen, Thomas,' he said, casting frightened glances over his shoulder.

'I fear they are,' Thomas said with a sigh, observing the Great Hall from the inner doorway.

Everything seemed to have been set out as per his instructions. The gold canopy of estate had been hung over the red and gold upholstered chair set on a dais reserved for the king while two other chairs, covered in cloth of gold and bearing cushions, were set to the left, behind a table covered with a Turkey carpet. These two chairs and table were for himself and Campeggio, where they would sit and listen to the evidence he had heard a hundred times already. Tapestries had been brought in from York Place to line the walls, and they brought a familiar feel to Thomas, though he could not find it comforting. Telling Campeggio to follow, Thomas entered the Great Hall.

Katherine's advocates were already there, he saw as he walked by them. She had amassed eleven men to speak for her and advise her, seven of them English, the remaining four foreigners. That was a shrewd move; Thomas admired her for arranging it. If she had stacked her supporters with foreigners, she might have lost the approbation of the people shouting for her outside. As it was, she had seemingly put her future in the hands of seven good Englishmen; she trusted them, she was saying with this choice of advocates, and Thomas knew the people, who were even now crowding into the hall, finding a standing space wherever they could, would love her even more for it.

The bishops occupied the front row benches opposite the cardinals' chairs. Bishop Fisher gave Thomas an unreadable look at he took his seat, arranging the velvet cushions behind him. Unreadable in that Thomas couldn't tell what the old man was thinking at that moment, but he had no doubt that Fisher would be on Katherine's side. Fisher had been her friend for too long, and had proved awkward when Thomas had sent out his men to get all the bishop's signatures for this trial to go ahead.

Then everyone was getting to their feet as Henry strode into the hall. His face was grim, set hard, and he gave a curt nod to Thomas as he took his seat. He had barely sat down when a great cheer could be heard from outside, and all eyes turned towards the doors, where a few seconds later, Katherine appeared.

She stood there, in the doorway, looking slowly around the hall. Then Thomas saw her take a deep breath and make her way to the chair set aside for her, far enough away from Henry to make conversation between the two of them impossible.

It took several minutes for everyone to settle, and even longer for the chatter in the hall to die down enough for the crier to be heard calling, 'King Harry of England, come into the court!'

'Here, my lords,' Henry called, stretching out one long leg to cross over the ankle of the other.

The herald then called, 'Katherine, queen of England, come into the court!'

Katherine did not answer. Instead, she rose from her chair, keeping her eyes firmly on the few feet of floor in front of her. She stepped down from her dais and crossed to Henry, where she fell to her knees.

'Sir,' Katherine said, in a voice loud enough to be heard by all, 'I beseech you for the love we have shared, and for the love of God, allow me to have justice. Take pity on me, for I am a poor woman, a stranger in this land, born out of your realm. I have here no friends, and no impartial counsel. I appeal to you now as this realm's head of justice. Pity me! Tell me, how have I offended you? What have I ever done that has been against your will or your pleasure and which now makes you want to be parted from me? Before God, and before all the world, I declare that I have been to you a true, humble and obedient wife, always conforming to your will and pleasure. I have never spoken a contrary word to you, it being my pleasure and delight to take pleasure and delight in the same things as you. I never found fault with your speech or your countenance, and have never showed the faintest hint of discontent. I have loved those whom you have loved for your sake, not for my own, even when these were men and women who have been enemies to me. For twenty years, I have been your faithful and true wife, and have borne you many children, though it has pleased God to take them from me, through no fault of mine.

'When I first came to your bed, I swear before God and all these witnesses that I was a true maid, having never been touched by a man. I appeal to your conscience in deciding whether I speak the truth or not. If you have a good, lawful reason to put me from you, I am content to leave you, to be shamed and disgraced forever. But if you do not have a good, lawful reason, then I beg you, allow me to remain in my rightful place. During your father's reign, he was held in high estate for his great wisdom, being called by many the Second Solomon. My father, Ferdinand, king of Spain, was held to be one of the cleverest princes that ever reigned in Spain. Were both these respected men at fault when they chose their councillors and bid them to judge on the lawfulness of our marriage and who said it was good?

'The answer can only be no, and therefore, I am astonished to learn of these new discoveries against me, or should I say inventions, for they were never thought of before this. How can you, the most goodly prince that ever reigned in England, allow for such cruelty to befall me?

'For my part, I can only provide insufficient responses to the questions put to me, for I have no counsel who does not foster desires contrary to justice. The men I have been given to counsel me are all your subjects, plucked from your Council, and who dare not disobey your will for fear of invoking your great displeasure. I therefore ask you, in the name of charity and God, to spare me the indignity of this court, at least until I can make contact with friends in Spain who will advise me how to proceed. But if you will not, and insist on me taking advice from men who love not me but you, then I can no longer stay here and submit myself to your creatures' interrogation. I will pray God gives me justice.'

Katherine got to her feet, struggling a little, trying not to stand on her skirts. She curtseyed to Henry and turned as the muttering in the hall grew louder. Then she raised her chin as high as it would go without threatening to topple her gable hood and walked out of the Great Hall.

Henry glared at Thomas.

Thomas gestured angrily at the crier, and the crier obeyed the unspoken instruction. 'Katherine, queen of England, come into the court.'

Everyone's eyes were on the doors, but Katherine did not reappear. The crier repeated the appeal to no avail. Thomas didn't know what to do, but Henry did.

'Never mind,' Henry almost yelled, drawing every eye to him. 'As the queen is gone, I will, in her absence, declare unto you all my lords here assembled that she has been as true and faithful a wife as any man could desire. She has all the virtues and qualities a woman ought to possess. She is, without doubt, a most noble woman.'

Thomas watched Henry as he spoke, and knew Henry hated having to say those words, but he couldn't focus on Henry's displeasure. He knew who Katherine had meant when she spoke of men who sought to please the king; she meant Thomas Wolsey, and her words stung his very soul.

He got to his feet. 'Sir,' he cried, addressing himself to Henry, 'I most humbly beseech you to declare before all these men and women that I have not been, as the queen has implied, the chief instigator of this most solemn matter. Without your assurance that this matter did not spring from me but from the torment of your conscience, it will be believed I am serving my own ends, whatever they may be.'

Henry nodded. 'I can well excuse you, my lord cardinal.' He looked around the hall. 'Indeed, I tell only the truth when I say Cardinal Wolsey has been rather against me in attempting to resolve this matter. And I will go further. I will explain why I have brought this matter to such public attention.' He cleared his throat. 'When we were in negotiations with the French some years ago, the legitimacy of the Princess Mary was called into question. The reason for this doubt? Why, the fact that the queen had been married to my brother before me. Once this doubt had been spoken aloud, I could not forget it. My conscience was pricked, my mind vexed and troubled. Had I offended God by marrying my brother's widow? This was the question that was with me every waking moment. Was he punishing me by not allowing any of my sons by the queen to live?

'My lords, let me make this point. The queen is in no way to be blamed for this burden on my conscience. She has been the best of wives, and if this worry of mine is shown to be false, then I will return to her as her husband most joyfully. But this I cannot do if you judge our marriage to have been against the will of God, and so this matter is put to you all and we have your seals on this document,' he gestured at a roll of parchment before Thomas on the table, 'to confirm that you agree to do so.'

Warham got to his feet. 'You speak the truth, Your Majesty,' he said, 'and I know all my brethren here have agreed the same.'

Bishop Fisher jumped up as fast as his aged bones would allow. Thomas felt his mouth go dry. *Sit down, you old fool, keep your mouth shut*, he silently begged.

'That is not the truth, archbishop,' Fisher declared. 'I did not sign any such document.'

There was a general muttering throughout the room. Warham leaned forward and looked down the row of clergymen at Fisher. 'Bishop, you did put your name to this act.'

'Indeed I did not,' Fisher said, shaking his head fiercely. 'When that document was presented to me, I said I would never consent to sign such a paper, for the whole substance of it went against my conscience.'

'I know you did say so at first,' Warham said, with a wary glance at the king, 'but at the very last, you agreed I should sign your name for you and seal it with your seal.'

'Archbishop, there is no thing more untrue than the words you just spoke.'

There was a silence as Fisher and Warham glared at each other. Thomas knew he should do something, say something, but he had no idea what.

'Well, well,' Henry said, waving his hand in the air, 'it doesn't matter, Bishop Fisher. You are but one man amongst many others who have given their consent and I will not argue with you. Sit down and be quiet.'

Fisher looked as if he was about to retort, but he did as Henry bid and resumed his seat. Thomas could feel Henry's eyes upon him. He dared not meet them.

A few heartbeats later, the trial began in earnest. The witnesses Thomas's commissioners had found to testify to Katherine's undoubted loss of maidenhood to Prince Arthur were brought before the court and made to give their statements. Many of them were old men who had served the prince and it was awful to watch them search their memories to recall what had been seen, said and done so long ago.

Sir William Thomas recalled how he had delivered Prince Arthur to Katherine's bedchamber, seen Katherine lying in the bed in her nightgown, and how he had collected the young prince the next morning, which in itself, Thomas knew, meant nothing. Who was to say what had happened once the bedchamber door was closed? The prince may have lain next to his wife and gone to sleep for all anyone knew!

Then the earl of Shrewsbury, fifty-nine if he was a day, and an old fool long before now, got up and declared he had consummated his marriage when aged only fifteen, so he was sure the prince had consummated his. Thomas swallowed down the sigh he felt rising in his breast.

Thomas's former master, the marquess of Dorset, affirmed he had seen Katherine in bed in her nightgown wearing the expression of a lady who had been subjected to copulation, while the duchess of Norfolk, being too ill to travel, had sent a written testimony that she had seen Katherine lying in her wedding bed.

Thomas knew how flimsy their case was. Unless the act of penetration had been witnessed, no one save Prince Arthur and Katherine was able to tell what really happened on their wedding night. Prince Arthur was long dead and unable to speak for himself, while Katherine... well, everyone knew what Katherine proclaimed. She had said so for all to hear not a few hours earlier in this very hall. She had been a virgin when she married Henry, she had declared, and the truth was neither Thomas nor the king had any way of proving she was lying.

And then, Bishop Fisher got to his feet again, and Thomas groaned.

'Your Majesty, you claim that we may never know the truth of this matter. I say to you, I know the truth.'

Thomas had had enough. He banged his fist down on the table. 'How do you know the truth, bishop?' he shouted.

Fisher turned cool, calm eyes upon him. 'I know, Your Eminence, that God is truth itself. What God has joined together, let no man put asunder. You know the quotation?'

'It's from the Book of Matthew,' Thomas said testily.

'Indeed it is,' Fisher nodded. 'And as this marriage was made and joined by God, I say that I do know the truth. And the truth is this marriage cannot be broken by the power of man.' He turned his face towards Henry. 'However exalted that man may be.'

Henry shot a look at Thomas, a look that ordered him to do something, anything, that would silence the bishop. But Fisher hadn't finished yet, and he wouldn't, Thomas knew, while he had an audience willing to listen.

'I will say more,' Fisher said, turning first to his fellow clergymen, then taking in the whole assembly, 'that I am ready to lay down my life to protect the sanctity of this marriage.'

There was a collective gasp. Fisher resumed his seat and stared at Thomas, as if daring him to speak. Thomas waited to see what Henry would do. Neither of them, he suspected, had expected the trial to come to this, that a man, a highly respected Churchman, would consider martyring himself in support of Katherine's cause. For the briefest of moments, Thomas hoped such defiance would make Henry think again, that all this trouble was too much, that bedding Anne Boleyn simply wasn't worth the effort, and call a halt to the whole affair.

Of all the people in the hall, it was Campeggio who came to Thomas's aid. His cracked voice called out clearly in the nearly silent chamber, 'This court shall adjourn for the day.'

All at once, there was a great bustle as people began to get to their feet, but they froze when Henry got to his. Henry stood on his dais for a long moment, his face growing more crimson with every passing second. He did not look at Thomas; he did not look at anyone. He strode from the chamber without a backwards glance.

'The king is not pleased,' Campeggio said, humour in his voice. 'The queen has her supporters, it seems, even though you would have preferred she did not.'

Thomas looked at Campeggio. 'Do you find this amusing?' he asked, and his voice was like steel.

Campeggio quailed. 'Not at all. Far from it, Thomas, I —' He broke off as a messenger wearing the king's badge on his arm presented himself before the table.

'Your Eminence,' the messenger said, 'the king summons you to attend him at once.'

The weather had turned. What had been a rather chilly morning had turned into a sweltering afternoon, and Thomas tugged his silk collar away from his neck as he hurried out of Blackfriars to answer the king's summons. The king had departed to Bridewell Palace, and Thomas made his way there, kicking his mule's sides to make it hurry. By the time he reached the palace, he was soaking wet with sweat beneath his silken robes.

When he reached the king's privy apartments, he paused to catch his breath, his heart hammering. When the doors opened, his stomach lurched as he saw Henry was not alone. Anne Boleyn was with him.

'You wanted to see me, Your Majesty,' he said, making

his obeisance.

Henry had been pacing up and down the chamber. When Thomas spoke, he halted, his hands went to his hips and he took a deep shuddering breath.

'What in God's name do you think you are doing?' he said in a low voice, and Thomas knew Henry was having to control his anger.

'If you mean Bishop Fisher, Your Majesty—'

'I do mean him, God damn you,' Henry yelled. 'How dare he stand up and throw his conscience at me like that, in front of everyone, in front of my people. In front of Cardinal Campeggio, who, I have no doubt, is already writing to the pope to tell him what Fisher said.'

Thomas nodded, knowing what Henry said was true. Campeggio wouldn't waste any time in letting Clement know how the bishop had opposed his king. *Play it down*, his brain told him. *Make out Fisher's words mean nothing.*

'Bishop Fisher is but one man, Your Majesty,' Thomas said, his voice trembling.

'One man who threatened to die to preserve my marriage. What is he saying I am? A tyrant who kills anyone who disagrees with him?'

'Of course not. Bishop Fisher was just…,' Thomas shrugged as he couldn't find the words to finish his sentence.

'Was just what, Your Eminence?' Anne asked innocently. 'What was Bishop Fisher just doing?'

Thomas swallowed. 'He is an old friend of the queen's, my lady. He was demonstrating his loyalty to her.'

'But surely, the bishop's first loyalty ought to be to the king?'

'I think,' Thomas began carefully, 'the bishop considers his first loyalty to be to God.'

'Meaning you agree with him. I see. You think the king's marriage is lawful.'

'I did not say so, lady,' Thomas said, wishing she would shut her mouth.

'You don't need to,' Anne said. 'The plodding pace of this whole matter is testimony to your distaste for it.'

Henry, who had been watching Anne as she spoke, turned back to Thomas. 'Is that true, Thomas?'

'I assure you, Your Majesty, I am doing all I can to secure your divorce.'

'I hope you're telling me the truth, because if I find out you're not…'

Henry didn't finish the sentence. He didn't need to. Thomas knew exactly what he meant.

'I am your most loyal servant,' Thomas said quietly, barely able to get the words out. 'I am doing all—'

'You can go,' Henry cut him off, moving to Anne and taking hold of her hand. Thomas watched as he raised it to his lips and kissed each of her delicate knuckles.

Anne let Henry kiss her fingers but her eyes were on Thomas. There was no mistaking the feeling conveyed by her look. *He's mine*, those eyes said, *and he'll do anything I want.*

Thomas bowed, though Henry had his back turned to him and didn't see it, and backed out of the room. He was shaking as he made his way down the corridor and into the Presence Chamber.

'Your Eminence,' an old, croaky voice called.

Thomas halted and looked around. Archbishop Warham was waving at him from across the room. *Go away, old man*, Thomas willed as he headed for the door, *I can't talk to anyone at the moment.*

'Thomas! Thomas!' Warham called again. 'Please,

wait.'

Cursing, Thomas stopped and waited for Warham to reach him. 'What do you want, William? I have much to do.'

Warham put a hand on Thomas's arm, gripping as he tried to catch his breath. 'I just wanted to know what the king said to you.'

'He is angry, William, but you don't need me to tell you that.'

Warham shook his head. 'I had no notion Bishop Fisher would stand up and say what he did. Did you?'

'Would I have allowed it if I did?'

'No, I suppose not. You weren't with the king long.'

'The Lady Anne was with him.'

'Ah,' Warham nodded understanding. 'The king is not the same since he met that lady, is he? I don't believe he is so kind as he was wont to be.'

'I will say nothing against the king,' Thomas said. There were too many ears nearby, too many people willing to report back to Henry or the Howards or Boleyns what he said. 'Now, if you will excuse me.'

'Where do you go?'

'Back to York Place. I have some work to do, and then,' he closed his eyes as black spots suddenly danced before them, 'I think I shall retire to bed for a few hours' rest.'

'In the middle of the afternoon? That's not like you.'

'I'm tired, William, and I need to get some sleep before we start all over again tomorrow at Blackfriars.'

Warham gave him a sad smile and squeezed his arm. 'It's going to be quite a battle, isn't it, Thomas?'

'Quite a battle,' Thomas agreed, 'and I fear we may not all survive it.'

CHAPTER TWENTY-SIX

Someone was shaking him.

Thomas opened his eyes, having to pull the lids apart, feeling crust crumble. It was dark but there was a triangle of light behind the dark shape bending over him.

'What is it?' he said, blinking.

'It's me, Your Eminence,' Cavendish said. 'I am so sorry to disturb you, but Sir Thomas Boleyn insists on seeing you.'

Boleyn. The name took a moment to register. Thomas threw the bedclothes back and allowed Cavendish to pull him upright. 'What's happened? Why is he here?' Thomas asked as Cavendish put slippers on his feet.

'I don't know. He just burst into the anteroom and said he would see you. I told him you were resting but he said he would drag you out of bed if I didn't fetch you. Forgive me, Your Eminence, but that's what he said.'

Thomas felt anger bubbling up inside his chest. That such a man as Sir Thomas Boleyn, a man he had helped to raise over the past decade, should use such language about him. Who did these Boleyns think they were?

'I shall call your body servant to dress you,' Cavendish said.

'No,' Thomas said. To hell with Boleyn. He wasn't about to put on a show for that popinjay. 'If he insists on seeing me, then he can see me as I am.'

Cavendish, wearing an expression that suggested he doubted Thomas's wisdom in granting Sir Thomas an audience in his nightgown, bustled out. Thomas pulled on his dressing gown and tied the belt around his middle before moving to his chair by the fire. He had only just sat down when Sir Thomas burst in.

'I come from the king,' Sir Thomas said, looking Thomas up and down contemptuously. 'He is very angry about how things went this morning, but,' his lip curled in an evil smile, 'you already know that.'

Oh, it hadn't taken long to get around, had it? Thomas mused unhappily. *What pleasure the Night Crow must have taken in telling her father and uncle what the king said to me.*

'You have a message from the king?' Thomas asked.

Boleyn put a heavily ringed hand to his hip. 'The king wants you and Cardinal Campeggio to talk to the queen again. He feels at least one more attempt should be made to persuade her to enter a convent.'

'Despite her obvious intransigence?'

'You are to advise the queen she must surrender the entire matter of their marriage into the king's hands and that she does so willingly, without proclaiming any kind of coercion or duress.'

'If that is the king's instruction, then, of course, I will go at once to the queen,' Thomas said, rising. Boleyn didn't move. 'You wish to see me dress, my lord?'

Sir Thomas gave Thomas a supercilious smile and sauntered out of the room.

'That man,' Cavendish said disapprovingly as he closed the door behind him.

'That man may very well be the king's father-in-law before long, George,' Thomas said as he handed Cavendish his dressing gown. 'You might want to curry some favour with him.'

'Never,' Cavendish said emphatically. 'I couldn't bear to pander to such a man.'

Thomas shook his head. 'Then you are a fool, my dear George. You must always be thinking of your future. After all, I won't be around forever, and you must needs then serve another master.'

Cavendish folded the dressing gown over his arm and shook his head. 'I wish for none other, Your Eminence.'

Thomas dressed and made his way down to the river steps where an unhappy Campeggio waited for him in his barge.

'I had not expected to be required again today, Thomas,' Campeggio grumbled as Thomas sat down beside him.

'Nor I, Lorenzo, yet the king orders we try once more to persuade the queen.'

'But the queen will not consent to step quietly aside,' Campeggio cried as the barge pulled away from the river steps. 'She was adamant when she told us that, and she said as much when she spoke at Blackfriars.' He tapped Thomas on the arm. 'And between you and me, I don't blame her. You know as well as I that the dispensation was good, the marriage was lawful.'

'I do not know that, Lorenzo.'

'Come, Thomas, there's no need to pretend with me.'

'The king questions the validity of his marriage. That is enough to make me work for it.'

'Do you always do what your king wants even when it is not good for him?'

Thomas fixed his gaze on the view ahead. 'He is my king, Lorenzo,' he said, and didn't say another word to Campeggio until the barge pulled in at the river steps.

He and Campeggio went straight to Katherine's Presence Chamber and told the usher on guard to tell Katherine they wished to see her. Thomas expected to be shown in to Katherine, but instead, she came out to them. She had been sewing; a skein of white thread was hanging around her neck. She was, Thomas mused, doing all she could to appear the perfect wife, even in private.

'My lords,' she began as her ladies formed a semicircle around her, 'what is the reason for this unexpected visit?'

'My lady,' Thomas said, gesturing at the ladies, 'it would be best if we could speak in private.'

'You may speak freely in front of my ladies, Your Eminence. I fear nothing you may say or alledge against me, and the fact is I would rather whatever you have to say is said in public. I want no secrets here.'

Thomas sighed. 'Madam, we have come to know your mind, how you are inclined to dispose of this matter between you and the king, and also to let you into our private thoughts on the matter, and to offer you our counsel.'

He met Katherine's eyes, and read there what she was thinking. Was this a trick, she was wondering, some ploy to trap her into saying something that would strengthen the king's case against her? He saw too the moment she decided how to act and knew his and Campeggio's journey here would prove a failure.

'My lords,' Katherine said, 'you have surprised me with this visit. I cannot give you an answer now, for my mind is on my needle and thread, not on such a great matter as my marriage. I must have time to consider whatever questions you intend to ask me and thereafter to consult with wiser heads than mine. You must understand, I have no Spanish Council to advise me. I must rely on the integrity of Englishmen to counsel me the way I should go, and I fear there are none who will go against the king's will in support of me. But I will tell you this. I will not step aside. I will never consent to enter a convent. So, I bid you good day, gentlemen.'

Katherine turned away, her skirts swishing, and disappeared through her privy chamber door, her ladies scurrying after her.

Thomas watched the doors close, a delicious fantasy entering his mind of bursting into Katherine's chamber and knocking some sense into her thick Spanish head. He couldn't understand why she was being so stubborn. She'd lost the king's love, the treasure she prized so greatly, and nothing would give that back to her, so why cling on? Was it really just for her daughter that she persevered, so the Princess Mary would not be called bastard? Or was it her sense of dignity that made her fight like this?

'There is no point in continuing the trial,' Campeggio said with a sigh, falling onto the bench against the wood-panelled wall. 'She will not relent.'

'We do not need her to relent for the sake of the trial,' Thomas said. 'If the verdict invalidates the dispensation, then the marriage will be annulled. Of course, it would be easier if she agreed to enter a convent, but if she refuses, then the trial must continue. We have no other choice.' He turned to face him. 'The pope must give the king what he wants. I know you have your orders, Lorenzo, and I know what is going on in Rome.'

'I don't know what you mean,' Campeggio said, horrified.

'Katherine is corresponding with the pope,' Thomas said sternly. 'I know he's ordered you to delay the trial as long as possible so he can get his orders from the emperor.'

'That is a scurrilous—'

'Enough!' Thomas said. 'For the love of God, I am tired of going back and forth like this. Do you not realise the pressure I'm under, Lorenzo?'

Campeggio didn't answer, just rose from the bench and shuffled out of the room. Thomas gave one last glance at Katherine's closed door and followed after him.

'What is it?' Anne asked languidly as Henry broke open the seal on the letter a messenger had just delivered.

'It's from Thomas,' Henry said. He made a noise of disgust, then screwed the letter up and threw it away.

Anne watched it as it flew through the air. 'Bad news, my lord?'

'Katherine won't go into a nunnery. She absolutely refuses.'

'Well, I could have told you that. She wants to make things as difficult as she can for us.'

'Why the devil can't Thomas talk sense into her?'

'I doubt he's even tried.'

Henry frowned. 'I wish you would try to get along with him, my love.'

Anne held up her hands. 'My lord, do not rail so. It is the cardinal who dislikes me, not the other way around. I would be more than willing to get along with him, as you call it, if I was convinced he had your best interests at heart.'

'He does have my best interests at heart,' Henry protested.

'You are too kind, my lord,' she said sadly, shaking her head.

'You don't know how much I owe him, sweetheart. Thomas has been my very good friend for many years, before even I became king.'

'I do not deny that, but a man may take loyalty too far, especially if he has been betrayed.'

'Betrayed?'

Anne threw her book aside and moved to Henry, letting her skirts brush against his hand. 'We have to ask ourselves how hard has he tried to get you a divorce? Cardinal Wolsey is supposed to be the man who can get anything done. Hasn't that always been his boast? So, why not this, the thing you want the most?'

Henry's brow furrowed. He sought her hand between her skirts and squeezed. 'You think he hasn't really been trying? That he's been stalling all this time?'

Anne's fingers stroked the inside of Henry's wrist. She shrugged and raised a dark eyebrow. 'You know him best, my lord. What do you think?'

The trial was over; there was nothing more to be said. Nothing more except the verdict.

Thomas sat in his chair, his foot nervously tapping. The room was full, curious spectators filing in even as he watched. So many people to witness his failure, he thought grimly.

A movement up in the gallery caught his eye. *Oh no*, he thought, his stomach sinking, *not him as well*. Henry had entered the gallery and was taking a chair to witness the verdict. Close behind him came Brandon, and Thomas saw his mouth moving, talking to Henry, though Henry wasn't answering him. Henry's gaze was on the people below. Not once, Thomas noted, did Henry look his way. Time was when Thomas would have been the first face the king sought in such an assembly, looking for that assurance that all would be well and giving a smile in return. *I won't receive a smile now,* Thomas mused. *It's long gone, wiped away by the Night Crow and her family of vultures.*

The crier banged his long stick on the floor and called the room to order. The chatter died down obediently. Campeggio rose from his seat and muttered his way through the preliminaries: why the court had been convened, the witnesses they had heard, and the deliberations that had taken place.

Oh, get on with it, Thomas urged, knowing what Campeggio was going to say. *Deliver the killing blow. I can't stand this much longer.*

Campeggio took a deep breath before his next words. 'I regret I am unable to give a judgement on this matter until I have acquainted His Holiness the Pope with the evidence gathered here. Great personages are involved and too much attention has been given to these doubtful allegations throughout the world for us,' he gestured at Thomas, 'to dispense with this matter hastily. I am, therefore, compelled to adjourn this court until October when the session in Rome resumes.'

He sat back down with a wince, lifting his swaddled

foot onto a footstool. There came a loud bang and everyone looked up towards the gallery. The noise had been caused by Brandon smacking his hand down on the gallery railing. His loud voice boomed out.

'I tell you, it was never merry in England while we had cardinals amongst us.'

A sudden rage swelled up in Thomas. He leapt to his feet. 'Sir, of all the men in this realm, you have the least reason to denigrate or find fault with cardinals. Have you forgotten how, not so very long ago, you came knocking at my door, begging me to help you regain the favour of the king you had so recklessly lost? And I helped you, my lord, though I need not have done, for until that point, you had never given me any reason to love you, far from it, in fact. And if I had not helped you then, know that you would have no head upon your shoulders now, for the king would have had it cut off.'

Brandon grinned and shook his head contemptuously. 'You hear that?' he said, half rising and appealing to the onlookers below. 'How's that for a man getting above himself?' He pointed savagely at Thomas. 'He was born a butcher's son and he dares speak so freely to a noble? Hear this, priest. Only one man in this realm has the right to speak to me so and I tell you, it isn't you.' He turned meaningfully to Henry.

Thomas too looked at the king. Henry's little mouth was pursed, the eyes narrowed, the cheeks a deep purple. For the first time that day, Henry met Thomas's eyes, and Thomas's blood ran cold at the look of hatred in them.

Henry rose slowly, straightened the chain around his neck, and walked out of the gallery.

CHAPTER TWENTY-SEVEN

There was bad news coming with the sound of Stephen Gardiner's footsteps in the corridor outside, Thomas could tell. Each footfall seemed to say a word: the king is displeased, the king is angry, the king will not forgive your failure. Thomas drew in a deep breath and squared his shoulders. He would be ready to face Gardiner, however, bad the news.

Gardiner entered. 'Your Eminence.' He gave a small bow, not so low as was customary, and that change told Thomas all he needed to know.

'I think you have come from the king, Stephen,' Thomas said.

'I have, Your Eminence. He is leaving London, going to Grafton and...,' Gardiner paused, putting two bony fingers to his pink lips.

Oh, don't pretend you find this difficult. I know the kind of man you are. 'And what, Stephen?' Thomas asked.

'The king has graciously asked me to go with him, as his chief secretary.'

Thomas saw the hint of a smile on Gardiner's lips. He

couldn't contain his pleasure at the appointment, not even now. 'I see,' he nodded. 'So, I must lose you. You have accepted his offer, I suppose?'

Gardiner shrugged. 'Your Eminence, an offer from the king…,' he began.

'Is as good as a command,' Thomas finished. 'Yes, I know. You need say no more. Well, God speed you to Grafton, Stephen. May you prosper in the king's service. I have no doubt you shall.'

'Thank you, Your Eminence.' Gardiner cleared his throat and Thomas knew there was more. 'The king has instructed me to inform you that there will be no further direct communication between him and yourself. If he wishes to convey anything to you, he will do so through an intermediary.'

Thomas forced himself to keep his eyes on Gardiner. He wouldn't look away, wouldn't do anything to suggest this news had delivered a blow to his very heart. He swallowed down the lump in his throat before speaking. 'Would that intermediary be yourself, Stephen?'

Gardiner inclined his head. 'Perhaps. I trust the message I have delivered is clear?'

'Oh, yes, very clear. Thank you, Stephen, for being so direct.'

There was an awkward silence which Gardiner broke. 'Well, I must be going.'

'Yes, you must not keep the king waiting. Goodbye, Stephen.'

Gardiner bowed and left. Not a word of gratitude for how Thomas had treated him while in his service, not a hint of sympathy for his current situation. *Why should he?* Thomas rebuked himself. *Did I worry about those I left lagging behind when I sought out better masters and more powerful posts? No, I took the opportunities that came my way and gave not a thought to those I had served. And now it's my turn, to be used and tossed aside. I never realised how cruel I was.*

'Oh, for heaven's sake, get out of my way and let me sit down,' Campeggio said, waving away the servant who tried to offer him a plate of sweetmeats. He limped over to the chair by the fire and fell into it with a loud groan.

Thomas gestured to the servant he could go and put down his pen. 'Your gout is bad today, Lorenzo.'

Campeggio made a face. 'This weather,' he said, staring out of the window at the rain that lashed the panes. 'I get no respite in this country of yours. I thank God I will soon be leaving.'

'Back to Rome?'

'Back to Rome. But first I must go to Grafton and take my leave of the king.' He looked sideways at Thomas. 'You have written to him?'

Thomas didn't meet his eye. 'I told you I am forbidden to do so, Lorenzo.'

Campeggio nodded sadly. 'I wondered if that was still the case. It's partly why I've come to see you. I take no pleasure in this discord between you and the king, and I know it will not please His Holiness either.'

'Well, of course,' Thomas said, a little sourly. 'For if I do not have the king's ear, neither does His Holiness.' He shook his head at Campeggio's shocked expression. 'You needn't pretend that's not what Clement is thinking. I would think the same myself in his situation. But I know you to be sincere in your feelings, Lorenzo, and I thank you for them.'

Campeggio leant forward. 'I want you to come with me to Grafton, Thomas,' he said. 'The king will not refuse me an audience, and so, he will have no choice but to see you also. I am sure once you two are face to face, a reconciliation will soon follow. It is this distance between you that has prolonged this breach.'

Thomas considered. There was sense in Campeggio's words. With his absence, the Howards and the Boleyns were at perfect liberty to pour their poison in Henry's ear.

But there was risk as well as sense in Campeggio's suggestion. Despite all Campeggio said, there was no guarantee Henry would agree to see him, and Thomas could just picture the scene of him being turned away. He wasn't sure he could bear the humiliation. But if there was a chance of reconciliation, he had to take it, whatever the risk. He reached out and grasped Campeggio's hand.

'Thank you, Lorenzo. I will come with you to Grafton.'

Henry drummed his fingers on his knee, annoyed he wasn't alone with Anne. Howard and Brandon had come into the privy chamber, and before he could tell them he didn't want their company, Anne had bid them take a seat. Henry watched her as she rose and took up the jug of wine and poured her uncle a cup, frowning as she set the jug down without doing the same for Brandon. Henry glanced at his best friend, noted the irritation and resentment on his face, and felt a pang of irritation himself. Could she not at least observe the courtesies? He knew Anne had no liking for his best friend, but that was no reason why she had to be rude to him. Katherine would never have treated Brandon so, and—

No, he chastised himself for his disloyalty, *do not think of Katherine*. It made no difference what Katherine would or wouldn't do. Anne was his only concern these days. So what if Brandon was offended? He had hands. He could pour his own damn wine.

'So, what now?' Anne asked, pulling her skirts out of the way of Brandon's boots.

Brandon took up the wine jug. 'You'll have to wait until October for the court to reconvene.'

'God's Death,' Howard banged his hand down on the arm of his chair. 'There isn't going to be any reconvening. Those red-skirted devils have seen to that.'

Brandon frowned. 'But Campeggio said—'

Howard cut him off. 'He's just following the pope's orders. The pope doesn't want there to be any progress with the divorce. He can't afford to offend the emperor, can he? The emperor's got the pope on a piece of string and he keeps tugging. Do this, do that, agree to nothing until I tell you to.' He waved his hand dismissively. 'Take my word for it, Campeggio won't be back.'

'So,' Anne said, flicking her long black hair over her shoulder, 'Wolsey has what he wanted. If you ask me, Wolsey told Katherine to walk out like that. He knew he can't openly oppose you,' she said to Henry, 'but this way, he thinks he's keeping both you and Charles happy. He can say to you that he's tried his hardest to get the divorce and blame the pope for his failure while saying to Charles he succeeded in keeping you married to Katherine.'

'How much does he get from the emperor?' Brandon asked, curious.

'Thousands upon thousands every year,' Howard said sourly. 'More than you and I get from our tenants, that's for sure. And that's just the pensions from Spain. What about all the others? The ones he gets from France and Portugal, the Netherlands? The fact is we have no idea just how many foreign kings' purses he has his hand in.' Howard caught Henry frowning at him. 'Well, how do you think he has come to be so rich, Your Majesty? A butcher's son, that's what he is, and here he stands, richer than he has any right to be, while fellows like me and Brandon must scrape to find every penny.'

'Not just you, Uncle,' Anne said. 'Do you know the fat cardinal is richer than His Majesty?'

Henry squirmed in his chair. There was no need for Anne to say that. Everyone already knew he was hard done by.

'You know what you should do, Hal?' Brandon said. 'You should cut him off.'

'My lord cannot,' Anne said. 'Wolsey's pensions come by way of his Church offices, and the king has no jurisdiction over the Church.'

Howard cursed. 'That's a damn liberty, as well. A king having no control over the clergy in his own country.'

Brandon laughed, not his bull roar of a laugh, but a little, sniggering thing. 'No, I don't mean cut off his pensions. I mean stop him being Lord Chancellor.'

'I can't do that,' Henry said doubtfully.

'Why can't you?' Anne asked sharply, staring down at him.

He looked up at her. 'Because we need him, my love.'

'For what, exactly? Has he done as you asked him and got you your divorce? Or has he delayed and prevaricated and said, "No, Your Majesty, you cannot have your divorce, I and the Church say you cannot"?'

Henry said nothing, just nibbled at a fingernail.

'But perhaps this pleases you,' Anne went on. 'Perhaps you do not wish to be divorced either.'

'Nan,' Henry chided and reached for her hand. He had to grab at it, for she did not offer it to him. 'Do not speak so to me. You know it's not true.'

'And God knows the fat cardinal has no reason to wish us to wed.' She tugged her hand out of Henry's and folded her arms tightly over her chest. 'He would like nothing more than if I were to disappear.'

'Why should he so?' Henry asked.

'Because he hates me,' Anne said. 'He has done ever since he broke off my marriage to Percy.'

Henry shifted uneasily in his chair. He had never told Anne it had been he who had insisted Thomas break off the match, and he wasn't about to disillusion her now.

'Well,' Anne said to Henry, 'has he ever said he is pleased at your wanting to marry me? No,' she said, before Henry could answer. 'In fact, he did all he could to persuade you not to do so.'

'Really, Anne?' Howard asked, playing along with his niece's efforts to drive the knife deeper into the cardinal's back.

'Oh yes, Uncle,' she nodded emphatically. 'He spent two hours on his knees before my lord begging him not to renounce Katherine.'

'Wolsey on his knees?' Brandon laughed at the very idea.

'It's where he belongs,' Howard growled. 'Butcher's son.'

Henry rubbed his forefinger along his beard. He had been thinking about what Brandon had said while the others talked. 'But if I dismiss him,' he said slowly, 'who would I appoint in his place?'

'My uncle,' Anne said.

Brandon laughed. 'Howard's not your man.'

'Would you suggest yourself, Your Grace?' Anne asked sarcastically.

'No,' he said, his face stony at her, 'not me. I don't want to be Lord Chancellor. But who's that fellow you like, Hal? The lawyer.'

'More, do you mean?' Henry said.

'Yes, Sir Thomas More, that's him. He could do the job, I suppose.'

'I'm sure he could,' Henry agreed, 'but I don't want to be too hasty. '

'Surely, haste is what we're after,' Howard cried. 'The longer we wait, the stronger Katherine's case becomes. Doesn't it?' he appealed to Brandon, who shrugged and downed his cup of wine.

'But Uncle,' Anne said, 'you are not considering my lord's generous heart.' She smiled down at Henry and he swelled with love. 'He cannot turn his back on the man he has loved all these years, no matter how greatly that man has failed him. I swear he could sooner turn me away than Wolsey.'

'Never, Nan,' Henry said, reaching out of his chair to grab her round the waist and pull her onto his knee. 'No one is more dear to me than you.'

'Well, then,' she said, fluttering her eyelashes at him. 'Shall we be rid of the fat cardinal?'

He wasn't ready to give in to her just yet. Henry ran his fingers over the top of her bodice, the tips brushing gently over her breasts. 'Thomas may still have his uses, my love. We will wait a little while longer.'

CHAPTER TWENTY-EIGHT

The steward shrugged and shook his head. 'I am sorry, Your Eminence, but no rooms are available for you.'

Thomas and Campeggio had arrived at Grafton, the journey an unusual one, for Henry had given orders that there was to be no ceremony for the two cardinals, no ostentatious display to draw the eyes of the people. They were to travel incognito had come the written instruction in Stephen Gardiner's hand, and Campeggio had raised his eyes at Thomas as if to say it was all his fault. Thomas had shrugged and said they would make better time without an entourage slowing them down.

But Thomas had not expected for no provision to have been made for him at the palace, and he had to swallow down his anger as the steward made his apologies. Perhaps the king was angry with him, but he was a cardinal still and that alone demanded respect. His resentment deepened when he discovered Campeggio had been provided with rooms. Henry couldn't have made his displeasure clearer than if he had told him he was out of favour to his very face. But that wasn't Henry's way, Thomas reminded himself. Henry was never one to do his own dirty work.

'Perhaps you could show me to a quiet corner,' he said to the steward, determined not to show how upset he was.

The steward looked around, as if a quiet corner was about to magically appear.

'Excuse me, Your Eminence.' A man stepped through the archway of the wooden screen and presented himself. Thomas studied the face; it took a moment for him to place it.

'Sir Henry Norris,' he said, recalling Henry's Groom of the Stool. Had he been sent to greet him? Was this all a dreadful mistake after all? 'How pleasant to see you again.'

'I couldn't help overhearing,' Norris said. 'It pains me no rooms have been made available to one such as yourself. It is an oversight, I am sure.'

Thomas nodded, as if he was sure of it too, and waited.

'You are welcome to use my room,' Norris said, a little uneasily. 'It is not what you are used to, I know, but it is all I have to offer.'

So, Norris was not here on the king's behalf. Thomas's heart sank. 'Thank you, Sir Henry. I gratefully accept your kind offer.'

'Then, please, do follow me,' Norris said, gesturing through the archway.

Thomas turned to Campeggio. Campeggio had the decency to look embarrassed but not enough to offer to share his rooms. They exchanged no words, just a nod to indicate they would meet later to go before the king. With that, Thomas followed after Norris.

. . .

It was time for Campeggio's audience with Henry, and Thomas was waiting outside the Presence Chamber for him to arrive. He had only been there for about five minutes but it felt so much longer; courtiers who would have bowed to him a month before now merely stared and whispered in each others' ears. *What a pitiful spectacle I must make*, he thought as he fixed a smile on his face. He turned at the sound of shuffling. Campeggio came up to him, shaking out his silk robes.

'Ready to see the king?' Campeggio asked.

Thomas nodded, though he wasn't at all sure he was ready. His heart had begun banging at his ribs.

Campeggio waved at the Yeoman Warders stationed either side of the Presence Chamber doors to open up. Half expecting them to cross their halberds as he tried to pass through, Thomas moved closer to Campeggio, almost treading on his heels. *Dignity, Thomas,* he reminded himself, *dignity.*

The Presence Chamber was as full as ever and he felt yet more eyes upon him. Thomas searched for Henry, and there he was, seated beneath his canopy of estate, talking with Brandon. He hadn't even noticed the cardinals, and Brandon had to draw his attention to them with a nod of his head in their direction.

Henry twisted in his chair to face the room and Campeggio stepped forward. For a moment, Thomas didn't know what to do. Follow after Lorenzo or stay where he was? His indecision took away any choice he might have made. It was too late now. To hurry after Campeggio would make him look ridiculous, so he stayed where he was.

Thomas stood tall, hands clasped behind his back, while Campeggio took his official leave of Henry. It seemed an age, but it couldn't have been more than a few minutes. Then Campeggio was walking backwards so as not to show Henry his back, and Thomas had to step to one side to avoid him. Campeggio nodded at Thomas and left the chamber.

Thomas fell to his knees, keeping his head down. It was so quiet in the chamber, Thomas could hear every breath being taken. Then there were footsteps, heavy, making the floorboards shudder beneath his knees, and a shadow fell over him. A hand touched his shoulder, moving down to cup his elbow, encouraging him to his feet.

'Your Eminence,' Henry said, his hand still on Thomas's elbow, and there was a look on his face that suggested he too was sorry they had quarrelled. 'Let us talk.' He guided Thomas over to the window, courtiers scattering left and right.

'I am most grateful for your seeing me like this, Your Majesty,' Thomas said, having to lick his lips because they were dry. This was more than he had hoped for. He was Henry's friend once again and Henry had let everyone know it. To be touched by the king and taken off by him to a private space to talk. Let anyone dare say Thomas was out of favour now.

'I was advised not to see you,' Henry admitted, and Thomas's joy dwindled a little. 'Brandon, Howard,' he laughed a little, 'even Nan said I should let you rot.'

He thinks that's funny, Thomas realised with horror. *My king actually laughing in front of my very face about abandoning me.* Thomas curled up the corner of his mouth. 'I'm very grateful you know your own mind, Your Majesty.'

'I cannot deny I am disappointed at how the trial

ended, Thomas,' Henry said with a sigh. 'I had hoped this matter would have been resolved by now.'

'That was my wish too,' Thomas said. 'But the pope and the emperor are determined not to allow the divorce. I really don't know what else can be done.'

'What use are you, then, if you can do nothing more?' Henry suddenly snarled. He took a deep breath and leant his head against the window. 'I must be free of Katherine, Thomas. I must marry Nan. Whatever it takes, I will do.'

And whatever I can do to make it happen, I must do, Thomas realised, for as he stared at the king's determined and unhappy profile, he really believed Henry would do anything to marry the Night Crow, and that anything might mean the death of Thomas Wolsey.

Anne pushed a slice of beef around her platter and looked across the table at Henry from beneath lowered lashes. He had been unusually quiet ever since they had retired to dine alone in his privy chamber, and Anne suspected she knew why.

'So, are you going to tell me what you spoke with Wolsey about?' she asked.

Henry licked his fingers and shrugged. 'Nothing of any consequence, my love.'

'Really? I heard the manner of your meeting was very friendly.'

'I wouldn't say very, but I greeted him as an old friend, yes.'

Anne pushed her food away. 'So, you're taking him back.' She folded her arms tightly over her chest. 'I see.'

'No, you don't.' Henry sighed, wiped his fingers on the napkin over his shoulder and leant back in the chair.

'Everything I do at court is witnessed. Everything. Even here, in private, there are people around.'

'I know that,' Anne snapped.

Her irritability made Henry smile. 'Then you also know that my meeting with Thomas will have been recounted a hundred times by now. "The king greeted His Eminence warmly", it will be said.'

'Where is this leading, my lord?'

'It is leading to us keeping our options open, Nan,' Henry said.

The patient way he spoke made Anne's skin crawl. 'But I thought we'd agreed you would cast him out. When my uncle and my lord Suffolk were here—'

'I told you then we may have need of him.' Henry held up his hands as Anne opened her mouth to speak. 'I will cast him off, but at a time of my own choosing, when I am ready and truly have no further use for him.'

'But I don't understand. Why not be rid of him at once? Of what further use can he be?'

'I don't know, and that's the point,' he cried out, his patience worn thin. 'Until I'm sure Thomas can do nothing more, he stays. If I cast him off, Nan, he has no reason to stay loyal. Now, do you understand?'

'I suppose so,' Anne said sulkily, 'but I wish you wouldn't grant him another audience, my lord.' She rose and moved around the table, sliding her hands around Henry's neck. 'For me?'

Henry kissed her neck. 'Very well, Nan. For you, I will not see him again.'

Thomas had woken early the next morning, having had a blissfully happy sleep in Henry Norris's bed. Where

Norris slept that night didn't concern him. All Thomas cared about was that the rift between him and the king had been healed. Lorenzo had been right. All it needed was for them to meet face to face for Henry's animosity to melt away.

Campeggio joined him after mass for breakfast. He was glad to hear how Thomas had been received and expressed the hope that the king's marriage would be settled one way or another before too long.

Thomas smiled as he waved goodbye, but the smile dropped from his face the moment Campeggio was out of sight. Thomas was not such a fool that he could be sure he and Henry would have the same friendship they had had before the marriage had ever been questioned. Even if that was what Henry wanted, the Boleyns and the Howards would see that it didn't happen. Thomas was in a better position than he had been but he knew he still had to tread carefully.

Henry had asked Thomas to meet him at ten o'clock in the privy chamber, and Thomas made his way there with his chin held a little higher than the previous day. The courtiers he passed still whispered, but he could tell their scorn had gone, as they were no longer sure it was wise to be scornful of the cardinal who was back in the king's favour.

The Yeoman Warders looked out of the corners of their eyes as he approached. Thomas wondered why they weren't automatically opening the doors, but perhaps they hadn't been told to admit him, still acting on orders from the day before. He came to a halt between them and still they didn't move. He was about to chastise them for their slackness when Henry Norris came running along the corridor.

'Your Eminence,' he panted as he came to a stop by Thomas, 'there you are.'

'Yes, Sir Henry,' Thomas said. 'I have an appointment with the king this morning, but these fellows,' he gestured at the Yeoman Warders, 'do not seem to know of it.'

Norris took a deep breath. 'You cannot be admitted, Your Eminence. The king is not in his privy chamber.'

'Well, where the devil is he?' Thomas cried. 'The Presence Chamber? The gardens? Where must I go?'

Norris stared down at his feet. 'You will not have a meeting with the king,' he said sorrowfully. 'The king has gone hunting and will not return until late today.'

Thomas stared at him. 'Gone hunting? No, no, Sir Henry, he specifically asked me to meet him this morning. He was most emphatic.'

'When did he tell you that?' Norris asked.

'Yesterday afternoon,' Thomas replied warily.

Norris nodded. 'He dined with the Lady Anne, Your Eminence.'

He said nothing more. He didn't need to say more. Thomas understood.

'She talked him out of meeting me, didn't she?' Thomas said quietly.

'I fear so,' Norris said, and Thomas heard sympathy in his voice. 'It grieves me to have to do this, Your Eminence.' He snatched his cap from his head and ran his fingers through his hair.

'Do what, Sir Henry?' Thomas asked helpfully.

Norris put his cap back on his head. 'The king's orders are that you return to London.'

'And do what once I am there?'

Norris's mouth opened, but then he shook his head and shrugged. 'I know not.'

'I see,' Thomas said. He sniffed back the tears, damned if he would cry before Norris and the Yeoman Warders. 'Thank you for telling me so kindly, Sir Henry. I do appreciate it.'

'Not at all, Your Eminence. I only wish I had not been the messenger.'

Thomas grinned ruefully. 'If not you, then I suspect it would have been Stephen Gardiner.' He put out a hand to touch Norris's arm. 'I am glad you were chosen and not he.'

His arm fell back to his side, then rose to clutch the gold cross over his belly. He gripped it tight. *God, sustain me in this time of trial*, he prayed, *for I know not what awaits me*. He bid Norris farewell and returned to his room to pack and arrange his journey back to London.

CHAPTER TWENTY-NINE

Carry on as if nothing has happened. That was what Thomas decided he would do on the journey back to London. He would head Privy Council meetings, he would despatch the business of the realm from his office at York Place, he would continue to communicate with King Francis and the emperor, and he would return to hear cases in Chancery. He would do his job, as Henry wanted, as he expected him to do. The king would not be able to find fault with him. And to his surprise, Thomas discovered he enjoyed being back in Chancery. He could almost believe he was a young man again, free of royal constraint and expectations, free to dispense justice in the way he saw fit.

That morning had gone well. He had dispensed with seven cases in just a few hours, cases that had been sitting around for months for want of a decent lawyer to take them up. *I've been remiss,* Thomas mused as he made his way back to York Place*, I've let justice slide while I've been caught up dealing with kings and emperors. Perhaps Henry's displeasure is God's way of telling me I should concern myself with the people and not politics.*

This notion had been on Thomas's mind ever since Grafton. It had been a long journey alone back to London, and he had had a lot of time to think. He thought mostly of his time at Magdalen College, when it had been expected, not least by him, that he would have either lived out his life as an Oxford scholar or else as a parish priest, only hearing about the deeds of great men at court, not being one of them. Would he have been happier then? he wondered, though he was smiling as he walked into his office. Cromwell was there, standing by the desk.

'You look glum, Master Cromwell,' Thomas said reproachfully. 'Careful. You will spoil my good mood.'

Cromwell stepped back for Thomas to pass, his face unchanging. 'There's a messenger from the King's Bench outside. He wants to see you.'

'Then why has he come here when he could have seen me at Westminster Hall before I left?' Thomas studied Cromwell's face, saw it had not altered, and asked quietly, 'What is it?'

Cromwell set his jaw. 'I fear it isn't good news he brings.'

Thomas sank down onto his chair, his good humour gone in an instant. 'When is the news good these days?' He sighed and nodded at Cromwell. 'You better bring him in.'

Thomas closed his eyes as Cromwell left to fetch the King's Bench messenger. He had started to think himself safe. What a fool he had been!

'This is him,' Cromwell said sourly as he returned. The messenger wore the king's badge on his arm and he held out a letter sealed with red wax.

'Your Eminence,' he said, 'I am here to serve you with this writ, by order of the king.'

Thomas gestured for Cromwell to take the paper. He watched Cromwell's face as he read it and knew he had been right. It wasn't good news.

'Well?' he asked.

Cromwell passed him the paper. Thomas unfolded it, his palms sweating, and read the writ. His blood ran cold.

'All right,' Cromwell said crossly to the messenger, 'you've done what you came to do, now piss off.'

The messenger hurried from the room. Cromwell watched him go, saw the door close, then turned back to Thomas. 'Your Eminence?'

'No need to fuss, Master Cromwell, I'm quite well.'

'You don't look well.' He snatched up the writ Thomas had tossed aside. 'Were you expecting to be charged with praemunire?'

Thomas snorted a bitter laugh. 'Was I expecting to be charged with putting papal law above English law and to learn that I must now stand trial for such a transgression? No, Master Cromwell, I was not expecting it.'

'What can we do?' Cromwell asked, chastened by Thomas's sarcasm.

Thomas shook his head. 'There's nothing we can do. I must answer this charge.'

'It has to be some sort of mistake. Some idiot at the King's Bench has got the wrong end of the stick. The king can't mean to put you through a trial.'

'Why not? You forget who's advising the king these days.'

'You mean the Howards?'

Thomas nodded. 'The Howards and the Boleyns. All one and the same.'

'But the king must be mad to accuse you of treason.' Cromwell stared at Thomas, saw the trembling hand that clutched the gold cross around his neck. 'Let me go to the king. Someone has to speak for you.'

'You're known as my man, Cromwell. I doubt if you would get past the Presence Chamber.'

'You must let me try, at least.'

'No,' Thomas said. 'The king will have his way.'

Cromwell sighed and sank down onto a stool by the desk. 'You could leave the country,' he said, only half-joking.

Thomas tried to smile but couldn't manage it. 'Well, let us get back to work.' He sat up and reached for his quill.

'Work? After this?' Cromwell gestured with the writ.

'What else would you have me do?' Thomas snapped. 'If I throw up my hands and stop doing my job, it would be yet another accusation of failure for my enemies to throw at me. And besides, it would not help to dwell on the matter. It will come. I will be made to stand trial.'

'The king will have his way,' Cromwell said.

'Yes,' Thomas said sadly, 'he will.'

Thomas shooed his secretary out of the room as he heard Cromwell's voice in the corridor outside, telling someone to take care of his horse. It had seemed an age since Cromwell had left for the new session of Parliament to discover exactly what Thomas was being charged with.

Cromwell entered the room, gave Thomas a grim look and closed the door.

'Well?' Thomas asked.

'It's not good,' Cromwell said, striding across the room and taking a seat opposite Thomas in front of the fire.

'Tell me,' Thomas sighed, fidgeting as Cromwell helped himself to wine.

Cromwell took a mouthful, smacking his lips. 'The king was there at Blackfriars. Sir Thomas More came in wearing his brand new robes. Rumour has it he told the king he had no desire to take over the Lord Chancellorship but he looked like he was enjoying it, if you ask me.' He set his wine cup down and took a deep breath. 'The charge of praemunire drawn up by the House of Lords is made up of forty counts.'

'Forty?' Thomas cried incredulously.

'Some of the charges are out and out lies, some are so petty I'm astonished the Lords had the gall to include them, but…'

'But? Out with it, Cromwell.'

'But some of the charges, I fear, may be true.'

'Such as?'

'You'll have to forgive me for repeating them.' He took out a piece of paper from his jerkin and read. 'That you exercised your papal legateship freely, thereby flouting the king's authority, that you made treaties with foreign powers without the king's knowledge, that you considered yourself equal to the king by including the phrase 'the king and I' in your letters, that you endangered the king by insisting on being in his presence when you were infected with a contagious disease, not allowing Privy Council members to voice their opinions, ugh…' He screwed up the paper and threw it in the fire. 'I shan't bore you with the rest.'

'No,' Thomas said quietly, 'you need not.'

'The bill of attainder was voted in without debate. All the charges accepted.'

'Did the king speak?'

'Not a word. He was just there to make sure More did as he'd been told. Not that he needed telling. I know for a fact More was the first to sign the letter that insisted on bringing the bill of attainder against you.'

Thomas didn't ask how Cromwell knew that; he had many sources at court, from spit-boys to nobles. 'Who else put their name to the letter?'

'Other than More? Howard, Brandon, as you would expect. Oh, and Dorset.' Cromwell eyed Thomas warily.

A leaden weight landed in Thomas's stomach. Dorset, his pupil back at Oxford when he had been a master at Magdalen College, the young man who had been so kind to him and treated him with the greatest respect. Even he had turned on him?

Cromwell leant forward, elbows on knees. 'I don't think you need to worry, though. An act of attainder is nothing without the king's will to proceed, and I think he will not see it through.'

Thomas looked at him in surprise, wondering at Cromwell's confidence. 'You sound very sure.'

Cromwell grinned. 'I am sure. I'm going to make the king realise he can't manage without you.'

It had been two days since the writ had been delivered, and Thomas had done his best to carry on as he had told Cromwell he intended to do. He went through the motions of checking ledgers, of reading ambassadorial letters, of replying to enquiries from people who still thought he had influence and could help them.

His household servants knew different. Some of them had already resigned their positions, the news of his indictment taking only a few hours to get around York Place, and Thomas expected more would quickly follow. No one wanted to serve a disgraced master.

Thomas was at his desk when he heard the sound of a scuffle in the clerks' chamber. He looked up expectantly, listening to see if he could identify the voices. Cromwell was out there, trying to calm down whatever was happening, but without much success. Thomas wasn't surprised. It was difficult to get Howard to calm down when he was worked up.

'Is he in there? Is Wolsey in there?'

'You cannot go in like this, Your Grace,' Cromwell said, but the door was flung open a few seconds later and Howard stood there, filling the aperture.

'You are here,' he said, grinning at Thomas.

'Where else would I be, Your Grace?' Thomas returned, not getting up. He wasn't sure he would be able to even if he tried, and anyway, he wasn't going to rise for Norfolk.

'If I had my way, you'd be in a dungeon in the Tower,' Howard said maliciously.

Thomas swallowed. 'Then I can assume that's not what you're here to do?'

Howard came into the room and Brandon took his place in the doorway. Both of them here. Why? Did they expect him to put up a fight?

'I'm here for the Great Seal,' Howard said, casting his gaze over the mess of Thomas's desk.

'The Great Seal?' Thomas repeated, not understanding.

Brandon strode in. 'Stop prevaricating, Wolsey. You've been removed from your post of Lord Chancellor and you're to hand the Great Seal over to us. By order of the king.'

Thomas saw Cromwell edge into the room. Cromwell was eyeing the two dukes warily, as if he half expected there to be a fist fight and he was readying himself to land a few punches of his own. *I'd like to see that,* Thomas thought as he drew his hands beneath the desk and clenched them, but only to stop them shaking.

'Excuse me, Your Eminence,' Cromwell said, coming into the room to stand by Thomas's desk, 'but if you will allow me?'

Thomas nodded for Cromwell to continue.

Cromwell looked from Howard to Brandon. 'His Eminence cannot deliver the Great Seal into your hands, Your Graces. He is its keeper, you see, by law, and by law, he cannot surrender it to just anyone who comes asking for it.'

'Anyone?' Howard sneered. He gestured angrily at himself and Brandon. 'We're not anyone, you insolent dog, we're—'

'Yes, Your Grace, I understand that,' Cromwell interrupted him, and Thomas wondered where he got the gall. 'But you must understand that His Eminence can only deliver up the Great Seal upon receipt of a written instruction from His Majesty. Signed Henry Rex and sealed with the royal seal. To do otherwise would be to risk the security of His Majesty's realm.'

The dukes frowned at each other. 'Do you mean to say you expect us to go all the way back to Windsor for a damned piece of paper?' Brandon asked.

Thomas watched Cromwell, conscious his servant was fighting this particular battle for him alone. Cromwell's jaw hardened and he stared straight at Brandon as if he had every right. 'I'm afraid I am, Your Grace.'

Brandon glared at Thomas. 'We could just take the seal and forget all this nonsense your man just spouted.'

'You could,' Thomas said, finding his voice at last, 'but consider whether you should.'

Brandon laughed. 'Why should we not? Who's to stop us?'

'Well,' Thomas said, glancing at Cromwell, 'my man Cromwell is very handy with his fists, I hear. But I do not wish to descend into violence, Your Grace, and I'm sure the king would not wish it either. A piece of paper, Your Grace, that is all that is required, as Master Cromwell says. And once I have that, I shall hand the Great Seal over to you.'

Brandon muttered something in Howard's ear. The creases in Howard's face deepened.

'Very well,' he said, when Brandon had finished. 'We'll come back with this piece of paper you insist upon.' He headed for the door, then turned back to Thomas. 'But be ready when we do come back. Nothing will stop us from taking it then, not even this brute you have here.'

The two dukes strode out of the office.

Cromwell moved to the door and shut it before turning to Thomas. 'Are you all right?' he asked.

Thomas nodded, but he felt far from well. 'They'll be back.'

'Yes, they will,' Cromwell agreed, 'and I won't be able to stop them next time.'

'Should you have stopped them this time? Was it true what you said, about the letter from the king?'

Cromwell smirked. 'It might be. It might not. Would you rather I hadn't said it?'

Thomas stared at Cromwell, then suddenly burst out laughing.

'What's so funny?' Cromwell asked irritably as the laughing went on and on.

Thomas took out a handkerchief and wiped his streaming eyes. 'Nothing,' he said truthfully. 'Nothing about this is funny.' His laughter stopped as quickly as it started. He took a few deep breaths, conscious of Cromwell's censorious stare. 'The king will be displeased.'

'Does it matter?' Cromwell asked. 'Your Eminence, you've lost the king's love, and I'm not sure you can win it back. You've got to look out from yourself now.'

'Are you not minded to desert me, Cromwell?' Thomas asked. 'I wouldn't blame you if you did.'

'I'm not ready to do that, Your Eminence,' Cromwell said.

'And when you are?'

'Then I'll be kind,' he promised.

Thomas nodded and smiled. 'I cannot ask for any more.'

The dukes returned a week later, all that time Thomas wondering what was keeping them. For a day or two, he nursed a hope the king had relented, that he had realised he was treating his beloved Wolsey unkindly, but Cromwell soon disabused him of that hope. Cromwell told him bluntly he didn't want another spell of Thomas's hysterical laughter. He wanted his master to be prepared for what was coming.

'A Tower dungeon?' Thomas had suggested with only a hint of humour.

Cromwell had shaken his head. 'I doubt if the king would do that. You're still a prince of the Church, after all. That he can't take away from you.'

Thomas had been ready when the dukes strode into his office. He no longer trembled, his voice did not falter when he greeted them. He handed over the white bag containing the Great Seal as Cromwell read the letter from the king the dukes brought without a flicker of regret. It was almost as if with the passing of the bag went the passing of his worries. A burden, undoubtedly, had been lifted, he felt.

Then Howard delivered a blow. 'You are to leave York Place and go to Esher. The king doesn't want you in London. And you are not to go with any ceremony.'

'No showing off, like you usually do,' Brandon added. 'And you're only to take what you need to be comfortable at Esher. Bedlinen, kitchenware, that's all.'

Thomas stared at him. 'But my tapestries, my silks.'

'They're to go to the king,' Howard said, not even bothering to hide his pleasure. 'He wants them for Hampton Court.'

Thomas knew the dukes wanted him to buckle, to show some desperate emotion, to prove they had broken him. He had given up so much, but he wasn't about to give up his dignity, too.

'He must have the tapestries, of course,' he said, 'because they are not mine. Everything I have, I have had by His Majesty's good graces, and it is right I give them back. Master Cromwell, will you oversee the packing and conveyancing of everything the king wants?'

'I will, Your Eminence,' Cromwell said, his voice implying he felt the slight of this looting far more than Thomas.

'We've got our own men to see to that,' Howard said, waving Cromwell away. 'Don't want you hiding any of the best things, do we?'

There was nothing else for it. Thomas left York Place, taking with him only a handful of servants and no more than five carts of household goods, and making an unremarkable passing through London. His small party was only a few miles from Esher when a figure was seen approaching. Thomas and his companions drew in their mounts and waited with apprehension as the figure drew near. Was this another messenger from the king, this one come to arrest and take him to that dungeon in the Tower Thomas had started to dream about?

It was dark by this time, the only illumination the torches attached to the carts, and Thomas only recognised the stranger when he had dismounted and stood by the side of his horse.

'Sir Henry Norris,' Thomas greeted him cautiously, 'what do you do here?'

'I had hoped to catch up with your party at Putney,' Norris said. 'I bring a message from the king.'

Thomas dismounted. 'What message?' he asked eagerly.

'That you must be of good cheer,' Norris said, smiling encouragingly. 'You are as high in his favour as you ever have been. I am to give you this.' He delved into a leather pouch hanging from his belt and brought out a gold ring with a large ruby stone.

Thomas's breath caught in his throat as he reached for it. It was the ring Henry always sent whenever he had a message of any great moment to deliver. He put it to his lips and kissed the stone.

'Could I have a word in private?' Norris asked, taking Thomas's arm and drawing him aside. He lowered his voice. 'The king also wanted me to tell you that all of this,' he gestured at the riders and the carts, 'is not sprung from his own unkindness, but is done to satisfy the minds of some, I'm sure you know who, and he plans to recompense you for the goods you have turned over to him to furnish Hampton Court. You must be patient, Your Eminence. You will yet be returned to your former state, perhaps be even better than you ever were.'

No message could have been more welcome. Thomas fell to his knees, the mud squelching around him. 'Sir Henry, I cannot but rejoice at these words. I have been so miserable, believing I have incurred the king's displeasure, but now I know it is not so and I have no greater joy than that.'

'Please, Your Eminence,' Norris said, embarrassed by this display, 'rise.' He bent to help Thomas to his feet, and then into his saddle, putting his hands on the ample back-side and pushing.

'Thank you, Sir Henry,' Thomas said. 'If I were a nobleman, I would endeavour to give you something worthy of your great news, but unfortunately, I have nothing but the clothes I wear on my back. The most I can give you is this.' The large gold cross he was accustomed to wear with his red robes had been packed away, but he lifted from around his neck a small gold cross on a chain. He handed it to Norris. 'Inside is a piece of the Holy Cross. Before this moment, I would not have parted with that for any amount of money, but I give it to you in grati-tude for the message you have brought me this night. Whenever you see it, remember me and speak of me kindly to the king. Assure him I am his obedient subject, vassal and poor chaplain, and that I love him better than I love myself.'

'I will, Your Eminence,' Norris promised and turned to get back on his horse.

'But wait,' Thomas called, and Norris halted. 'Take my fool back to court with you. He always pleased the king and I will willingly part with him if he will afford the king any joy.'

His fool, mounted on one of the carts, called out to protest but Thomas held up his hand to silence him. 'You do not know what a great favour I am doing you. Get down and go with Sir Henry.'

The fool did as he was told, his face mutinous, taking one of the spare horses. Thomas watched the pair ride away believing his situation was not hopeless, after all.

CHAPTER THIRTY

Thomas and his party arrived at Esher late the following evening. It was not a warm welcome. The house had been shut up for months and the messenger Cromwell had sent on ahead had not yet arrived. Thomas was left shivering on his horse while Cavendish went off to find someone to unlock the front door and let them in.

Thomas looked up at the façade, his amateur builder's eye noting the crumbling windowsills, the broken panes of glass, the weeds creeping up the walls. They all should be put right, the place tidied up, but there was no point worrying about such matters now.

Cavendish came up to his horse. 'I've found someone to let us in, but I don't have high hopes for what we'll find inside.'

'It will be preferable to spending the night out here,' Thomas said, climbing down from the saddle stiffly.

An old man scurried around the corner of the house, jangling a huge iron ring of keys. He fumbled the largest key into the front door keyhole and it swung open with an ominous squeal.

Cavendish shooed Thomas inside, muttering His Eminence needed to get out of the cold air. 'Oh, this is intolerable,' he said after a hasty look around the house. 'There isn't any furniture, not even a bed for our master, no bed sheets even if there was one. No tablecloths nor cups nor dishes—'

'George,' Cromwell cut into his complaining, 'we must make do with what we have. There are mattresses on one of the carts. We will throw them on the floor if we have to and sleep there.'

'His Eminence cannot sleep on the floor,' Cavendish protested.

'It's too late to make the house good tonight,' Cromwell said, glancing at Thomas.

Thomas nodded, understanding, though the thought of sleeping on the floor was as abhorrent to him as it was to Cavendish.

'You have your writing case, George?' Cromwell asked. 'Then take out your quill and ink and write to the bishop of Carlisle and to Sir Thomas Arundel – they have houses nearby – asking them to send us some of the most necessary items.'

'What if they refuse?' Cavendish asked, heading for the front door.

Cromwell glared at him. 'Then I'll go and take what we need and bang some heads together while I'm about it. Go on. You write the letters and I'll sign them.'

'Very well, Master Cromwell.' Cavendish went out and Thomas heard him asking which cart his writing box was on.

'George is a good man,' Thomas said, perching on a wide windowsill. 'You shouldn't be so rough with him.'

'He can be an old woman at times,' Cromwell muttered.

'Don't disparage old women,' Thomas said, giving him a wry smile. 'They have their uses.' He looked out of the window. 'George is not happy at our lot.'

Cromwell kicked at a sheaf of dried-up rushes. A beetle scuttled out and hurried to find cover. 'He's right, though. This is a disgrace.'

'It is the king's will,' Thomas said. 'Ours not to reason why.'

'I'll tell you why. The Lady Anne wants to humble you.'

'I hope to disappoint her. My situation may have been humbled, but I believe it is only a temporary state of affairs. You look doubtful, Master Cromwell.'

Cromwell raised an eyebrow. 'I'm considering what I've seen and heard, Your Eminence.'

'You forget I now have this.' Thomas held up the ring Norris had delivered. 'The king wouldn't have sent this ring if he did not still love me. I understand his situation. The Lady Anne and her family insist on his enmity towards me, but they cannot erase all that he owes me.'

'Owes you?' Cromwell repeated in a surprised tone. 'Should a king owe a subject anything, Your Eminence?'

Thomas nodded. 'You're right to question me like that. Owe is the wrong word, but I am right, too. Henry knows what I have done for him since he became king, and even before then. This ring is proof—'

'Of nothing,' Cromwell cried, taking Thomas aback with his vehemence. 'It's all piss and wind. Forgive me for speaking so plainly, Your Eminence, but if you ask me, that ring is symbolic of nothing more than the king keeping you dangling.'

Thomas rose from the windowsill. 'I don't understand you,' he said indignantly.

Cromwell sighed deeply. 'Forget I spoke.'

'I can't forget it,' Thomas said, his indignation draining away as he considered what Cromwell had said. 'Do you really think that's what he's doing?'

Cromwell met Thomas's eye. 'Yes,' he said grimly, 'I do. I'm sorry, but I do.'

'No,' Thomas said, 'I know you mean well, but you're wrong.' He returned to the windowsill. 'Yet, even so, perhaps I should leave England. Go to Rome, be a cardinal there.'

'The king would never let you go.' Cromwell rubbed his forehead. 'I wasn't going to tell you, I didn't see the need, but—'

'Tell me,' Thomas insisted, not at all sure he wanted to know.

'When you left Grafton, the king was worried you might flee with Campeggio back to Rome. He ordered a watch put on all the southern ports in case you tried to get on a ship. If you did, the port authorities had orders to arrest you.'

His words made Thomas's blood run cold. Could it be true? He looked into Cromwell's worried, dark eyes and knew he did not lie.

'Thank you, Cromwell. It's best I know the truth. It never pays to build on false hopes.'

Cromwell kicked at the rushes again. 'I'll get these swept up and new ones laid down.'

'Yes, please do,' Thomas said, knowing Cromwell felt awkward and wanted to get away.

When he had gone, Thomas held up his hand and

stared at the king's ring. He had placed so much faith in the gesture, but Cromwell had proved it meant nothing. *I really have lost the king*, he realised.

CHAPTER THIRTY-ONE

1530

Thomas was finding it difficult to break the habit of a life-time and sleep in a little later than five o'clock in the morning, but as Cromwell had pointed out, there was very little for him to get up for now. He had tried to rest, to turn over and keep his eyes closed, but often found himself staring up at the tester of his bed – no longer silk, just a cloth cover – as the dawn turned into day.

He was just finishing his breakfast when Cromwell announced that Stephen Gardiner was waiting outside to see him. Thomas wiped his hands on his napkin and nodded for Cromwell to bring him in. Gardiner didn't even bow as he stood before Thomas, a slight that made Thomas want to throw something at him. There really was no such thing as gratitude, he was coming to realise.

'Good morning, Stephen,' Thomas said, swallowing down his anger.

'Good morning, Your Eminence,' Gardiner gave his oily smile. 'I trust I find you well?'

'Better than I was,' Thomas said.

'His Eminence was ill over Christmas,' Cromwell explained.

'So I understand,' Gardiner nodded. 'The king sent you his doctor.'

'He did,' Thomas said, 'and I was most grateful for his attendance.'

'His Eminence needs to move to a better place,' Cromwell said. 'This house is damp.'

Gardiner looked around the room, eyebrows rising. 'Is it?'

'You stay here for a month or two, then tell me it isn't,' Cromwell sneered. 'Have you brought any news about us being allowed to move to Richmond?'

'I have not,' Gardiner said, and gestured at a chair. Thomas nodded and Gardiner sat. 'I am come with the terms the king offers.'

Thomas glanced up at Cromwell, whose expression had hardened since announcing Gardiner. He knew Cromwell had been working hard to have the praemunire charge revoked, and though Cromwell had only given him vague reports, Thomas had learnt Henry was willing to listen. Thomas hadn't wanted to know all the details, content to leave it to Cromwell to sort out, but he knew there had been weeks of intense negotiation between Cromwell and the Privy Council. Thomas bid Gardiner continue, anxious as well as eager to hear the terms the king offered.

Gardiner laid out his papers on the table. 'The king has agreed to issue a formal pardon for the charge of praemunire on the following terms. That you renounce all titles and land with the exception of the archbishopric of York. You may keep all the lands and revenues associated with the archbishopric saving York Place, which is to remain the property of the king. You will resign as bishop of Winchester and abbot of St Albans, and all your properties will be made over to the king.'

Thomas's mouth had fallen open as Gardiner spoke. 'But…,' Thomas began, perplexed, 'I thought we had agreed that I would plead guilty to the praemunire charge and then the king would allow me to keep more of my properties and revenues. The archbishopric of York is not enough to sustain me. Why, I would need at least…,' he looked up at Cromwell for help.

'Four thousand pounds per annum,' Cromwell supplied promptly.

'Yes, four thousand pounds. How am I supposed to manage on so much less, Stephen?'

Gardiner paused to consult his papers. Thomas waited anxiously. 'The king is very generously gifting you three thousand pounds as well as a considerable amount of plate and furnishings. Also, horses fully apparelled, and oxen. All told, a value of over six thousand pounds. This, in addition to a pension of one thousand marks. I think you will find that the king has been most generous, Your Eminence, all things considered.'

Thomas let out the breath he had been holding. Yes, all things considered, Henry had been generous, although the pension and the other items in Gardiner's papers didn't come close to a reparation for what he had lost. All those properties, all those revenues he had enjoyed for years, gone.

'Will you please convey my very great thanks to the king, Stephen?' Thomas said. 'He has indeed provided me with more than I could have hoped.'

'I will tell him,' Gardiner said, shuffling the papers and holding them out to Cromwell. 'Your copy of the terms.'

Cromwell snatched the papers from his hand and Gardiner's mouth twitched in amusement. 'I shall wish you good day,' he said, and left.

'It's a good deal,' Cromwell said when he had gone. 'It may not seem it, but considering what you were facing, it is.'

'I understand,' Thomas said. 'You've done well for me. Thank you, Cromwell. I am in your debt.'

Cromwell grunted. 'I'm going to write to the Privy Council again about moving to Richmond. You can't stay here.'

'Do not make a nuisance of yourself, though,' Thomas warned. 'I won't have you pushing for more concessions. The king may grow angry and change his mind.'

'Don't worry,' Cromwell said, 'I won't push too hard.' He poured himself a cup of wine and took a mouthful, wiping his lips with his sleeve. 'Just hard enough.'

Thomas closed his Bible as Cromwell strode into the room.

'A letter's come from the Privy Council,' Cromwell said, snapping open the red seal and unfolding the paper he held. His dark eyes quickly read.

'Well?' Thomas asked impatiently. 'Am I allowed to move to Richmond?'

Cromwell sighed. 'No. You're to go to York.' He held out the letter to Thomas, who took it and read for himself. Cromwell began pacing. 'This is the dukes' doing, I just know it. They're worried that if you moved to Richmond, you'd only be a stone's throw from Windsor, and the king might allow you to visit him. And they want to prevent you two from meeting because they know if you did, the king would take you back, and that's the last thing they want.'

Thomas refolded the letter. 'I am archbishop of York, but I've never been there.'

'I have, and you haven't missed much. It's cold and damp, the people are surly and the food inedible.'

'I don't suppose we can refuse to go?' Thomas asked hopefully.

Cromwell shook his head. 'The king's signed that,' he said, nodding at the letter Thomas held. 'You shall have to go.'

'Perhaps you will be able to convince the king to allow me to return to London,' Thomas suggested. 'After a few weeks or so.'

Cromwell looked at him. 'Aye, maybe, but I can't do that from York.'

'You mean to stay in London?' Thomas felt strangely upset at the prospect of losing Cromwell's company.

'It would be best. If I go with you to York, the dukes will be able to say what they want with no one to speak in your defence.'

'Are you really the only man who will speak for me at court, Cromwell?'

'There are others, but at the moment, I have the king's ear and I mean to use it. I'll get you back in London before too much time has passed, Your Eminence, don't worry.'

Thomas smiled at him. 'Then I won't worry, Cromwell. I know you'll do your best for me.'

Thomas took his time leaving Esher, hopeful that out of his window he would see a messenger come from the king informing him the royal mind had altered and he need no longer go to York. But no such messenger arrived. Instead, Cromwell brought back a conversation he had had with Howard, who threatened to tear Thomas apart with his teeth if he delayed leaving any longer.

Thomas was surprised by how quickly his reduced household could be ready to leave. From having over four hundred servants, he now had no more than one hundred and sixty, the others having been taken by the king into his service, including Thomas's cooks and his choir. More than anything, Thomas missed his choir. He felt that if he had need of anything other than the king's love, it was the beautiful sound his chapel choir had made. But they had been too accomplished, and the king had always coveted them.

And what the king wanted, he got. *Funny*, Thomas thought, *it used to be whatever I wanted, I got, and what I wanted was usually what was best for the king, so where was the harm?* It would have stayed that way had it not been for the Night Crow. If he'd known all those years ago how Anne Boleyn would destroy him, he would have let Percy marry the bitch and good luck to him.

Thomas had come to the conclusion that Anne Boleyn was God's way of punishing him for being too much the king's man and not enough of a priest. So, en route to York, when he and his party stopped to spend a few days at a monastery, he asked the monks to furnish him with a hair-shirt. He had always viewed a hair-shirt with disdain – he remembered shaking his head when one of her ladies had informed him Katherine had taken to wearing one – but he was beginning now to understand the point of them. He had erred. He saw it now. All those years making and unmaking alliances, acquiring revenues and pensions… it was not what a priest was supposed to do. Well, he would make amends. He would become a true priest, and made what he considered a good start by washing the feet of fifty-nine beggars on Maundy Thursday.

He felt better for this change. It gave him something else to think about rather than brooding on his relationship with the king. Until, that was, he arrived at his house at Southwell, a few miles from York. It was a shock, after what he had been used to, to enter the dilapidated property. It was in an even worse state than Esher had been. He had not made any provision for its maintenance, and he discovered that the roof leaked, the panelled walls were spotted with black mould, and mice ran in and out of the wainscoting.

Cavendish tutted and shook his head, then hurried away to make what he could of the bedchamber while Thomas and his secretaries found a cold parlour in which to wait. A secretary brushed debris off a chair and offered it to Thomas. Thomas sank into it, watching as his page bent to light a fire. Fortunately, the wood store was dry and the page adept. He had a fire warming the room in less than a quarter of an hour.

The hair-shirt was rubbing painfully, the coarse hairs prickling into the scabs already forming on his shoulders. *Our Lord suffered far worse*, Thomas reminded himself, and shut his mind against the pain. If only he could shut his mind to his resentment against the king and his nobles that had been steadily growing with each step taken towards York. The page, pleased with his handiwork, asked Thomas if he wanted anything else.

'Fetch my secretary,' Thomas said. 'I want to write a letter.'

The secretary came into the room a few minutes later carrying his writing box. He set it down on the rickety table, set out his ink pot and a few blank pages, then trimmed the nibs of his quills with his penknife.

'Are you ready?' Thomas asked impatiently.

'Yes,' the secretary said, brushing shavings onto the floor. 'Ready.'

'Then write this. "To your most gracious Majesty." No, leave out "most gracious". Begin, "Your Majesty. As you so desired me to do, I have arrived in York, and find a welcome entirely without cheer or comfort. It is my greatest hope that my misery in this place so far from you may not last too long, and it is my greatest desire to be once again standing by your side, your humble servant once more." Sign it, "Thomas Cardinalis", and send it with all haste.'

The secretary hurried from the room to find a messenger to take the letter to London. Thomas sank back in the chair, wishing he had a cup of his finest Burgundy in his hand. That was perhaps the shortest letter he had ever sent to Henry. He hoped its abruptness would alert the king to how miserable he truly was and so lead him to relent and allow Thomas to come home.

CHAPTER THIRTY-TWO

'Pitiful, isn't it?' Anne tossed the letter aside. 'That he should criticise you so.'

Henry took up the letter and studied it again. 'Is that what you see in it, my love? I thought Thomas sounded penitent.'

Anne laughed. 'I can read between the lines even if you cannot, my lord. He grovels very well, I'll give him that, but what he's really saying in that letter is that you have been wrong to send him to York.'

'Really?'

'Obvious. Why?' she asked sharply. 'You're not thinking of bringing him back, are you?'

'No,' Henry assured her, setting the letter down, 'of course not.'

'I hope not, my lord,' Anne said, her dark eyes glaring at him. 'If you only knew…'

'Only knew what? What, my love?' he prompted when Anne's mouth opened, then shut again.

'I wasn't sure I should tell you,' she said, affecting an air of innocence. 'I didn't want to upset you.'

Henry grabbed her hand. 'You must tell me. What is it?'

'Well,' she said slowly, as if Henry was dragging the words from her, 'Wolsey has been writing to the Spanish ambassador asking how the divorce is progressing and whether he can help to hinder it further.'

'What?' Henry roared, vaulting from his chair to tower over her.

Anne forced her smile away and put a look of fear on her face. 'This is why I thought it best to keep this knowledge from you. I knew you would be angry.'

'He's helping Katherine? After the assurances he gave me that he was doing all he could to get the divorce?'

'You cannot believe a word that man says,' Anne nodded. 'My father and my uncle have told you so often enough.' She watched as Henry charged up and down the chamber, his face growing darker with each step.

'Is he plotting against me, do you think?' Henry asked. 'Up there in York?'

'What has being in York to do with it?' Anne wondered.

'Plantagenet country, Nan,' Henry said. 'They have never been for Tudor.'

Anne rose, genuinely alarmed. 'You don't think there might be a rebellion?'

The very word made Henry's eyes widen. 'Thomas could be rousing the populace up there. The reports I've had tell of how the people have welcomed him, for they have never had a prince of the Church venture so far north. He is a novelty, balm for their souls. Oh Nan, what if he is planning to unite with Charles and Katherine against me? He could be helping to plan a Spanish invasion.'

Anne had not wanted this, Henry alarmed beyond

reason. It would take all her powers of persuasion to soothe the temper she had roused, and she wasn't sure she had the energy. It was tiring always having to please him; his demands on her person were growing greater by the day.

'I think it unlikely Wolsey has the influence now,' she said calmly. 'Besides, Charles loathes him, you know that. He will not enter into an alliance with Wolsey.'

'But we have no idea what he is getting up to in York,' Henry said, shaking his head. 'Oh, God's Blood, why did we send him so far away? He should be close, where we can keep an eye on him. I will bring him back.'

'To the Tower?' Anne asked sharply.

Henry stared at her. 'The Tower?'

'Well, if you're bringing him back, then surely you're bringing him back because you're charging him with treason, no? After all, communicating with a foreign ambassador without the consent of the Privy Council or your prior knowledge… I am not mistaken, am I, my lord? That is treason, is it not?'

'Yes,' he nodded slowly, 'it is treason.'

'Then you will send men to arrest him?' she prompted.

'Men? Yes, at once. Your uncle shall go.'

That didn't suit Anne at all. She wanted Howard at court in case she had need of him. An idea entered her head, one that made her thin lips curve in a smile.

'No, not my uncle. My lord Percy. Why not? He is already in the North, is he not? He can arrest Wolsey much sooner than my uncle, being here in London, could. Why, it might take several weeks for my uncle to even reach York, and who knows what mischief Wolsey might get up to in that time.'

'Percy?' Henry repeated, watching Anne with curiosity.

'Yes,' Anne nodded emphatically, 'Percy.'

Thomas was reading when his servant announced he had a visitor. Pleased at the prospect of company, Thomas closed his book and looked expectantly towards the door. His smile faltered a little when he saw who his visitor was.

'Why, my lord Percy, how pleasant to see you once again after all this time. Won't you please join me?' Thomas gestured at the chair opposite.

'No, thank you, I won't,' Percy said, and Thomas wondered at the young man's unease. He was also shocked by the change in him. Percy had been tall and well built when he served Thomas at York Place, but in the few years he'd been gone, he had withered. Yes, that was the very word. Percy had withered.

'Well, then, if you will not sit, can I offer you a cup of wine? It is not very good, but it does.'

'No, thank you.' Percy looked down at his feet, and there was something in the way he shuffled that put Thomas on his guard.

'Is it on your own business you come to see me or the king's?' Thomas asked warily.

Percy looked up. 'On the king's, Your Eminence.'

Thomas's heart beat faster. 'I see. What have you to say to me, then? Come, out with it, my lord, I cannot bear delay when it concerns the king.'

'Your Eminence,' Percy said suddenly and a little too loudly, 'I am come to arrest you of high treason.'

Thomas's hand gripped the pommels of his chair. Treason? Was it possible? What treason had he committed?

'You have a warrant from the Privy Council?' he asked.

'I do,' Percy nodded, 'but I have been ordered not to show it to you.'

'Have you, indeed? Then I refuse to accept the validity of your warrant.'

'Your Eminence, please,' Percy begged, and Thomas saw beads of sweat pop on his forehead.

Thomas held up his hand. 'I do not wish to make things awkward for you, my lord, but every man, even the most base, has the right to read the charge laid against him.'

Percy glanced at the man he had come in with who had so far hidden in the shadows. Now he stepped forward and Thomas recognised him as an officer of the king's privy chamber, one Master Walsh. With a great sinking feeling, Thomas realised there was no point pursuing the matter of the warrant, for Master Walsh came from the king and had the authority to arrest Thomas with or without a warrant.

'You will come with us, Your Eminence,' Master Walsh said, showing none of the awkwardness Percy obviously felt.

'Yes,' Thomas nodded, 'I see I must. Very well.' He rose, feeling his legs shaking a little, and he put out a hand to steady himself. Percy stepped forward and Thomas felt his shadow fall over him. Withered though Percy was, his shadow felt oppressive.

'I am sorry for this, Your Eminence,' Percy said in Thomas's ear, 'but I was ordered to come. I did not wish to.'

'Could you not have pleaded illness, my lord?'

Percy shook his head. 'I don't think Anne would have shown any pity for that.'

'The Lady Anne,' Thomas nodded. 'Now, I under-stand.' This was Anne's little act of revenge, sending her former lover to arrest the man who had parted them. She didn't care that she hurt Percy almost as much as she hurt him by doing this. She really was a bitch. 'May I bid my servants farewell before we leave?'

Percy hesitated. 'I suppose that will be all right,' he said to Walsh, asking permission.

'As long as you're not too long about it,' Walsh told Thomas. 'I want to be on the road before nightfall.'

Thomas and Percy had been on the road for three days when they reached the house of Percy's father-in-law, the earl of Shrewsbury. Here, Percy bid Thomas farewell, unable to hide his joy at being relieved of his charge. The young man had done his best to make Thomas comfort-able, had tried to take his mind off his impending fate, but his efforts had been in vain. Both men knew there was not going to be a happy ending to this journey. Percy kissed Thomas's ring as he left, but could not meet his eye.

Thomas was now in the custody of Sir Anthony Kingston, the Constable of the Tower. 'I am to see you to London, Your Eminence,' Kingston said. 'I trust I am an acceptable escort.'

Am I actually being asked for approval, Thomas wondered, *or are you merely being polite?* 'I could ask for none better, Sir Anthony. But tell me, if you can, the details of this latest charge against me.'

Kingston cleared his throat and then gestured with a jerk of his head for Thomas to step to the side so they could talk privately.

'You should be of good cheer, Your Eminence. While

the charge against you is grave, I am assured it has only been brought so you have the opportunity to clear your name. There are so many rumours bruited around court, that you are in league with the French and Spanish to force the pope to excommunicate the king if he does not renounce the Lady Anne, that you are planning to leave England and set yourself against the king by aligning yourself with the pope in Rome, and I know not what else.'

The rumourmongers had been busy, Thomas mused, realising he had acted foolishly by communicating with foreign ambassadors. It was madness to have believed he would not be found out; madness, too, not to realise how bad it would look in the eyes of the king. Why had he done it? he scolded himself, but he knew the answer. He had been desperate.

'Lies, Sir Anthony,' he said vehemently, 'all lies. I would never do such a thing.'

Kingston seemed in earnest, genuinely believing what he said, that the arrest was merely for show, but Thomas could hardly believe that to be true. He was under no illusions now. Despite his penitence, despite all Cromwell's efforts, he had lost Henry's love and he would not have it again. Kingston could believe what he wanted. Thomas knew he was on his way to London to die, whether by the king's hand or by God's.

They had reached Nottingham, and George Cavendish was far from happy. Not that he was ever happy to be travelling from place to place, but that wasn't what was concerning him. He had noticed, if no one else had, that his master's health was failing.

'His Eminence is extremely ill, Sir Anthony,' he said

desperately to Kingston. 'He cannot keep on being moved in this way. His body cannot take it. And that is not to mention the effect the treason charge is having on him. I've never seen him so unsettled, both in mind and body. Please, can you not write to the king and ask him to forgive the cardinal for his wrongdoings? The king's displeasure is killing my master.'

Kingston drew himself up. 'Master Cavendish, I cannot write to the king. I am a lowly servant. I have no such influence, not with His Majesty nor with his Council. My orders are clear. I am to escort His Eminence to London to stand trial—'

'But he is desperately ill,' Cavendish cried. 'My master can hardly sit up in bed. He cannot move without pain. It is agony for him to mount his mule. He cannot be far from a close stool because his bowels have turned to water and his doctors despair of his life. Indeed, I overheard one of them say my master will be dead within these five days.'

'I hear you, Master Cavendish, and I am sympathetic to His Eminence's plight, but your master himself has just told me he means to resume the journey on the morrow.'

'What? No, he cannot have said so. You have got it wrong.'

'I assure you, I have not. Now, I will do what I can to see he is comfortable on the journey, but I can do no more than that. Excuse me.'

Cavendish watched Kingston leave the room, no doubt to continue the preparations for their removal. Cavendish wished there was something he could do to stop them going, but he knew there was nothing. He sank to his knees and prayed for a miracle.

CHAPTER THIRTY-THREE

Cavendish got him to bed, but not even the soft mattress, sent on ahead for his comfort, eased Thomas's body. He ached everywhere. Every bit of pressure was as if a bruise had been pressed hard.

'Is that any better, Your Eminence?' Cavendish asked.

'Some,' Thomas lied, and sank into the pillow. There was a noise outside. 'What is that?'

'I'll see,' Cavendish said, and slipped out into the corridor. Thomas could hear him talking, his voice growing unusually loud. Then the door burst open and Cavendish had his hands pressed against Kingston's chest, trying to hold him back.

'What is it?' Thomas asked, wincing as he forced himself to sit up. 'Sir Anthony? You know I have retired, so why are you here again?'

Kingston looked embarrassed. 'A message has come from the king, Your Eminence. It seems you owe him fifteen hundred pounds, and he instructs me to take possession of it.'

'For the love of Christ, you talk of money?' Cavendish

cried incredulously. 'Can you not see His Eminence is gravely ill?'

'That has no bearing, Master Cavendish,' Kingston said angrily, and Thomas sensed Kingston's anger was not directed at Cavendish but at the king for making him do this. 'The king demands the money. Where is it?'

Thomas closed his eyes and tried to think. Had it really come to this? The king demanding such a measly sum as fifteen hundred pounds when he had taken everything else Thomas owned?

'George,' Thomas said, 'did not David Vincent have the care of such a sum?'

Cavendish was still looking indignant. 'I think he may have, Your Eminence, but he is not here.'

'Then where is this Vincent?' Kingston asked impatiently.

'I shall discover that for you, sir, in a little while, if you will but leave my master alone,' Cavendish said with some force.

Kingston left reluctantly, and Cavendish fussed around the room, shaking out blankets and setting out the medicine chest.

'That the king should send after you for money,' he said, shaking his head. 'Has he forgotten what you once were to him? Has he forgotten all you have done for him ever since he became king?'

'The king has grown used to getting what he wants,' Thomas sighed. 'That is my fault. I have always tried to give him what he wanted, and until recently, I had always succeeded. I have failed the king, George.'

'And he has abandoned you for it,' Cavendish said bitterly. 'This money. Does he really need it? Is your need not greater than his now? You are so ill provisioned here. We need the money for decent food and—'

'The money was for my funeral, George,' Thomas said.

'Your fune—' Cavendish broke off as the word stuck in his throat.

'My death is coming,' Thomas said. 'When the clock strikes the eighth hour, I shall meet my Maker.'

'You may yet rally, Your Eminence,' Cavendish said.

'Do not place your faith in that, George. You will be disappointed.'

'The eighth hour? Why are you so sure of the time?'

'I don't know. I just feel it.'

'But not tonight?' Cavendish sounded fearful.

'Perhaps,' Thomas conceded. 'If not tonight, then tomorrow, or the day after. But soon, George. It will come soon.'

Thomas woke at four o'clock in the afternoon just as the church bell was ringing. *This is the day I die*, he thought as he lay there, unable to open his eyes.

He wasn't sorry or afraid. The truth was he didn't want to live any longer. It wasn't just the constant bodily pain he was tired of; it was the pain he felt in his heart knowing he had lost the king's love that hurt the most and which he didn't want to feel any more. No, he didn't want to feel anything anymore.

He heard George snoring on the pallet at the side of the bed. George had been up most of the night, on hand should Thomas need him, but Thomas reasoned he was a young man who could afford to lose a little sleep.

'George,' Thomas called, his voice barely audible, even in the quiet of the room. He forced his eyes open, licked his dry, cracked lips, and made a feeble attempt to clear his throat. He tried again. 'George.'

He heard a rustling, and then a tousled hair appeared at the side of the bed. 'Yes, Your Eminence?'

'Fetch my confessor.'

Cavendish scrambled to his feet and hurried out of the room. He quickly returned with his confessor, and Kingston, too.

'Why are you here, Sir Anthony?' Thomas asked, wondering why he had come. 'I would have my confession made in private.'

'I came to see how you are,' Kingston said, glancing at the confessor.

'I am dying,' Thomas said, 'and that worries you. You worry the king and Lady Anne will be disappointed of their revenge.'

'Nonsense,' Kingston gave an embarrassed laugh. 'The king has no personal enmity towards you. You'll see that when you are back on your feet and you and he meet. I'm sure you will have nothing to fear.'

'You mean to be kind, Sir Anthony,' Thomas said, glancing at the priest who had donned his vestments and was waiting to hear his confession, 'but you're not sure at all. Do not fret yourself,' he added, as Kingston opened his mouth to protest. 'I see how it is framed. My only regret is that if I had served God as diligently as I have done the king, He would not have given me over in my grey hairs as the king has done. I would have you do me one last favour, Sir Anthony.'

'What favour?'

'Commend me to His Majesty. Beseech him to remember all that has occurred between him and me from the beginning of our time together to this very day. And regarding his secret matter, have him know I did my best, though it was not enough. I beg him to search his conscience to discover whether I have truly offended him and so deserve his hate. Tell him what I have said, Sir Anthony, please. And now, let me be alone with my confessor.'

Cavendish, sniffing as he tried to hold back his tears, shooed Kingston out of the room, closing the door behind them both.

'Come closer,' Thomas said to his confessor, and the priest knelt by the bedside. 'I'm afraid you may be on your knees for some time.'

'I will hear all,' the confessor said.

Thomas nodded. 'I shall start at the very beginning,' he said, and confessed his sins until his tongue failed him and he could speak no more. His eyes closed. He heard the priest groaning as he got to his feet, heard the latch of the door lift and the squeal of the hinges as the door opened. He thought he heard the priest say, 'Master Cavendish,' but then he heard no more.

'What is it?' Cavendish asked quietly, looking towards the window as the church bell tolled. He turned back towards his master in the bed, his silent, unmoving, most beloved master.

'It is eight o'clock,' he said in astonishment.

CHAPTER THIRTY-FOUR

Cavendish rode through the night to tell the king of Thomas's death.

He rode into the Base Court at Hampton Court Palace and handed his reins to a stable-boy who had arrived to take care of his horse.

'I must see the king,' he told a steward who stepped forward and stared disdainfully at the badge on Cavendish's sleeve. 'I have news of the cardinal. The king will wish to hear it.'

'The king is shooting at the butts in the gardens,' the steward said. 'I'll get someone to show you—'

'I know where to go,' Cavendish said over his shoulder as he hurried away.

'But you have to be announced,' the steward called to his retreating back.

Cavendish ran to the gardens, unmindful of the curious stares of courtiers he passed on the way. He spotted the king easily, standing head and shoulders higher than the men and women clustered around who were clapping his every shot.

He slowed as he neared the group, making his way around the back until he stood at the edge where the king could not fail to see him. Cavendish bowed. Henry looked him up and down, his forehead creased, then looked away, bringing up the bow and drawing the string.

The onlookers shot him disapproving looks. He was a non-entity now, Cavendish knew. Where once he had been welcomed with enthusiasm by courtiers eager to curry favour with a servant of the great cardinal, he was now an outcast, a leper, disgraced along with his master. They disgusted him, and he kept his gaze firmly on the king.

Henry shot his arrow, waited for the applause, then held his hand out for another arrow. 'What do you do here, Master Cavendish?' he asked.

'I have news of the cardinal, Your Majesty,' Cavendish said. 'Important news.'

Henry had been fitting the arrow to the bow. At Cavendish's words, he lowered both. 'Step forward,' he said, and waved the courtiers away. They went, muttering.

Cavendish, feeling less brave than he had, moved towards Henry and waited for the king to speak again.

'What news?' Henry asked.

Cavendish felt tears prick at his eyes and there was a lump in his throat. He swallowed. 'His Eminence died last night.'

Henry's mouth twisted. 'Thomas is dead?'

'Yes, Your Majesty.'

Henry drew in a deep breath. 'That saddens me, Master Cavendish. Was it peaceful?'

'His passing was, though his last days were fraught with worry. About you, Your Majesty.'

The creases in Henry's brow deepened, and he looked

away, back towards the palace, his eyes squinting against the sunlight.

'He let me down, Master Cavendish,' Henry said, fingering a pearl on his doublet, 'when I needed him the most.'

'He did what he could,' Cavendish protested. 'In everything, he served you faithfully.'

'He served himself as well,' Henry said, and his voice had become hard. 'Let us not forget that. But now is not the time for recriminations. Thomas was a great man, and I would have him with us still. By God's Blood, I would pay twenty thousand pounds to see him alive again. I shall miss him.'

Cavendish lowered his head. 'I shall miss him too.'

Female laughter punctuated the silence between them, and the king spun around to face the path Cavendish had hurried along. The laughter had come from Anne Boleyn. There she was, coming towards them, the breeze blowing strands of black hair across her face which she pulled back with a long, slender hand.

Cavendish looked up at the king. Henry's expression had softened, his face was positively glowing, and a smile was tugging at his lips as he looked upon his heart's desire. Cavendish's face hardened with loathing as he stared at the woman who had ruined the final years of his master's life.

Henry dragged his eyes away from Anne and back to Cavendish. 'I thank you for bringing me this news personally.' He took a step in Anne's direction, then halted and turned back. 'What of the fifteen hundred pounds I sent Master Kingston to fetch? Did that ever turn up?'

'The fifteen hun…' Cavendish's voice tailed off. Was the king really asking after money at such a time as this?

He'd just said he would pay thousands to have Thomas alive again.'No, Your Majesty, it has not yet been found.'

Henry frowned. 'Well, see to it, Master Cavendish, and with haste. I want that money.'

Cavendish watched Henry as he hurried over to Anne, his arms spread wide to take her in an embrace, which she shook her head at, a coy smile playing on her lips. She held out her hand for the king to take, and Henry pressed his lips to the slim fingers, then whispered in her ear.

Anne Boleyn's dark eyes settled on Cavendish and her own mouth spread in a wide, triumphant smile.

AUTHOR'S NOTE

With the previous books in this trilogy, *Master Wolsey* and *Power & Glory*, I focused as much on Thomas Wolsey's political career as I did on his personal life. In this novel, I wanted to focus mainly on the personal challenges he faced, most notably his deteriorating relationship with King Henry. That is not to say that this last decade of Wolsey's life was devoid of politics; these years were busier than ever in terms of his involvement in domestic and international affairs. Indeed, there were so many foreign alliances made in this period, that if I had covered them all, this would have been a much longer novel and I fear I would have risked boring and confusing the reader. I chose to dramatise only those that offered the greatest insight into Wolsey's life and career.

I have also used dramatic licence in some scenes. For instance, Wolsey did not witness the duke of Buckingham's trial, although he would certainly have received a report of the proceedings, and I have chosen to place Thomas Cromwell in his service earlier than some historians would agree with, but also later than others would agree with.

Lastly, there is some debate over whether Wolsey ever truly wanted to become pope. Some historians believe it was always his ambition, while others believe he was content as Henry VIII's chief minister and only contemplated the papal crown when he thought it was the only way to give the king his divorce. For the purposes of writing this novel, I decided to adopt the latter point of view.

ALSO BY LAURA DOWERS

The Tudor Court

The Queen's Favourite

The Queen's Rebel

The Queen's Spymaster

The Queen's Rival (short story)

The Queen's Poet (short story)

Master Wolsey

Power & Glory

The Rise of Rome

The Last King of Rome

The Eagle in the Dovecote

Standalone Novels

The Woman in Room Three

A Deadly Agreement